Was he seducing the wrong woman?

Without knowing how or why, he could feel the warmth of her body next to his, smell the faint, sweet fragrance of her perfume, sense the motion of her hips and arms pressed too close to his as they danced.

Without thinking, Alex tightened his arm around her waist, propelled her nearer, whirling her in a new direction. It was a basic fox-trot, but it felt like the hottest tango in history. What the hell was happening to him?

They swayed together, feeling the music, the night, the nearness. Alex wanted desperately to bend and cover her mouth with his. He wanted to make love to her, with all the rhythm of the damn song.

"Meg..." he whispered.

Meg? Alex went still. *Oh, God.* This was the wrong woman. He was being seductive, all right, perfectly according to plan, but with *the wrong woman!*

ABOUT THE AUTHOR

Julie Kistler has been reading books and imagining herself as part of the adventures as long as she can remember. She is happy to report that writing books is almost as much fun as reading them, although it's a lot more work! An avid film buff, Julie has a special fondness for old black-and-white screwball comedies; these movies have provided the inspiration for many of her books, including *Fantasy Wife*. Julie and her husband live in Bloomington, Illinois, with their cat, Thisbe.

Books by Julie Kistler

HARLEQUIN AMERICAN ROMANCE

JULIE KISTLER

FANTASY WIFE

Harlequin Books

TORONTO • NEW YORK • LONDON
AMSTERDAM • PARIS • SYDNEY • HAMBURG
STOCKHOLM • ATHENS • TOKYO • MILAN
MADRID • WARSAW • BUDAPEST • AUCKLAND

ISBN 0-373-16593-5

FANTASY WIFE

Chapter One

When it comes to dealing with a misbehaving child, patience is indeed a virtue. It can also be exceedingly hard to come by, especially when the little dear begins to wail and scream and turn an appalling shade of purple, right there in the gourmet foods section of the corner market. But you will prevail, never fear. Remember that you are in charge. Remember that you, too, were once a youngster and *your* parents somehow muddled through. Remember that no one at the corner market will long remember you were the one with the purple child.

And if things get too far out of hand, never fear to seek outside help from an expert . . .

—*The Sabina Charles No-Fuss Guide to Parenting*

His life was a complete and total disaster.

Alex Thornhill had always said, with a great deal of satisfaction, that his life ran like a well-oiled machine; it took effort and organization, of course, but he was up to the task. Of course he was. He was the hottest of the hot up-and-comers at the sprawling media conglomerate, Dateline/Dynasty. In fact, he was in line to run the whole place one of these days. He could handle anything. Until...

Until Alex's well-oiled machine had ground to a screeching halt, spewing gears and gizmos every which way.

"It's a bloody disaster!" the woman on the other end of the telephone cried in his ear.

Rose Cotten, who held the dubious distinction of being thirty-fifth in a series of nannies, housekeepers and au pairs he had tried to retain in the past year, had been ranting at him for a full five minutes now. If Mrs. Cotten's hysterical tone was any indication, Alex had the impression he would be looking for her successor all too soon.

No one had lasted longer than two weeks, although one formidable German woman had made a valiant effort to persevere. But after the children tried to set her shoes on fire, she, too, marched her scorched brogues out the front door of the Thornhill residence.

So here he was, on the second day of number thirty-five's employment, more desperate and confused than ever.

Could it get any worse? The lights on his phone were all flashing, indicating that his secretary wanted his attention in the worst way. He'd missed a lunch meeting with the VP for print media, his chief rival. He had a stack of unread memos and reports piled chin-high on his desk. The limo had been waiting downstairs for half an hour to take him to La Guardia for a flight to L.A. And the shopping network he had pushed to acquire was in the red for the third straight month.

All in all, he felt it was fair to assume that his stock as Dateline/Dynasty's golden boy was plummeting by the moment.

And he still had his housekeeper on the phone, screaming in his ear.

He was almost afraid to ask. With a sense of foreboding and the first pangs of a piercing headache, he inquired, "What did they do this time?"

"What *didn't* they do?" trumpeted Mrs. Cotten at the top of her lungs.

And she'd seemed like such a calm, unflappable lady. Alex was at a loss. He just couldn't understand how two tiny little girls could create such a fuss.

Business he could handle, with all the wheeling and dealing, intrigue and backbiting that went along with it. He could pacify his secretary, smooth over the missed lunch date, plug holes in the shopping network, schedule a later flight to L.A., and do it all without breaking a sweat.

But his children . . .

Ah yes, his children. His Achilles' heel. He honestly felt there must be some foolproof and tidy way of getting them to behave, if only he found the right help. But he had to admit it—to him, the girls were like an alien species. They left him utterly mystified.

Still, Puff had never had any trouble dealing with them. When Puff was there to run the house, the children were perfect angels. When he came home, they appeared on cue to politely kiss him good-night before they toddled off to bed.

So why were they so impossible now?

"The fire department?" he asked suddenly, shocked out of his musings by Mrs. Cotten's latest complaint. If they had set anyone's shoes on fire again, he swore he'd send them to military school. "Did you say the fire department was there?"

"Yes, and I'll tell you why," Rose said smartly. "Because your precious little darlings rang them, that's why. After Sydney tied me to a chair, Lolly perched on the counter and called up the fire department, and she said the kitchen was aflame. Out came all those nice young men with their sirens and their hoses and—"

"So there really was no fire this time?"

"*This time?* Do you mean to tell me there've been fires before? And you hired me on anyway, knowing I might be set ablaze by the little devils?" Rose Cotten shrieked.

"They promised me they wouldn't set any more fires," he told her quickly.

"And you believed them?"

"Well, they didn't actually do it this time, did they?"

"No, they just tied me to a chair, the little heathens!"

"But Sydney is only eight, and Lolly's barely six," Alex managed to say. "How could they possibly...?"

"It doesn't bear telling," she groused.

It didn't really matter, although he had a pretty good idea that Mrs. Cotten had dozed off and the children had taken advantage. Whenever the girls were feeling ignored, they pulled tricks like this. God help him, he was getting used to it.

"So, tell me," he said wearily, "what happened with the firemen?"

"They were actually quite nice, considering," she allowed. "They gave the girls a talking-to, about how they could be arrested for filing false reports and such, then they left instructions for you to call them."

"I'll take care of it." He and the fire department were becoming the best of pals. After all, this wasn't the first time this month they'd been out to his apartment.

"But what with the sirens and the ladders and the muddy footprints all over the hall, Mr. Tompkins next door said to tell you this is the last straw."

"Mr. Tompkins?" Oh, damn. Emery Hopwell Tompkins ran the co-op board with an iron fist.

The board had been very iffy about having children in the building to start with. And they weren't all that certain about Alex. Sure, he held a good steady job at an impressive large company. But the board members were, quite frankly, snobs.

In the end, the only reason they'd let in the Thornhills was that Puff had the right connections. She, at least, was old money. She was one of them.

But now Puff was gone, and Alex's patina of privilege was slipping. With all this hubbub, it seemed likely he was going to be out on the street after the next directors' meeting at the co-op.

His headache intensified. "Anything else?"

"Just that you'd better get home right away, because I don't plan to stay here any longer than it takes me to get a taxi," she said smartly. "I've cleaned up most of the mess from the firemen, I've gathered my things and I'm leaving, whether you're here or not."

"Mrs. Cotten," he interrupted quickly, "you can't leave. Not until I can find someone to replace you. I have business out of town and I won't be back till Friday. You do remember that, don't you?"

"I don't care what business you've got. I'm not staying. Those children are possessed! They threw half my clothes off the balcony," she sputtered. "While I was rescuing my things out of the bushes down on the street, Sydney called the police and claimed I had tried to poison her. And after that—"

"I get the idea."

No hope. There was no way he was going to convince Mrs. Cotten to stay tonight. Rapidly, he ran through his options. He really didn't like the idea of her staying there five minutes longer, given her attitude toward his children, but he couldn't think of anyone to call who could fill in.

So Rose Cotten it would have to be.

"I'll come home as soon as I can. And, Mrs. Cotten, you'd better be there when I get there," he warned. "If you leave them alone, I'll have you charged with child endangerment."

"Child endangerment! It's *me* who's in danger."

"I'll be there as soon as I can," he said curtly.

"Oh, and, Mr. Thornhill... If you're looking for a replacement, don't bother calling my agency," she told him smugly. "I've already tipped them off about you and your girls."

"You did what? Then how am I supposed to—"

But she had already hung up.

The pounding in his head took on a calypso beat. Alex stood and made his way to the door. Leaning into the outer office, he called to his secretary, "Helga, get Peter Beckett in here on the double. He's going to have to cover for me in L.A. And get on the horn ASAP to any employment agencies you haven't already used who handle nannies or housekeepers."

"You lost another one?" She stopped in midscribble on her notepad. "How many does that make?"

"Thirty-five."

"Good grief."

"Well, it doesn't matter," he said briskly, "because I need a new one. On the double. As soon as I meet with Peter and brief him on the trip, I'll have to go right home, so tell the new nanny to meet me there."

"But, Mr. Thornhill, where am I going to get another one? I've already used up every agency in town. Housekeepers, nannies, au pairs, maids, butlers..." She added delicately, "And they all told me not to call back. Nicely Nannies threatened to sue if I ever called again."

"*Every* agency? You're sure there's not one more?"

"Not unless a new one has sprung up since yesterday."

A long pause hung in the air between them. "I don't suppose you would consider... ?"

"Baby-sitting?" she queried, with an air of absolute horror. "Don't even ask." She held up a hand. "I mean it, boss."

"Just for a few days..."

"No way," she said with determination. "Look, I'll call Mr. Beckett, okay? Maybe he can think of something."

He couldn't blame Helga. He didn't want to deal with the thorny issue of his children, either.

Alex began to pile up documents to hand over to Peter, but he was too preoccupied with his dilemma to concentrate on what he was collecting.

"What's up?" Peter Beckett asked calmly, strolling into the room with his hands in the pockets of his custom-made suit. "God, you look awful."

"Thanks." He began to sort through the papers more quickly.

Peter, too, was a rising young exec at Dateline/Dynasty. Not rising quite as quickly as Alex, but he had potential. Even so, he wasn't as cutthroat as a lot of the other stars at D/D. In fact, Peter Beckett had integrity and loyalty, which was exactly why Alex had added him to his staff in the broadcast media division.

"I'm giving you the L.A. deal," Alex said abruptly, handing over the files. "If you go over this on the plane, you ought to be able to bluff your way through the fiber-optic meetings. Helga will call and let the Kyoto people know I had a family emergency and you'll be filling in. If you have any problems, you can call me at home."

"Got it." Peter narrowed his eyes. "Family emergency, huh? Your kids again?"

"Yeah." He swung his briefcase off the desk and headed for the door. "This time they tied up the housekeeper and threw her clothes off the balcony. Then they called the fire department. And the police. Just for fun."

"Ouch," Peter said with obvious sympathy. "So what are you going to do?"

"I haven't got a clue."

"Got any relatives who'd take them for a while?"

"Nobody on my side. Puff's parents... Well, even if they would take them, which I doubt, let's just say I'm not sending my kids off to live in the casinos at Monte Carlo."

"Boarding school?" Peter suggested.

"Tried it. Six schools have sent them back."

"Well, I'm out of suggestions."

"Yeah," Alex said gloomily, "me, too." His briefcase bulging with papers, he strode out the door.

"Alex," his friend called, "there is one other thing..." He turned back. "Yeah?"

"Well, I hesitate to bring this up, but what the hell?"

"Anything, Peter, anything."

"Okay." Peter shrugged. "Before I was transferred to broadcast, I did some PR work in the print division, and I saw the endorsements for this woman. A lot of people say her approach really works."

"I'm desperate," Alex vowed. "I'll take anything."

"It's Sabina Charles."

"Who?"

"Oh, come on, you must've heard of her." Peter plucked a fat hardcover book off one of Alex's shelves. The books had been provided by the company for decorative purposes; Alex didn't even know what was up there. "She was a big soap star, then did her own makeup line, some kind of infomercials. A few years ago she started writing these books, guides on just about every subject under the sun. The *No-Fuss* guides have put Daybreak Books, which just happens to be a wholly owned subsidiary of our very own Dateline/Dynasty, on the map. Big-time."

He held up the book, displaying the front of the dust jacket.

The Sabina Charles No-Fuss Guide to Parenting, it read, with the author's name in swirling pink script above the title.

Alex's hopes dwindled. Peter's big solution was no more than a lousy self-help book. "I don't have time for books," he said, hefting his briefcase, ready to go.

"I don't know, Alex." Peter gave him a shrewd look. "Do you really have time to turn your back on an answer to your prayers?"

"Oh, come on. How can one book fix my life when thirty-five nannies and housekeepers have already failed?"

His friend shrugged. "People all over America think Sabina Charles walks on water. They plan their weddings with *The Sabina Charles No-Fuss Guide to Modern Marriage,* and their divorces with *The Sabina Charles No-Fuss Guide to Breaking the Ties.* They cook with *The Sabina Charles No-Fuss Guide to Low-Fat Cuisine.* They decorate their houses with—"

"Let me guess," he said dryly. *"The Sabina Charles No-Fuss Guide to Home Decor."*

"Something like that."

"I've never stooped to self-help books."

"What have you got to lose?"

That was indeed the question. With his business concerns on hold, his household in chaos and the threat of expulsion from his co-op looming before him, what did he really have to lose?

Alex dropped his briefcase back on his desk. "Give me the book," he said wearily.

Peter handed it over and Alex took a seat long enough to flip it open to the table of contents. "Let's see what we've got here. 'Tranquillity in Infancy,' 'Incomparable Christenings,' 'Ten Steps to a Terrific Toddler.' Who cares? Ah, here we have it—'Taming the Tantrum: How to Instill Discipline with Decorum.' "

"Sounds like what you need," Peter put in hopefully.

But as he skimmed the first few paragraphs, Alex saw one thing written all over the book. Patience, it said. Which was the one thing he couldn't afford.

He slammed the book closed and pushed it away. "Good try, but slow and steady is just not my style. Not me, Peter. I don't have time to read the book, and I certainly don't have time to start some system. I need results *now,* immediately." He frowned. "There has to be some way to slice right through all the gobbledygook and solve this thing—" he snapped his fingers "—like that."

No solutions presented themselves. Until his eyes fell to the picture on the back of the dust jacket in front of him.

"Sabina Charles," he murmured.

"Beautiful, isn't she?"

"Perfect," Alex said slowly. Her shiny blond hair fell into a sleek pageboy, skimming just below the chin. Her soft blue eyes seemed calm and wise, infinitely soothing, as if she had answers to all the questions that plagued him.

Classy, elegant, impeccably groomed. She was the very image of the perfect wife and mother.

And she bore a striking resemblance to the late Puff Thornhill.

Alex yanked open the back cover, searching for her bio.

Sabina Charles is best known for her role as Serenity on the daytime drama "Hope Springs Eternal." Miss Charles has been nominated for four Emmy awards, and is also the creator of bestselling makeup, jewelry and clothing lines. Now retired from television, this single mother spends her time sharing her solutions for coping with today's busy world through her fabulously successful series of *No-Fuss* guides, which have brought "serenity" to the lives of millions of readers worldwide. Sabina Charles lives in New York City with her young son, Remington, and five Welsh corgis.

Balancing makeup, jewelry, clothing, writing, a young son, five dogs... Bringing serenity to the lives of millions...

And she was single.

Was there anything this woman couldn't handle?

Still staring down at the flawless photograph, Alex sat up straight in his leather chair. He smiled for the first time that day—for the first time in a good long while.

"What's with the grin?" Peter asked. "Decided to give Sabina Charles a try, after all?"

"Precisely," Alex announced with a certain smugness.

"Well, good. But I thought you didn't have time to read the book."

"I have a simpler idea in mind."

"Yeah?" Peter asked slowly, narrowing his eyes.

Alex shrugged. "She's single. I'm single. And she's the one person who can handle all my problems." He saw understanding break over his colleague's face.

"You're going to ask her out? Alex, you can't—"

"Of course I can." Once again, he gathered up his briefcase, but this time with a bit more aplomb. "And I'm going to do more than ask her out. I need a permanent solution."

"Permanent? What are you saying?"

With all the confidence of a man who had been named number three on a list of New York's most eligible bachelors not two months before, he declared, "If I want a wife, I don't think I'll have any problem getting one. And Sabina Charles is quite obviously the perfect wife for me."

"A wife?" Peter choked. "A bit more goes into it than picking somebody off the back of a book. Think about this, Alex."

"I have. And this is the solution I was looking for." His smile widened. "You said yourself she's an expert on absolutely everything. So I just superimpose her on my household and my life goes back to clear sailing. A nanny can quit, but a wife is around for the long haul."

Peter shook his head in disbelief. "But you've never even met her!"

Alex shrugged. "Details," he said, as easily as if he were discussing his plans to buy another network. He hadn't gotten where he was by allowing himself to be bogged down by details. "She writes for Daybreak Books. We own them. How difficult can it be to arrange a meeting?"

"Don't you think you should find out if you like her, if you can love her, before you decide to marry the woman?"

"I'll like her. What's not to like?"

"But marriage, Alex—"

"Is a partnership. A contract." He took a step toward the door. "So what if there's no grand passion? That kind of thing just gets in the way. It muddies the waters."

"But, Alex—"

He shook his head. "No, Peter, I'm sure on this one. What you really need is a basic understanding of the rules of the game. Tolerance, space, the ability to look at the situation dispassionately—that's what's important. If this Sabina Charles is anything like I think she is, and she must be to write those books, then she's exactly what I need."

As he passed through the outer office with Peter sputtering behind him, Alex added, "Helga, put together a file on Sabina Charles. I want more than the usual PR stuff. Go as in-depth as you can. Call whomever you have to at Daybreak Books. I doubt it will be a problem when they know the request is coming from this far upstairs."

"Sure, boss. Anything else?"

Alex gave her an arrogant smile. "No, I think that will do it."

MEG KACZMAROWSKI SLAMMED down the receiver with a vengeance. "Who is this guy?" she demanded. "Who the heck does he think he is?"

"I haven't the slightest." Sabina Charles, idol to millions, examined her manicure intently. "Oh, dear. This color is much too pink. I wanted peach. Peach is my trademark color."

"Yeah, I know." Meg glanced around at the luxurious living room of the three-story town house that comprised Sabina Charles, Incorporated. The place was entirely decorated in shades of cream and peach, with just a hint of apricot for variety. The Sabina Charles signature. "You always dressed in peach when you played Serenity, so peach it must be, forevermore."

"I didn't play Serenity," Sabina corrected. "I *was* Serenity."

"Sorry." Meg was busy looking for the corrected galleys on the upcoming *No-Fuss Guide to a Glorious Garden,* and she didn't have time to fool with Sabina's nail polish problems. Especially when some high-muckety-muck from the company that owned the company that owned Daybreak Books, their publisher, was driving her crazy. "Sabina, are you sure you don't know this guy?"

"What guy?"

"This..." She found the slip of paper with his name scrawled on it. "Alexander Thornhill. I guess he's some major player at the top of the Dateline/Dynasty hierarchy. Right up there in the stratosphere. Vice president of broadcast media. Broadcast media—what would he want with information about you?"

"Maybe he likes my books." Sabina shrugged her slender shoulders, encased this morning in a lovely silk caftan—peach, of course, washed with subtle streaks that almost made it to orange. "Or maybe he was a big 'Hope' fan. It's not unusual. Men want to meet me all the time."

"Well, this one is a real pain."

"Alex Thornhill, did you say?" She narrowed her exquisite sapphire blue eyes. "I may have heard of him, actually. I've never met him, but I think I saw his picture in some magazine article about Manhattan's most eligible bachelors." Tipping her chin up to catch the light at a more flattering angle, Sabina smiled her patented pearly white smile. "You know I keep my eye out for single men with money. Let me think—not terribly social, too busy doing whatever he does to rake in the bucks to make the scene. And quite adorable, if he's the one."

"He may be Robert Redford in the flesh—"

"No, he has dark hair. More like, oh, I don't know, Pierce Brosnan, Timothy Dalton, that type."

"Oh, yeah?"

Intrigued in spite of herself, Meg paused. Many of her own fantasies involved that precise type of man. She blamed it on her mother letting her stay up late to watch too many Cary Grant movies when she was a kid.

Resolutely, she put the delicious images of tall, dark, elegant men out of her mind. "Well, forget about it, Sabina. Whether he's good-looking or not, the last thing we need is some vice president from Dateline/Dynasty nosing around."

"I don't see what you're so upset about." Sabina glided over to the window seat to pour herself a glass of expensive mineral water. "The books are selling like hotcakes—Lord knows I'm wearing myself out doing publicity appearances—and Daybreak seems to be simply thrilled with the product we're giving them. So what is there to worry about?"

Usually, Meg really enjoyed working for Sabina. The hours were good unless they were close to deadline, the pay was great, and the town house where they toiled, putting together all those sinfully successful how-to books, was absolutely fabulous. Sabina herself was nice enough, even though she was undeniably vain and not all that bright.

But sometimes, every once in a while, the overwhelming composure and tranquillity that clung to her employer were a bit annoying. Like today.

"This guy has asked Daybreak for photos, bios, press releases and copies of every interview you've ever done. Well, you can imagine what Daybreak's PR department did with the request," Meg said sharply. "They passed it on to me. And I don't have time for this nonsense. Besides," she added with more than a hint of irritation, "I want to know why he wants all this stuff!"

"Oh, they probably want to send me off to their shareholders meeting to make nice with the bigwigs or something." She brightened. "You said he was in the broadcast department, right? Maybe they want to give me my own TV show. Everyone who's anyone has a talk show these days."

"I really doubt that's it." Meg could just imagine Sabina with her own talk show. What a concept... *Mr. President, I'm so glad you could join me. Have you ever seen 'Hope Springs Eternal'? And what did you think of me?*

Meg shook her head. "I keep wondering if maybe something is up. Maybe the powers-that-be have heard something, you know, about *you.*" She chewed on her thumbnail. "Do you think that's it? Do you think they found out?"

"No, of course not." Sabina adjusted the sleeve of her caftan. "How could they know?"

"Have you said anything to anyone?"

"Of course not. Have you?"

"Why would I? I'd be out of a job!"

"They don't know anything," Sabina assured her. "You're being paranoid, Meg. And you know, all this anxiety is very bad for you. Worrying adds wrinkles."

"I know. It was in the *No-Fuss Guide to Less Stress.*"

"So don't worry."

But then the phone rang.

Meg looked at Sabina, and Sabina looked at Meg. The phone kept ringing.

Meg finally picked it up. It didn't take long to find out what the caller wanted. Hanging it up slowly, she tried not to panic. "And you think I'm being paranoid. That was *him* again."

"Same guy? Alex Thornhill?"

"Yes. Or his secretary, anyway. Do you know what he wants this time?"

"I haven't the slightest."

"He wants a date," she said darkly. "With you."

"Oh, well then, that's all right."

"It is not all right. I told the woman there was no way."

Sabina shrugged. "I'll go out with him."

"You will not. It's too dangerous."

"Oh, don't be silly. He's a man, isn't he? I can handle *men.*"

"Sabina, he's also a vice president at Dateline/Dynasty," Meg said with spirit. "If he finds out—"

"He won't find out."

"You don't know that."

Sabina frowned down at her manicure. "I'm going to have to get this fixed before I see anyone. This is entirely too pink." And she swept off, gliding along with her trademark Serenity stride. As she neared the double doors to the hall, she turned back to Meg. "If he calls again, accept, all right?" She smiled. "As long as he wants to take me somewhere nice."

But Meg had no intention of setting up a date between Sabina and such an obvious threat to their security. "If he calls again," she said under her breath, "I'll tell him where he can go. And it will not be anywhere near Sabina Charles."

Chapter Two

If you are feeling a bit nervous about facing a first-date situation, never fear. Keep the following three simple rules in mind and all will go smoothly.

1. Show up. It is never polite to spot a blind date from across the room, decide you don't like what you see and then bolt. On the other hand, if you have good reason to suspect your date is married, a fugitive from justice or a member of a cult, a plausible excuse accompanied by a discreet exit is acceptable.

2. Plan ahead. You may even wish to prepare a list of conversational topics. Going so far as to write them on your shirtsleeve or the palm of your hand is probably excessive, however.

3. Be yourself. Pretending to be a celebrity, puffing up your résumé, hiding the fact that you are married, a fugitive from justice or a member of a cult, or otherwise obfuscating the truth will only cause you problems in the long run...

—*The Sabina Charles No-Fuss Guide to Dating*

Alex awoke with a jolt. Where was he? What time was it?

He rubbed his eyes with a nagging sense that all was not well. Sofa. The sofa in the living room.

Okay, he knew where he was. And it was daytime. It was also very quiet. Too quiet.

Sitting up, Alex looked around the still room, wondering why he was so groggy. This was very unlike him. He never took naps. And he certainly didn't remember starting this one.

He'd been watching that damn shopping network, trying to figure out why it was going over so poorly, while the girls—

The girls. He leapt to his feet. He was supposed to be watching his daughters this afternoon. All by himself.

He had way too much work to do to spend a whole day at home, but he didn't have any choice. Helga had found him a new nanny, bless her soul, but the woman was coming from Prague and she wouldn't arrive in the U.S. for another twenty-four hours. Which meant that Alex was alone with his children until she got there.

Pretty scary stuff.

The last thing he remembered, Lolly and Sydney had been sitting on the love seat across from him, quietly dressing and undressing a series of dolls, while he took notes on what exactly the dimwits at Shop-Net were doing wrong. He had been congratulating himself on how well it was going—the girls were presenting no trouble at all—and wondering why all those nannies had failed so miserably.

There was nothing to this child care stuff. You made it clear that they were to create no noise or other disturbance, you ordered food to be brought up every once in a while and you provided them with a nice variety of toys to keep them occupied. Nothing to it.

Except, where were his children? And why was it so quiet?

His unease was growing by leaps and bounds as he stood and looked around the large formal living room. But Sydney and Lolly were no longer there. There was no mess, either—the red Italian love seat was spotless, the Louis XVI chair was still standing on its beautiful little gilded legs and the Renaissance tapestry over the mantel hadn't been touched. The television had even been turned off and the armoire doors closed in front of it.

In fact, the living room looked as lovely and immaculate as it always had when Puff was running the show.

Alex quickly checked their bedrooms and bathroom, but the girls weren't there, either. His room? No. Master bath? No, although his bathtub was full of strange green streaks, which gave him pause.

On closer examination, he discovered a tiny green handprint on the wall and a mostly empty jar of poster paint tipped into the wastebasket. Paint. At least he had some idea of what they'd been doing, although why they were painting in his bathroom, he had no idea.

Further search yielded no clues. They were not in the kitchen, the dining room, the maid's room; they were not even hiding in the pantry.

Where were the girls? Had they run away while he was napping?

Just when he was about to get really frantic, he heard a flapping noise coming from the balcony. What could that be? Surely even his children wouldn't have strung sheets together and climbed down twelve stories!

Quickly, he strode to the French doors on the Central Park side of the living room. He peered out at the plants on the terrace. Were the girls hiding out there, tucked behind a pot of geraniums?

He took a deep breath and opened the doors. No, they weren't on the terrace. It was empty except for the planters and the flower pots—and that damned flapping noise, which was much louder now.

But they'd been there. Grimly, Alex leaned out past the knots of white fabric at the ends of the long flower box, far enough to get a glimpse of his daughters' latest handiwork. It was a long, wide banner, splashed with hideous, glowing green paint. Help! it read, with a large arrow pointed back up at his apartment.

As he reeled it in and untied it, he couldn't miss the cluster of people gathered on the street twelve stories below him, all staring up at his terrace. Pointing and whispering no doubt, wondering what kind of lunatics lived up there. And then he heard the whir of a helicopter.

Oh God. A police helicopter was circling his building, no doubt on the lookout for kidnap victims or something. He was ruined.

And he was going to kill his children. If he ever found them.

Then he heard the French doors click behind him. He whirled.

They'd locked the damn doors.

"Lolly! Sydney!" he shouted. "Open these doors at once. Do you hear me?"

They were giggling. With her blond curls in disarray and a splash of green across one cheek, Lolly was rolling on the floor on the other side of the doors. Sydney's sleek blond bob was perfectly in place, as always, just as her mother's had been, and her giggles were much more refined, behind her hand. But she was still laughing. At her own father.

He really was going to kill them.

Alex pounded on the glass. "Either let me in now or I'll send you both to military school in Switzerland!"

Was that even a legitimate threat to throw at female children? He had no idea. He was too furious to care.

But his daughters were too young to fully appreciate just how angry their father was. And he felt that familiar dizzy, floundering sensation he got whenever he was around them. He had no idea what to say or what to do or how to make them obey.

Out of control. Alex Thornhill was out of control.

He wished he had that damn parenting manual out here with him, although he doubted it had a chapter on what to do if your kids locked you out on a twelfth-story balcony while half of Manhattan gawked and a helicopter circled. But at least maybe he could have used the damn thing to throw through the door and break the glass.

Oh God. He was losing his mind. He had once thought there was nothing he could not handle, or tame, or make his own.

He was wrong.

"Sydney," he said in a low, fierce voice, appealing to the more mature of his two children. "If you do not open this door within the next ten seconds, you will never see the outside of your room again."

No response. But he could tell by the speculative look in her china blue eyes that he had her attention.

"If, on the other hand," he continued in that same no-nonsense tone, "you do open the door, I will send you to FAO Schwartz with a platinum credit card. Anything you want is yours."

Click. While Sydney stood there, considering, Lolly leapt off the floor and unlatched the door.

It appeared he had discovered the secret. Bribery. But what was he going to do once they had everything they wanted? He decided not to think ahead that far. The implications were too troubling.

As he raced back into the apartment, dragging the damn sheet, he herded both children down the hall. "Your behavior has been terrible," he told them. "I am very disappointed in you."

And he was showing it, wasn't he? Sending them to the toy store with a blank check. Oh yeah, he was showing them.

But what could he do? He'd already promised.

"You promised," Sydney said quietly, staring up at him with those serious blue eyes of hers. She took her sister's hand.

"You promised," Lolly added.

They looked like orphans of the storm. Poor, motherless children, with a father who was clueless.

"Go sit in your rooms until I can get someone to take you," he said lamely.

Oh God. He was a disaster as a father and he knew it.

"I need help and I need it now," he said to himself with feeling. And he only knew one way to get it.

He picked up the phone. "Helga, this is Alex. I know you don't want to baby-sit my children, but here's the deal. I'll give you two hundred bucks to get a limo and take them to FAO Schwartz."

There was a pause. "For how long?" she asked finally.

"Long enough for me to run an errand at Beekman Place, wherever that is."

"But isn't that the address I found for—"

"Sabina Charles," he said with determination. "She won't take my calls. So the only thing to do is show up on her doorstep."

Come hell or high water, he was going to talk to Sabina Charles. And he was going to charm her, fascinate her, reel her in until she was so smitten she'd agree to whatever he wanted. Until she'd agree to save him from his own children.

THE PHONE WAS RINGING off the hook this afternoon and Meg was having a tough time getting anything done.

"One more call," she said under her breath, "and I'm going to quit."

She didn't mean it, of course. Actually, she loved her job. Participating in a life like Sabina's, even from the sidelines, was pretty exciting. It was life lived at a faster pace and a higher style than she'd ever dreamed possible. For an ordinary, uneducated person with a certain literary flair, this job was a dream come true.

It was just that sometimes . . .

Sometimes she had way too much to do and way too little time in which to do it. Sometimes she wanted to throw all of the research notes she'd compiled for Sabina's books out the window. Sometimes she wanted to turn off the computer and the phone and take a breather.

And sometimes, just every once in a while, she wanted to be the one in the spotlight, the one who wore the beautiful dresses at the fancy parties, who chatted and laughed with Regis and Kathie Lee, who had dishy vice presidents from multinational corporations calling and begging *her* for dates—

"Oops. Where did that come from?"

Meg didn't have time to consider her wayward thoughts. Instead, she set aside a list of Sabina's publicity appearances she was double-checking and reached for the phone. If it was some secretary calling for that damn Thornhill man again, Meg thought she might scream.

"Sabina Charles's office. What is it?" she said a little more sharply than she'd intended.

"Jeez, are you having a bad day or what?" her favorite sister, Joannie, asked.

"Terrible," Meg said with a sigh.

Of all the people in all the world, Joannie was the only one who might actually understand why Meg was cranky today. The rest of her family just didn't get it. They were so in awe of the famous Sabina Charles that they thought working for her must be a constant party.

Anytime Meg tried to complain, her mother said, "Oh, Meggie, honey, you should be so thankful to have such a terrific job. Count your blessings."

Her other sisters just gave her dirty looks for being uppity enough to live on her own and work in the city, never mind being the assistant to a *celebrity,* for heaven's sake!

Except for Anne-Marie, third from the oldest, who would say, with smug superiority, "You never should've moved out of Brooklyn. You need to find a man and get married and make babies."

Meg had very little tolerance for Anne-Marie.

But Joannie was another matter. Joannie was the fourth of the seven Kaczmarowski sisters, and Meg was number five. Being stuck in the middle as they were had made them allies. And Joannie was the only one among the Kaczmarowski brood who knew the real truth about Meg's job.

"I'm so glad you called," Meg told her. "I needed to hear a friendly voice right about now."

"Oh, poor kid. What's up?" Joannie dropped her voice, as if she thought the phone might be bugged. "Is her highness giving you problems?"

"No, she's fine. I think she's taking a nap." She listened intently for a moment, but she didn't hear any sounds from upstairs. "She's resting up—she has a big party at the Rainbow Room tonight. Sabina needs to zone out with slices of cucumber on her eyes at least five hours before any public appearance."

"So if it's not her, then what's the prob?"

"The usual." She was beset by the normal barrage of details that filled Sabina's world. That plus this Thornhill thing, of course. "I've been trying to get her schedule for next week firmed up, plus type up two new *No-Fuss* proposals and call one more time to find out where her last advance check has run off to, since Daybreak promised me yesterday they'd send it out by messenger. There's also a stack of unanswered fan mail that's so big we could put ropes around it and charge admission."

"And?"

"And what?"

"And what's really bugging you? That stuff is nothing new. I want to know what else there is."

Joannie knew her too well. "Okay, okay. There is one more thing that's kind of been bothering me."

"Yeah?" her sister prompted.

"It's just that it's hard sometimes to sit here and work my buns off while she gets all the glory." Spoken aloud, the statement sounded really petty.

"So quit," Joannie said sensibly. "Forget the *No-Fuss* books and work for somebody else. Or better yet, work for yourself. You're just wasting your time making phone calls and signing somebody else's name to eight-by-ten glossies."

"And if I quit, what would I do?"

"I don't know. Whatever you want. Books, I guess, now that you've worked on Sabina's," Joannie said logically. "Not the self-help kind, but something else. Something better."

"Oh, right, Joannie. Like it would be that easy." Meg sighed. "Do you know how many people in the world think they want to write a book? Millions!"

Like even if she could get anyone to buy what she wrote, the name Meg Kaczmarowski blazoned across the front of a book was never going to get it anywhere. Sabina had the name, the image, the connections—she was the total *No-Fuss* package. Meg was just hired help.

"Besides," she went on, "even if I did write this amazing book and somebody actually bought it and it was a runaway bestseller, what then? You know how Sabina is always schmoozing at charity balls and having cocktails with the rich and famous."

She shook her head. "It's like tonight at the Rainbow Room, where she'll be with a whole bunch of VIPs. That kind of stuff is all part of the package. Can't you just see me at the Rainbow Room?"

"You'd be great!" her sister protested. "You're so funny and cute, they'd love you."

"Do you know last month she had tea with the Queen of England?" Meg swung her red cowboy boots up on the desk and leaned back into her chair, making herself a lot more comfortable. When she and Joannie got going on the phone, it could take a while. "Turns out the queen is a big fan," she said confidentially. "She told Sabina she just loved the *No-Fuss* low-fat cookbook."

"Of course she's a fan. She probably read Sabina's bio, and once she saw the bit about the Welsh corgis, she was a goner!" Joannie laughed into the phone. "I remember when you were trying to decide what kind of dog you should put in the bio. English sheepdogs? Nah, too big to be believable for Sabina. Apricot poodle? Right color, but everybody has poodles. 'I know,' you said, 'Welsh corgis—Queen Elizabeth has those—it's perfect!' Jeez, Meg, that is just too funny.''

She had to admit, it was pretty amusing. But that was years ago, back when she was frantic to finish Sabina's bio before they marketed the very first *No-Fuss* book. Amazing how something that dopey helped garner Sabina an invitation to Buckingham Palace.

"Can't you just imagine me at Buckingham Palace?" Meg asked dryly. "I'd probably step on one of the dogs and spill hot tea on Prince Chuck."

"You're too hard on yourself. I mean, come on, people like Jerry Lewis have been to visit the queen." Joannie added loyally, "You have a lot more class than he does."

"Jerry Lewis? I certainly hope so." They were interrupted by an insistent buzz from the front hall. "Wait a sec, Joannie. There's someone at the door. I've been waiting for Sabina's advance check and that's probably it."

Setting the receiver on her shoulder for the moment, Meg leaned over her desk far enough to hit the buzzer for the front door. She called out, "Come in. Door's open. Just leave it on the desk, will you?"

"Leave what on the desk?" snapped a male voice from the hallway. "What desk?"

"In here. Leave the package, the envelope, whatever," Meg said loudly. "Sorry, Joannie," she whispered into the receiver, "I've got the world's stupidest messenger standing in the hall."

"Do you need to go?"

"Nah." She refused to cut short her personal conversation, which was the most fun she'd had in this pitiful day, just to baby-sit some messenger boy. He could drop his package and scat, just like everybody else.

Except, come to think of it, he didn't sound like a messenger *boy*. More like a man.

"I hope it really is a messenger," she said suddenly. "What if I just buzzed in some religious fanatic or somebody who wants to sell us a vacuum cleaner?"

"Or a crazed crack addict or something," Joannie added helpfully.

Meg twisted her head around to see more of the hall. "Are you out there? What are you doing?" she called out.

"Whatever you do, stay on the phone," her sister commanded.

And then *he* walked in the door. Strolled really, with that easy, bred-in-the-bone elegance that characterized all the movie stars Meg loved best, the ones who just sauntered into the heart of the screen and took your breath away.

Tall, dark, with everything in the right places, head to toe...oh, he was gorgeous all right. Gorgeous and powerful and arrogant. And he was no messenger.

He had an armful of roses—pale *peach* roses—and a scathing look in his eyes that could have melted the Chrysler Building into a pile of warped metal. Blue eyes. The color of sparkling water in a clear stream. Devastating blue eyes.

Naturally. Didn't all the really dreamy ones have blue eyes?

His dark hair was perfectly cut, and his clothes reeked of money and good taste, of peerless shops on Madison Avenue where the customers were treated like royalty.

Alex Thornhill. She knew it the minute she laid eyes on him.

First she closed her mouth and stopped gaping at him. Then she scrambled to get her feet off her desk and find some semblance of dignity, mumbling, "I'll call you back," as she dropped the phone.

"Meg? Meg?" her sister squealed.

"It's not a maniac—I'll call you back." She hung up quickly.

He just raised a dark eyebrow.

"Can I, uh, help you?" she asked, pulling her jean skirt down over her thighs, wondering how much leg she'd been flashing when she'd had her boots up on the desk as he strolled in from the side.

Oh hell. Alex Thornhill, suave man-about-town, grand high pooh-bah at the company that owned the company that owned Daybreak Books, had gotten a real good look at her little red cowboy boots.

"Can I help you?" Meg asked again. Taking a note from Sabina's book, she put what she hoped was a serene and competent look on her face.

"I'm here to see Sabina Charles," he announced.

Of course he was. After his secretary had tried several times to get through without success, the great man himself must've decided to storm the barricades.

Stalling for time to think of something better, she asked, "Do you have an appointment?"

Smooth as silk, he said, "Yes, as a matter of fact, I do."

The man was shameless. Pointedly, Meg glanced down at the empty appointment book and then back up at him. "I don't think so."

"Since her calendar appears to be empty, it wouldn't seem that I'd need one."

"Well, you know, I can see how you might think that. But the thing is . . ." With a sudden burst of inspiration, Meg fixed a thin smile on her face. "She's not in."

"She's not?"

"No, she's a very busy woman. You know, public appearances and research trips—constantly on the go." Brightly, Meg added, "Here, there, everywhere."

"And when does she write her books?"

"She makes very productive use of her time." Nodding sagely, she asked, "Have you read the *No-Fuss Guide to Time Management*? It's all in there."

"Uh-huh. I'm sure it is."

As he regarded her with a baleful stare, the sound of footsteps came thumping from the floor above them.

Trust Sabina to pick this one time to forget to use her patented ladylike, noiseless glide. Trust Sabina to choose this exact moment to wake up and take off the cucumbers.

"So that's not her?" Alex Thornhill asked, leaning in a bit closer.

Meg would have backed up, but she was trapped at her desk. Meanwhile, he smelled wonderful, with just a hint of expensive cologne wafting over the heady scent of all those roses. Peach roses. For Sabina.

Get rid of him before Sabina spots those roses. She'll be on him like a rottweiler with a T-bone.

"No, that must be the . . . dog. Er, dogs. Five of them, you know."

"The dogs?"

"Right. That's Sabina's room right above us and the dogs are probably, uh, romping around."

"Aren't they Welsh corgis?"

Someone had been reading Sabina's bio. Meg braved it out. "Yes, that's right."

"That sounds a lot bigger than a Welsh corgi."

"Well, sounds can be deceptive in an older building like this." She paused. "The echo, you know."

"Right."

Tap-tap, tap-tap.

Crisp, rhythmic and very audible. Meg knew what the noise was.

Sabina typing. She had an old manual typewriter that clacked louder than Santa and all his reindeer, which she used for her personal notes. She said the old thing made her feel like a real writer, like Hemingway or something. But did she have to use it *now?*

"And what's that?" Alex asked in an oh-so-casual tone that let her know he didn't believe a word she said. "Sounds like a typewriter. Do the dogs type?"

"I'm sure one of them is just...standing on the keys or something. Those little devils." Meg smiled bravely.

"Uh-huh."

Balancing the roses as if they were the merest trifle, he rested one hip on the desk, bending in even closer. About another inch and he'd be breathing on her.

"Listen, Miss..." He picked up her nameplate with his free hand. "Miss Kaczmar—"

"Kaczmarowski," she said delicately. "It's not really that complicated."

"Yes, well...Meg," he said, obviously surrendering to the impossible syllables of her last name, "I'm sure you are a very loyal employee, and I'm sure you think you're just doing your job, playing watchdog for your boss. But it's not necessary. In fact, it's rather foolhardy."

"I'm not—"

"Oh, yes, you are." He smiled. She really wished he wouldn't. His smile made her want to fall to her knees and promise him anything, if only he'd keep smiling at her that way.

Meg stared at the pencil she was holding, pretending it was something very interesting.

"Meg, do you know who I am?"

What am I? An idiot?

Luckily, righteous indignation won out over the drool factor. As a little person herself, from a long line of little people, Meg found it really annoying when fat cats tried to pull rank.

"As a matter of fact, I know exactly who you are." She lifted her chin. *Power to the people!* "And it doesn't make any difference. Sabina isn't interested, and she doesn't want to go out with you."

"I'd like to hear that from her, if you don't mind."

Meg stared him down. "Well, you aren't going to because I told you—she's not here."

"Meg dear, is there something wrong?" Sabina's mellifluous voice asked from the doorway. She was lounging there, lovely and cool and definitely present, in body as well as spirit.

Meg stifled a groan. Her goose was cooked.

Fresh from her nap, wrapped in a peachy robe, Sabina looked like every man's fantasy. And Alex Thornhill was showing every sign of lining up with all the rest of the guys. "I'd recognize you anywhere," he said with a lazy smile, striding right over and offering the roses.

"For me?" Sabina preened. "And in my color, too."

"Of course. When I want a lady's attention, I do my research."

Oh, puh-leez. Meg was about ready to lose her lunch.

"Sabina, having read your books, I feel as though I already know you."

Meg tried not to choke too loudly. Anybody who judged Sabina by her books was in for a big surprise.

"I hope you'll agree to have dinner with me," he murmured.

"She can't," Meg said loudly. "She's busy."

"Is she busy the way she wasn't here?"

"What?" Sabina asked, clearly perplexed by the murky currents running past her in the room.

"Nothing," Meg snapped.

Alex just smiled, all calm and arrogance. She wanted to smack him.

"I'd love to have dinner with you," Sabina said sweetly.

"The Rainbow Room," Meg said pointedly, aiming her words in Sabina's direction and ignoring that Thornhill man. "Reception for the governor's wife. Tonight. Remember?"

"Oh, yes. Unfortunately, I have a prior engagement," Sabina cooed. "But some other night..." She proffered a hand to be kissed.

"Tomorrow?" he murmured.

This was going too far. Meg felt as if she were watching "The Dating Game," right here in the living room.

"You're going to Atlanta in the morning," Meg put in with determination. "You'll be gone for the rest of the week."

"Call me next week, first thing," Sabina whispered in his ear. "We'll find you a spot on the schedule."

"Next week?" He looked momentarily taken aback, as if it were on the tip of his tongue to protest that he couldn't wait that long. He was going to ask her to postpone her trip; Meg could just see the thought forming in that clever, manipulative brain of his.

"Sabina," she reminded, "better go get ready." She tapped her watch, indicating there were only a few hours left before the Rainbow Room gig.

"Adieu," the woman whispered, and Alex reluctantly backed away.

"Soon," he said softly. And then, with a last malevolent look at Meg, he took off.

She waited for the front door to close before she turned on Sabina. "What do you think you're doing?" she demanded. "You're crazy to even consider going out with him."

But Sabina didn't turn a hair. "I'd have to be crazy to pass him up."

"You can't do it." Meg stood her ground. "When he calls, you'll have to make some excuse to get rid of him."

"I don't think so," Sabina said coolly.

"He'll find out, Sabina. You know he will. He's smart. No offense, but you're not." Her boss sent her a mildly irritated glance, but that was it. They both knew who was in the right here. Unfortunately, Sabina's ego was now involved. And when it came to a battle between Sabina's common sense and her ego, the latter would win hands down.

"Please," Meg implored, appealing to whatever reason her boss had left. "Don't go out with him. We stand to lose everything."

"He won't find out," Sabina replied breezily.

"How can you stop him?"

"If I go out to dinner with that man," America's most famous advice-giver purred, "the last thing we'll be doing is talking about my books."

"But, Sabina—"

Meg was talking to thin air. Sabina was already waltzing up the stairs, humming some romantic tune, paying no attention whatever to Meg's commonsense objections.

"This is a disaster in the making," Meg called after her, refusing to give in. "You know it as well as I do."

Even though there was no answer from up above, Meg sat back down at the desk and resolved to think of some way to pull the fat from the fire.

"It's not too late," she said to herself, trying to stay calm. "I'll think of something. Because there's no way I'm going to let those two get together. No way."

Chapter Three

Many people are frightened by social occasions such as dances and balls, no matter whether it's a gathering of Astors and Vanderbilts or your twentieth high school reunion in Flatbush. Chin up! Be brave! Consider this a new challenge to be met and mastered. Simply stride right in and make yourself part of the party. And remember, it's a new age—if you lack for partners, whether you are male or female, do not be afraid to reach out, to look the likeliest prospect in the eye, and ask this paragon to dance...

—*The Sabina Charles No-Fuss Guide to the Social Life*

Ensconced in the privacy of her own apartment, with the TV in front of her, her feet up on the couch and her cordless phone at her ear, Meg related the afternoon's events to Joannie.

"And then, even though I had already reminded her that she was busy, she said to him, in this really mushy voice, 'Oh, Alex, I'd love to go with you.'" She paused for effect. "So then I told her, in no uncertain terms, that she absolutely, positively, no way in hell could go with him."

"You told her that?" Joannie gasped.

"Well, yeah." A little defensively, Meg continued, "She has to go to the Rainbow Room tonight. It's a reception for the governor's wife, for crying out loud. I just told her what should've been obvious, even to her. So then he asked for tomorrow, but," she said with satisfaction, "I put the kibosh on that, too."

"Meg, I can't believe you!"

"This is serious stuff. I couldn't fool around, could I?"

"But doesn't she get mad when you boss her around like that?" Joannie asked, still obviously agog over these latest developments in the Sabina-meets-Thornhill incident.

"Well, no." Meg shook her head. "For one thing, Sabina never gets mad at anything. And for another, we both know I'm right this time."

"But, Meg," Joannie protested, "if you're not careful, you could ruin the whole deal. I mean, how many times have you told me you're sitting pretty there?"

At the moment, she really was sitting pretty in her cozy apartment with a new TV and VCR, nice furniture, a fridge stocked with premium ice cream and Chinese takeout... all the things she stood to lose if she screwed up her job. Meg sat up straighter on the couch. "Weren't you the one who told me just today that I should ditch Sabina and go out on my own?"

"Well, yeah, but I didn't think you'd really do it," Joannie said lamely.

"Don't worry. I wasn't planning on it." Gaining confidence, she added, "But Sabina won't fire me, no matter how mouthy I get. She can't."

"But what if she—I mean, couldn't she find someone else to do your job?"

"No way." Of that Meg felt sure. "That's why this is so infuriating. She has as much to lose as I do—maybe even more. I mean, she's a public person. The fallout could ruin her, or at least make her a joke in Letterman's monologue. Remember what happened to those singing Milli Vanilli guys with all the hair?"

"Huh?"

"Never mind. All I'm trying to say is that it would be terrible for Sabina. Whereas I'd just be out of a job."

"That's the worst that could happen?" Joannie asked dubiously.

With a sigh, Meg faced reality and answered the question. "The worst? No books, no job, no rent money, and I end up in Brooklyn living with Ma, working at the bakery, with Anne-Marie two houses away."

Joannie shuddered. Although they'd both had jobs at their parents' Polish bakery when they were growing up, it wasn't something they wanted to go back to. "That's pretty scary."

"I know." Shaking her head, Meg added, "I can't believe Sabina is being this foolhardy. She's willing to risk everything for a couple of laughs with a stiff like Alex Thornhill."

"Oh, so he's a stiff?"

"No, he's not," she said gloomily. "That's the problem." Still cradling the phone, Meg got up off the sofa and took a walk to pick up the remote control for the TV. She switched off the tape of her soaps, unable to handle the distraction. Normally, she could do three things at once, but right now she needed all her wits about her. "You see, Joannie," she explained, "this guy is trouble.

You just look at him and you can feel *trouble* in the pit of your stomach."

"The pit of your stomach, huh? Are you sure trouble is what you're feeling?" Her sister's tone took on a hint of mischief. "It might not be, say, lust or something?"

"No way," she returned. "Okay, okay. So he is definitely your basic A 1 dreamboat."

"I thought so," Joannie said with a sigh. "Trouble in the pit of your stomach . . ."

"But still," she argued, "when you think about losing everything, is it really worth it to Sabina, even if he is the most gorgeous, the most brilliant, the most—"

"Are you kidding? If he's half as fabulous as you say he is, of course it's worth it," Joannie interjected.

"I don't need to hear this." Meg began to chew on her thumbnail, which was something she never, ever did. She had great nails, long and hard and polished bright red at the moment to match her cowboy boots. "Even worse, he's read the books," she said, narrowing her eyes. "Five minutes alone with her and there's no way he wouldn't catch on to the whole thing."

"Okay, so he's a threat. But you said you put the kibosh on it, right? I mean, there's no date, right? No date, no danger."

"For now. Luckily she was busy tonight and she's leaving for Atlanta in the morning." She reflected moodily for a moment. "But Mr. Steamroller Thornhill wasn't happy about it. I know he'll call her as soon as she's back. And then we start all over with me running interference. How long can I keep it up?"

"As long as you have to," Joannie contributed. "But what I really don't get is why he's pushing this. Do you really think he's that much of a goner over Sabina?"

"I don't know. I don't think so," Meg confided, pacing more quickly now.

Men were always interested in Sabina, and Alex Thornhill was a man, wasn't he? But no matter what his motivation, it didn't seem warranted. Sure, Sabina was beautiful, but she was also a first-class flake, with her breathing exercises and her cucumber slices and her entire world of peach. Weren't vapid thirty- something beauties a dime a dozen? If he was really attracted to one-dimensional beauty, there were tons of twenty-year-old supermodels clogging up the airwaves.

And why would he want someone just for beauty anyway? Because it sure seemed as if a guy like Alex Thornhill could get anyone he wanted—somebody who was beautiful *and* smart. But then Meg had never understood men. Maybe skin-deep beauty was enough for Alex Thornhill.

Still doubtful, she said, "I guess it's possible he's really interested in Sabina. I mean, he could be deluded."

"But you don't think so."

"No," Meg concluded, "he's too smart for that. And that's what scares me. If he's not going after Sabina in a romantic way, then what's in it for him? I'm afraid somebody at the top of Dateline/Dynasty is suspicious of our operation and they sent Mr. Steamroller to get the scoop on Sabina, up close and personal."

"So he's, like, going undercover?" Joannie asked, shocked.

"Exactly."

"Ooh, Meggie, that's dangerous."

"I know."

"And if he's as stubborn and pushy as you say," Joannie continued, picking up speed, "I bet he won't wait till she comes back. He'll just follow her to Atlanta!"

Meg sat back down on the sofa, bringing the phone with her. "Oh, jeez. I hadn't thought of that."

"No, Meg, wait! It's worse!"

"How could it be worse?" she lamented.

"Didn't you say you told him she had to go to the Rainbow Room?"

"Yeah, but—"

"And you mentioned the Rainbow Room specifically, by name?"

"Well, yeah, but—"

"I'll bet you anything," Joannie declared in a really excited voice, "right now, that man is headed for the Rainbow Room!"

"You're right," she whispered in horror.

"At this moment, the only thing standing between him and her is *you*. And you're not there!"

"Oh, no. What am I going to do?"

"Throw on a dress and get your bootie to the Rainbow Room," Joannie said sensibly. "Do whatever you have to. Just remember how you could end up—making rum babas and cheese kolachky for the rest of your life, living with Ma, two houses from Anne-Marie."

"But—"

"No buts. You said yourself he'll figure it all out. Your career will be history, Meg," her sister reminded her sternly. "Up to your elbows in flour and yeast and oven mitts, Ma, Anne-Marie..."

"I know, but—"

"Meg, just do it."

Flour, yeast, Ma, Anne-Marie... Did she have a choice?

"THORNHILL," HE ANNOUNCED. "Alex Thornhill."

"I'm sorry, sir, but I don't see…" The girl at the door tipped her head down as she studied her clipboard. All Alex could see was the top of her ridiculous little bellboy hat. But then she glanced up, got a good look at him and her eyes widened. She smiled tremulously. "G-go right in."

It was Alex's credo: If you looked and acted as if you belonged, you belonged. Tonight, he looked like just the sort of affluent businessman they expected at this little soiree. Therefore he was in, whether he was invited or not.

He gave the room a quick once-over, taking in the spectacular view of Central Park and the famous art deco details, none of which really interested him. Soft music, something that brought to mind old black-and-white movies, drifted through the air, sung sensually by a chanteuse in a sequined evening gown. Alex blocked that out, too.

He was a man with a mission.

His gaze swept over clusters of well-dressed party-goers, some chatting, some eating, several couples dancing here and there around the floor. Alex waved away the passing waiters, armed with flutes of champagne and luscious little hors d'oeuvres, unswerving in his quest to find Sabina.

It wasn't hard. She was dancing with an elderly man in a white jacket, smiling and chuckling as he waltzed her around in uneven circles. She had her hair up in a sleek twist, and her dress was a wispy masterpiece of peach chiffon. She looked the very picture of a gracious hostess or an elegant lady about town. Perfect.

With a determined smile, Alex strode right up and cut in, taking her elbow, disposing of her escort, ushering her aside.

The man in the white jacket made some noises of protest, but Sabina just smiled, going along for the ride. Of course she did. Women loved men who took charge.

"Dance?" he asked, not wasting time on excess verbiage.

"Love to," she murmured, batting her eyelashes over crystal-clear blue eyes.

With one swift motion, he pulled her into his arms, moving smoothly to the music, not saying anything for a moment.

"You dance divinely," she purred.

He offered a slow smile, calculated to set her pulses pounding. "Thank you."

But her pulses didn't seem to be pounding. In fact, she didn't seem to be anything at all. Her half smile never wavered, her cool gaze never lost its tranquillity as she sailed through the dance as easily as if she were doing it at home by herself.

Alex was a bit taken aback. He usually had more of an effect on women than that.

Like this afternoon, for example, with Sabina's little brunette watchdog. Meg Kaczma-whatever-it-was. A very odd young woman. Yet she'd reacted to him, hadn't she? He had to admit, however, that her reaction was a lot more unpredictable than most. One look at him and she'd dropped the phone, muttering something about a maniac.

He never had figured out what that was all about. Weird little thing, anyway, what with those goofy cowboy boots, long red nails and generally uncooperative attitude. Everything about her mystified him.

He frowned. He didn't like being mystified. It wasn't in his game plan. But still . . . He wouldn't have minded fixing that miniskirted little wagon once and for all.

"Who was that Meg woman at your office?" he asked suddenly. "Why was she so hostile?"

"Meg is my assistant. She worries too much," Sabina said delicately, "but she's rather sweet. And very smart. Invaluable, you might say."

"But why did she—"

Then it struck him that he finally had the woman he needed right there in his arms and he was talking about somebody else. He shook his head. Even when she wasn't there, that Kaczma-what's-it woman was driving him crazy.

"Don't you think so?" Sabina asked, and he snapped back to attention.

Unfortunately, he had no idea what she'd just asked him. He decided that a compliment would probably smooth things over, no matter what the question. So he murmured, "I'm really enjoying the music and the beautiful woman in my arms."

Sabina gave him a satisfied smile. "Of course you are."

Except that he wasn't. *Keep your mind on the woman in front of you,* he ordered himself. Why was it so difficult? She was beautiful, charming and a skillful dancer. And she might as well have been a hat rack for all the enjoyment he was getting from dancing with her.

But she didn't say anything, just stood there in his arms, sliding along, the perfect dance companion. If you were a department store dummy.

Alex knew he bored easily. It was one of the drawbacks of living life at the pace he did; he was so used to racing from project to project that nothing held his attention for long. But he needed Sabina Charles and he couldn't afford to start yawning on her. So he vowed to make the effort to find her more interesting.

He asked her a few questions about her books—how long she'd been writing them, how she got started, that kind of thing. He knew the basic details from the information Helga had gathered for him, but he thought the real woman might make the cut-and-dried résumé come alive. Instead, her answers were nothing special, delivered in that same soporific style.

"A few years," she said with a wave of one slender hand. "It seemed like a natural outgrowth of my life-long desire to help people."

"Ah. A lifelong desire to help people. How generous of you."

"Thank you."

And then there was silence again. It was very strange how much the gaping silence annoyed him and didn't seem to bother her in the least. He found himself humming along with the singer, who had begun a smoky version of "Let's Face the Music and Dance." At the moment, he was wondering whether facing a firing squad might be more fun.

"And what did you do before the books?" he asked hastily.

"I was Serenity, of course."

"Serenity?"

Sabina flashed him an astonished glance. "Serenity, on the daytime drama 'Hope Springs Eternal.' I won five Soapies and was nominated for an Emmy award four times."

"Oh." Right. He remembered reading that in her bio. But what did he say to that? "Congratulations. I'm sure you were wonderful."

"Yes, I was." She eyed him curiously. "Are you saying you never saw me on 'Hope'?"

"I'm afraid not. I've never seen a, uh, daytime drama."

"You're joking."

"I'm afraid not."

"Oh." She seemed momentarily nonplussed. Since it was the most interesting reaction he'd gotten out of her so far, he wasn't sure he was sorry. "So how do you know me?"

"From the books," he reminded her. "The *No-Fuss* guides. They're wonderful."

"Thank you." She inclined her head gracefully. "We all do what we can."

"Of course." What the hell did she mean by that? "Quite a wide range of topics you've covered. A real Renaissance woman. What's your background for that?"

"I attended a small college in Pennsylvania," she said daintily.

That much was in her bio. Only child of an upper-class family, good schools, undistinguished educational record, moved to New York to take a part on the soap and never looked back. But still... How did a soap opera actress turn into an expert on absolutely everything?

"You must've picked up a lot about human nature along the way."

"Oh, right. I'm an actress. It's part of the job." Again, she waved her hand, this time in the direction of greater Manhattan, visible through the windows. "There is so much out there to be learned, don't you think? And, of course, I rely heavily on experts in the various fields."

From what little he'd actually read from the *No- Fuss* guides on his bookshelves, he would also have said that she relied heavily on her own common sense and rather acerbic wit. Funny she wasn't demonstrating any of that tonight.

"You dance divinely," she said again in that same kittenish tone, as if she hadn't already said it before.

"Thank you," he told her. "You, too." He searched his brain for another topic of conversation. "Peach," he said out loud. "Your signature color. How did that start?"

God, if that wasn't a lame way to spark a rapport.

Just as Sabina opened her perfect lips, no doubt prepared to offer words of wisdom on the general topic of peach as a metaphor for life, a small hand with extremely red fingernails tapped Alex on the arm. Alex recognized those fingernails. And the tension level in the room rose by about a hundred percent.

"Excuse me," Sabina's watchdog interjected. "May I cut in?"

He turned, prepared to give her a piece of his mind. But his words died in his throat.

She looked great. But she didn't look at all as if she had an urge to dance. She was wearing a red halter number that was a few inches too short to be respectable, paired with sheer stockings and tall red heels. As small and curvy as she was, she looked great in the dress.

It was the attitude that needed work. As she raised her chin and stared him down, there was an air of challenge hovering around the slim shoulders of Meg Kaczma-whatever-it-was.

Her short cap of dark curls looked as if it had been tousled by the wind rather than styled, and her ripe, red little mouth, painted in a color to match the fingernails, was curved into a saucy smile. Her round brown eyes sparkled with spirit, as if she were daring him to turn her down and make a scene.

No, she didn't look ready to dance. More like itching to start a fight.

With him. That was a given. And he felt more than ready to fight back. There was something about Miss Kaczma-whosis that brought out his combative instincts. Suddenly he had the urge to grab her and do something ruthless—like dance her around the floor until she dropped or gave in and admitted he was in charge. Whichever came first.

"Hello, Meg dear. What are you doing here?" Sabina inquired with just as much sweet serenity as she'd directed at him.

But the feisty little interloper didn't answer. "What happened to the CBS exec who brought you?" she asked instead.

"He's around somewhere." Sabina waved her hand yet again. "Charming man."

Those vacuous gestures of hers were starting to get on his nerves. "What are you doing here?" Alex asked point-blank, doing his best to glare at Meg, when he had the insane urge to smile at her.

"Cutting in." Her own smile widened as she stood there expectantly, waiting for Sabina to clear out.

Alex spared a glance at his current partner—lovely, perfect Sabina—before sending a helpless gaze back at feisty little Miss Meg, who seemed determined to screw up his plans. How annoying that he was actually looking forward to her interference.

"Are you supposed to be here?" he asked, dredging up a hint of sharpness. "As in, were you invited?"

"Well, not exactly. Just like you, I decided to crash the party," she said sweetly. "Right, Alex? About crashing, I mean?"

"I'm always invited, sooner or later," he returned.

"And this one was later? As in, maybe tomorrow?"

"Do you really think they wouldn't have invited me if they'd known I wanted to come?"

"Do you really think I couldn't get an invitation just as easily as you?"

"Yes, I do."

"Well, I could."

"How? Steal one from your employer?"

Her eyes narrowed. "I never steal."

"Except other people's dancing partners."

Sabina's gaze bounced back and forth between them as the volleys came fast and furious.

"Well," Meg said finally, "are you going to dance with me or not?"

"I don't believe in cutting in," Alex told her, conveniently forgetting that that was how he'd gotten to Sabina in the first place. "Especially not by women."

"Oh, please," she scoffed. "Come on, Thornhill. Get with the nineties, will you?"

Alex raised an eyebrow, not moving an inch. Who told her she could act this way, taking him on, trying to bully him? Normally, people were afraid of him, they deferred to him, they jumped as high as he told them to. But this little snippet of a woman had just called him *Thornhill.* She was ordering him around!

"People are starting to stare," she put in. "And besides, there's the governor's wife, sailing through the door in the purple organza. Don't you think you ought to say hi to Mrs. Guv, Sabina?"

"Oh, I must," Sabina murmured. "She's a big fan from my Serenity days."

As Alex watched, astonished, Sabina glided away in search of the governor's wife. Leaving him with Meg.

"You might as well dance with me," she told him. "You look kind of silly standing there with your mouth open."

Grimly, he caught her hand and swung her into a wide turn. "This is outrageous," he muttered. But he was stuck with her, all in the name of politeness.

When she spun back from the turn, she fitted very nicely into the circle of his arms. Very nicely. And somehow his body had roared to life; all of a sudden, he was positively seething with energy and steam. He set his jaw, determined to ignore the feeling.

"What is this really all about?" he asked darkly, leading Miss Kaczma-whatever backward with a strong hand.

"Excuse me?"

"What are you trying to do?"

"I thought I was trying to dance with you." She gave him a crooked smile. "It's tough when you lead like a Mack truck, but I think I can keep up."

"What you are very obviously trying to do is keep Sabina away from me. I'd like to know why."

"It's what she pays me for." Helpfully, she added, "You know, keep away the pushy fans, the nuts, the potential stalkers."

He almost laughed. "Neither of us thinks for one minute that I'm a stalker."

But Meg just tipped her head to one side and gave him a sardonic look. "Well, you know, that's what a lot of people would call someone who starts phoning someone he's never met and trying to get a date, just because he saw her picture on the back of a book. And then he starts showing up without an invitation wherever she goes. Sounds like a stalker to me."

"Showing up without an invitation wherever the object of her pursuit goes. Hmm," he murmured. "Are you stalking me?"

"Stalking you?" she shot back, her mouth dropping open. "In your dreams, buster."

Alex grinned. It was kind of fun to get a rise out of Little Miss Meg. He picked up the tempo of their dance. "So you crashed this party just to scope me out as a potential crazed fan, hmm?"

"Something like that."

He swung her around into a sudden turn, enjoying the determination on her face as she tried to keep up with him.

"How am I doing? Am I crazed enough for you?"

"I can take it."

Alex led even more fiercely, sliding them between two couples who clearly didn't know what they were doing, heading for a darker corner.

"So how about you?" she asked abruptly. Her cheeks were flushed and the light in her eyes had grown brighter. Was she getting winded? Or just intrigued? "Why are you doing it?"

"Dancing with you?" Alex smiled. "I didn't think I had a choice."

"Very funny." Moving to the music, battling him for the lead, Meg stared up at him, almost as if she were trying to read his mind.

"What?" he asked finally. "What is it?"

"I just can't figure out what you want with Sabina." She pulled her hand off his shoulder long enough to tap a finger against one luscious red lip. "A guy like you. I wouldn't think you'd need to pick people off book covers to get dates, if you know what I mean." Her eyes narrowed. "Not unless you have ulterior motives."

Damn the woman. Ulterior motives? How about two uncontrollable kids in dire need of a mother figure?

All he needed was for Little Miss Big Mouth to go telling Sabina that the only reason he was interested in her was to step in as his new hausfrau and baby-sitter. It was such an attractive image...

He spun Meg faster, twirling her out and back, double-timing the more languid tempo of the music. Thank goodness he could think and dance at the same time. He sincerely hoped Meg had more trouble with it.

"Well?" she asked breathlessly. "Do you have ulterior motives?"

She might be breathless, but he hadn't steered her off course at all. "What can I say? I saw her picture and I was...smitten."

"Uh-huh." She chewed on her lip. "This isn't like some corporate deal, is it?"

"I'm afraid you've lost me now." It was beginning to be a familiar feeling.

"You know, family values and all that," she explained, pressing onward with this latest brainstorm. "Like the bigger bigwigs than you want everybody to be settled down and married, or at least dating somebody presentable. So you decide Sabina is presentable, get a few dates and, bingo, you're in good with the brass."

She was totally on the wrong track. What a relief.

But in his relief, he got careless. As the music swelled, as the singer hit some particularly sultry lyric, Alex tightened his embrace.

Not a good idea. Not a good idea at all.

Suddenly, Meg seemed to be standing a whole lot closer than Sabina had, although their relative positions should have been roughly the same. But this was nothing like dancing with Sabina.

Their eyes met. And held.

This was a whole new ball game.

Out of nowhere, his heart pounded against his ribs. "Moonlight and music and love and romance..."

The singer sailed on, oblivious to his distress. Meanwhile, Alex had the terrible feeling that for the first time in his life, he knew exactly what she was singing about.

Chapter Four

Don't mistake chemistry for compatibility. In the scheme of things, finding someone you can get along with through bad plumbing and male pattern baldness is a lot more important than a sizzle of synapses here and there...

—*The Sabina Charles No-Fuss Guide to Love*

He had the wrong woman and the wrong impulses.

With a supreme effort of will, Alex brought himself back to the subject at hand. Except he couldn't remember what the subject at hand was.

What had they been talking about? Something to do with Dateline/Dynasty. Some harebrained notion that he was pursuing Sabina to make brownie points with the company brass. *Harebrained* was the word for it, especially since he *was* the company brass.

"Dateline/Dynasty doesn't run that kind of operation," he said forcefully, putting some distance between them physically as well as emotionally, spinning her off-balance and away from him. "We don't interfere in employees' personal lives. Besides, even if we did, my image is secure." He shrugged. "I was married. I have two children. So my family values are just fine, thanks."

"You were married?" she asked with obvious curiosity. "So you're divorced now?"

"No." He paused, unwilling to start the onslaught of pity he knew he was going to get. He never spoke about Puff with anyone. But Meg was waiting, still watching him, and he didn't seem to have a choice. "My wife died," he said finally, awkwardly. "A little more than two years ago."

Meg's eyes widened. He saw the light of sympathy there, but something else, as well. Warmth, maybe. "I'm so sorry," she said quickly, catching his arm. "I didn't mean to ask—"

"No, it's okay."

She squeezed his hand gently, and he was surprised at how nice it felt, that quick little jolt of human contact. He was also surprised at how much information he was volunteering here. He never told anyone anything about himself, and yet he'd already displayed his most personal side to Kaczma-whatever, of all people.

She was breezing on, obviously determined not to dwell on something that bothered him. "Two kids, huh?" she asked brightly. "Girls or boys? How old?"

Wound up in their little discussion, he had to think for a minute. "Girls, six and eight. Sydney and Lovell."

"Cute, uh, names. Sydney and Lovell... Well."

"She's called Lolly. Lovell, I mean." He got the distinct impression that children in her neighborhood were not named things like Sydney and Lovell. Were those unusual names? He had no idea. Puff had named them, of course. Everything to do with the children was her domain, not his.

"So, do they look like you? Got any pictures?"

"No, no pictures." What did she think, he was going to carry photos of his children in his suit pocket? Did the men of her acquaintance do that? Shaking his head, feeling again as if he were tripping delicately through a mine field, he said dubiously, "You seem to be awfully interested in my children."

"Sure. I like kids. Who doesn't?"

"Sometimes I'm not sure I do," he said under his breath.

"Oh, all parents feel that way every once in a while." Now the sympathy was out in full force. What was it about her that was making him say these personal things that were none of her business? "I'm sure you have it harder than most, too, since your wife died."

"Things were perfect then," he said moodily. "Perfect."

"Gee, I'm sorry."

Alex just shrugged. "So what about you? Family?"

"Tons of family," she said cheerfully. "I have, let's see, sixteen nieces and nephews at last count. No, wait, seventeen. I forgot to count Kim's new baby. Kim is my youngest sister and she just had her first. Emily Rose, isn't that pretty?"

"Seventeen? Wow." Two seemed overwhelming to him.

"Yeah, I know." Meg grinned, speeding up as she went along. "My sisters have been busy. Teri is the oldest and she has five, three from her first marriage and two from her second. Her first husband, Tony, was a real jerk, but the new one, Phil, is a doll. He's a pediatrician, isn't that great? Darla is second youngest, but she already has four, and Anne-Marie, who's third, has three. Joannie and Rhonda each have two—they're fourth and second oldest—and then Kim just has the one."

Names and numbers were flashing by so fast he felt dizzy. How many sisters did she have? It sounded like about fifteen. And they all had children—lots and lots of children.

When he didn't say anything, Meg added with a great deal of enthusiasm, "It's great at Christmas and holidays. My mom just loves it."

Christmas was great? It sounded like a madhouse.

"So, do your kids look like you?" she asked with a definite spark of curiosity.

Alex peered at her. This conversation was jumping around like a jackrabbit. Besides, she'd started to lead while they were dancing and he was having a hard time wresting back control. "Look like me? My girls? As a matter of fact, no. They both look just like Puff."

Her eyebrows shot up. "Did you say Puff?"

"Yes." He paused. "Why?"

"Look, I'm sorry. I don't mean to bring up painful subjects or anything…" Pulling him along, veering close to another couple, she hazarded another glance his way. "But did you say your wife's name was *Puff?*"

"Yes." He was baffled again. What was this all about?

"I've never heard of anyone named Puff," she said thoughtfully. As she spun him into a turn, she leaned in a bit more closely. "For a person, I mean. There was that cat. You know, Run, Puff, run. See Puff run."

"It was a nickname," he told her, firmly guiding her back in the direction he wanted to go. "For Pamela."

"Oh, right. Well, that's good. I would hate to think that anyone purposely named their child Puff." She laughed, but seemed to catch herself almost immediately. "Oh dear. Look, I'm really sorry," she said in a stricken tone. "I didn't mean to, you know, insult your wife or anything. I didn't mean to make a big deal of it. That's just me, foot-in-mouth disease. I'm sorry."

"I accept your apology," he said finally, mostly because he didn't have a clue how else to respond. He could honestly say he had never had a conversation or a dance partner like this in his entire life.

Off-balance, off guard, being led around by a curvy little woman with big brown eyes and a very short red dress. This whole evening was a new experience.

"Oh, I love this song, don't you?" she whispered.

He hadn't even noticed the song until she mentioned it.

"'Night and Day,'" she prompted, tapping one hand against his chest, over his heart, in soft rhythm. Her eyes were alight with warmth as she began to move to the music, dragging him with her again before he had a chance to object. "'The beat, beat, beat of the tom-tom, that repeats and repeats in my ear...' No, wait, that's not right. How does it go?"

He had no idea. As her hand touched his heart, he could feel the mood suddenly shift around them. Her gaze met his, the song washed over him and Alex was lost in a place he'd never been. Behind Meg, the skyline of the city sparkled, a glittery backdrop for her soft, shiny hair and luminous eyes.

He was suddenly aware of the warmth of her body next to his, smelled the faint, sweet fragrance of her perfume, sensed the motion of her hips and arms pressed so close to his own.

Without thinking, he tightened his arm around her waist, propelling her nearer, whirling her in a new direction. Meg trembled. Her eyes, so deep and dark, framed with spiky lashes, went wide with surprise.

He was pretty damn surprised himself. The dance was a basic fox-trot and it felt like the hottest tango in recorded history. What the hell was happening to him?

But he knew. It was so simple. Their bodies were in tune.

It was bizarre, inexplicable, unthinkable... and happening just the same.

He closed his eyes. They swayed together, feeling the music, the night, the nearness. Alex rubbed his chin against the top of her head, breathing in the soft, irresistible fragrance of her sleek dark hair. He wanted desperately to bend down and cover her mouth with his. He wanted to make love to her, all to the building rhythm of the damn song.

"Meg..." he whispered.

Meg? Alex went still. This was the wrong woman. He was being seductive all right, perfectly according to plan, but with the *wrong woman.*

"What is this?" he asked, and his voice came out huskier, a bit more desperate than he'd expected. But, damn it, this was crazy.

"I—I don't know." She glanced up and he saw innocence, sweetness, the same sort of awe and panic he was feeling, mixed in her eyes.

How had this happened? By design, maybe? Lull him into a false sense of security talking about babies and sisters until, *whammo,* she unleashed the big guns? He knew it wasn't fair, but he couldn't help wondering. "Is this all part of the scam, Meg?" he asked slowly.

She stiffened. "What scam?"

"To keep me away from Sabina."

Her cheeks grew pinker.

"I hit the nail on the head, didn't I, Meg? When the obnoxious act didn't work, did you decide to throw yourself in between us bodily?" he asked. "Keep me away by cozying up to me yourself?"

"I can't believe you would say something like that," she whispered.

"Am I right, Meg?"

Raising her chin, she took a step backward. Her words were clipped and cold when she tossed them at him. "Forget it, Alex. Go slobbering after a pretty picture on the back of a book if that's what you want. I couldn't care less."

And then, with one last look that sent daggers at him, she marched off into the crowd of partygoers around the governor's wife.

"Meg..." he called out, not sure why he was bothering. So what if he'd made her mad? She continued to infuriate him.

But she was gone.

"Sorry it took me so long to get back to you," a honeyed voice whispered from behind him.

He whirled. Sabina, of course. Damn it all to hell. He had completely forgotten about Sabina.

The night was getting older by the minute, he was no closer to achieving his goal, and he had completely forgotten about Sabina.

Alex ran a hand through his hair. He was an idiot. A shortsighted idiot.

When this party was over and he went home, nothing would be changed. Once again, he would face his adorable daughters and their terrible discipline problems. Alone. Meanwhile, he had wasted an entire evening on a very odd little troublemaker who seemed every bit as uncontrollable and exasperating as his daughters.

He needed cool tranquillity, not constant confusion. He needed Sabina—not Meg.

"You are so lovely you simply take my breath away," he said suddenly.

"How sweet," the lady in peach murmured.

Strike fast, he told himself. Before Kaczmarowski had a chance to throw up any more roadblocks. He couldn't risk any more delays, any more missed opportunities. He simply didn't have the time.

And so he jumped. "I think we should get to know each other better, Sabina, away from all these distractions. What do you say to spending the weekend with me, at my house in Connecticut?"

"What a lovely idea."

He gave her his most charming smile. "It will be wonderful."

And if not, well, at least it would be peaceful.

"You're *WHERE?*" Meg shot up in bed, pressing the receiver closer to her ear, as if that would make things clearer. "And with *whom?*"

"I told you—I'm in Connecticut with Alex Thornhill," Sabina returned rather petulantly.

"But you're supposed to be in Atlanta." She flashed a glance at the clock. "I'm supposed to send a car to pick you up at the airport at five this evening. And what in God's name are you doing with Alex Thornhill? Haven't you had enough of that man yet?"

"Oh, I flew in last night." Meg could almost hear the shrug on the other end of the phone. "I'm here for the weekend. He has a lovely place." She paused. "There's just one little problem."

"One?" Meg said with as little hysteria as she could manage. "Aside from the fact that you've completely lost your mind?"

"Meg, everything is fine. Besides, I didn't see you avoiding him at the Rainbow Room the other night." Slyly, Sabina added, "Are you saying it's okay for you to talk with him, but not me? What's the difference, Meg?"

"The difference is that I wasn't just talking—I was working. I was trying to figure out what he's up to," she said defensively.

Oh, yeah. Right. Like she was some paragon of virtue. Like she hadn't just said whatever popped into her mind, not bothering to be careful or crafty at all. Like she hadn't rambled all over the place about his kids and her family... and the fact that his wife was named Puff.

Meg winced. The whole evening had been a disaster.

"Alex told me you didn't object anymore," Sabina went on sweetly. "He said that was the last thing you told him before you left."

"Well, actually, that's technically true," she admitted reluctantly. "I did say..."

But it was hardly fair for him to take her literally when she was just trying to toss out a good exit line. What had she said? Something unkind about slobbering after a pretty picture. She winced again. Why hadn't she kept her mouth shut and stayed away from Alex Thornhill in the first place?

"Well, Sabina, I suppose you couldn't possibly do any worse than I did." Actually, she could. As clumsy as Meg had been, she still hadn't let anything important slip. At least she didn't think so. But Sabina...

A vision of Sabina, arm in arm with Alex Thornhill, gazing at the sunset, filled her mind. She wanted to throw up. And it had nothing to do with the potential threat that Sabina might say more than she ought to about their little *No-Fuss* operation.

No, nothing like that. What this was all about was the fact that she had danced with him and chatted with him and basked in the warmth of his lovely blue eyes.

What this was all about was that she found Alex Thornhill wildly attractive herself. And now, more than ever, she didn't want him anywhere near Sabina.

And it had nothing to do with job security.

Resolutely, she pulled herself back from that precipice. He was after Sabina, he was way out of her league and he was a very dangerous man. Staying away—far, far away—was the only reasonable choice.

Now if she could only get Sabina to agree.

"Meg, are you still there?"

"Yes, I'm here." Whatever Sabina spilled or didn't spill, there was nothing Meg could do about it, she told herself firmly. There was no way she could step in again. It was too humiliating.

And if Sabina lost them both their jobs, so be it.

"So I'm back to rolling out mazurkas and frying doughnuts at five in the morning," she mumbled. "Me and Anne-Marie, side by side, up to our necks in powdered sugar and poppy seeds."

"What?" Not waiting for an answer, Sabina swept on. "Meg dear, never mind that now. I have a teensy-weensy problem, and I need you to fix it for me."

"That's my job," she murmured. For as long as it lasted.

She could just imagine what this was going to involve. Tracking down a weekend's worth of peach nail polish and having a messenger schlepp it out to Connecticut, maybe? Nail polish, okay, but if it was lingerie or anything remotely erotic, there was no way...

"The thing is, Meg," Sabina said, dropping her voice, "I need a baby for the weekend."

"A what? Did you say a *baby?*"

"Yes, that's right."

Either Meg was going crazy or this was a very bad connection. "A human baby? As in bottles and diapers and bibs?"

"Yes, that's right," Sabina repeated, with a little more of an edge this time. "A baby. Any old baby will do. But I need it right away. Out here in Connecticut."

Meg tried not to get too upset too soon. She didn't want to blow the big buildup. "Putting aside the question of what you need it for, just for the moment, how in God's name did you think I would come up with one?"

"Well, I'm not blind. I've seen all those pictures on your desk, and I've seen a whole parade of your sisters and their children waltzing through the office." With a hint of annoyance, Sabina added, "It isn't as if you don't have twenty or thirty of them to choose from."

"There are seventeen," Meg retorted. "And most of them are well past the baby stage."

"So bring me a toddler instead, if you can't get a baby. He won't know the difference."

"Sabina! I can't just borrow my sisters' children like a dress or a pair of shoes," she protested.

Sabina heaved an extravagant sigh. "I don't see why not. You baby-sit all the time, don't you? So instead of you, it will be me. I'll baby-sit one of them at a beautiful house in Connecticut. Why is that so difficult?"

Meg rubbed her forehead, wondering how to keep the headache at bay. "Okay, Sabina, let's go back to the beginning. Why exactly do you need a baby?"

"Oh, I told Alex I would bring my son," she said dismissively, as if she actually had a son. "You know, my son, Remington. The one in the bio."

"You told Alex you would bring your *son?*" Meg echoed.

"Yes, I just said that, didn't I?" Sabina asked tensely.

Meg swallowed. *Stay calm,* she told herself, although she really felt that a good shriek would make her feel much better. This was outrageous! Aside from the fact that this was the most anxiety she had ever heard in her employer's voice, there was also the small fact that Sabina had promised to bring her son to Connecticut.

Except she didn't have a son. They'd made him up for the bio.

At the time, it seemed like a good idea, so that her advice on parenting would seem reliable. And anytime anyone asked to see him, for magazine covers or TV interviews or whatever, Sabina was supposed to say that she didn't want him to suffer the glare of publicity, that she was keeping that part of her life private.

So why in the name of all that was holy had she offered to bring this nonexistent child to Connecticut?

"Alex seems to be very interested in the maternal side of my personality," Sabina said weakly. "He insisted I bring little Remy."

"Sabina, there is no Remy, little or otherwise."

"I know that, and you know that, but Alex doesn't," she responded sensibly. "I told you, Meg, any baby will do. Just pop it out here for a few hours and then you can take it right back home."

"Sabina, this is crazy." With a surge of inspiration, she suggested, "You can tell him the baby is sick and you don't want to expose him to the germs."

"I can't."

"Why not?"

"I already told him the nanny was bringing out the baby," Sabina said stubbornly. "I said they were on their way. I can't change stories now."

Meg set her jaw. "Well, I don't see any way I can get you a baby."

"Oh, yes you can. Call up one of your sisters, give her some money to go shopping or get her hair done and offer to baby-sit while she's gone. And then you bring the baby out here to me. That's it, it's done." She muttered, "I can't imagine any one of your sisters wouldn't be thrilled to get a few hours away."

"Sabina..."

"Just do it, Meg. It isn't that hard. Besides, it's your job to solve my problems and this is a problem. You're very good at your job. Don't disappoint me now." Sabina might not be a brain surgeon, but she had a lot of natural guile. She also knew Meg well enough to know that her assistant had a great deal of trouble saying no when pressed to the wall.

"Sabina..."

"Our livelihoods are on the line here. Do it."

"I'll try," she said finally.

After all, what could it hurt? She baby-sat frequently for all of her sisters, and only last week she'd taken Joannie's little boy, Jamie, shopping for toys and out for ice cream, just the two of them.

Maybe Joannie wouldn't care if Jamie had a little outing to Connecticut. "I'll try," she said again.

"Great. Oh, and, Meg, while you're at it, could you stop by Dean & Deluca's and get something fun for dinner? Alex thinks I can cook, too."

"I wonder why he thinks that," Meg said with a sigh. "Maybe because you supposedly wrote two cookbooks?"

"I guess."

"So you need a baby, a gourmet dinner and what else, Sabina? Maybe I should bring a circus and a few elephants while I'm at it? Sabina," she said wearily, "listen, if I come out there with one of my nephews, you have to keep Alex Thornhill away from me, okay? Because I really don't want to run into him again."

"Gotta go," Sabina said gaily. "Alex is waiting. We want to get in some tennis before the baby gets here."

Meg just sat there for a moment, staring at the silent receiver. What had she just agreed to?

"I only agreed to try," she reminded herself as she dialed Joannie's number.

Oddly enough, her sister said, "Sure. No problem. How long do you want him for?" the minute she asked the question.

"You're kidding. It's really okay for me to take Jamie to Alex Thornhill's house in Connecticut for the day?"

"Sure. Why not?" Joannie said calmly. "Jamie is being a real terror this morning—he threw Froot Loops all over the dog and spit orange juice at his sister. I'll be happy to farm him out for a while."

In the background, Meg could hear one child wailing while the other one beat pots and pans together, with a dog barking to keep time.

"I'll bring him right over," Joannie said quickly.

Figuring she was better off burying herself in details instead of worrying about the insanity of this whole operation, Meg busily organized the trip to Connecticut. First she called in a quick order for prefab food to a convenient market, although she really didn't understand why Sabina couldn't have called her usual caterer if she was going to pretend to cook. Meg was good with baked goods—no surprise, considering her parents ran a bakery— but she was pretty dicey when it came to the rest of the meal. Somehow she doubted rye bread and cinnamon rolls were what Alex Thornhill had in mind when he asked Sabina, Queen of Hostesses, to cook for him.

"Well, he's getting Meg the Handmaiden, instead, isn't he?" she grumbled. "I should bring a few cans of soup and some SpaghettiOs."

The delivery boy arrived with the groceries just moments before Joannie got there, dragging her son, her daughter and a variety of bags and boxes.

Jamie was squawking, so Meg didn't even try to greet him, letting him run around the apartment and burn off some excess energy. Instead, she took the baby, giving her namesake and goddaughter, MaryMeg, a big, sloppy kiss. The baby giggled and shook her head back and forth.

"Isn't this the most beautiful baby ever?" she cooed, choosing not to notice the fact that MaryMeg's wispy hair stood straight up and that there were bits of dried food stuck to her chin.

"Yeah, she's great," Joannie agreed. "At least until she learns how to talk. Jamie knows a lot of swearwords already, and it's really getting out of hand."

As if on cue, the little boy launched into a list of all the nastiest words he knew, while his mother ignored him.

"Is this the 'Don't show a reaction, that's what he wants' stage?"

"You got it," Joannie said grimly.

Meg began to realize just what an ordeal this trip was going to be. Not only did Jamie seem to be on his worst behavior today, but she had no guarantee that he wouldn't act that way all day. She had a feeling he was not going to be quite the angelic little "Remington" Sabina envisioned.

"Well, let's hope he falls asleep on the way to Connecticut," she mused as he continued to shout swearwords, "or I may have to stop and get earplugs."

"Good luck." Joannie took back her daughter, handing over a tote bag in exchange. "Jamie's toys, treats and a change of clothes," she explained. She held up a big white bakery box, as well. "Ma sent you a poppy seed hedgehog for dessert."

"Just what I need is a poppy seed hedgehog." That kind of cake was actually very tasty, but it was more of a kids' thing than a dessert for a fancy dinner for two. She had forgotten about dessert, actually, so it might come in handy. Maybe Sabina and Alex would be so enamored of each other they wouldn't notice their dessert was shaped like a small forest creature.

Enamored. Now that was a disgusting thought.

Dubiously, she looked through the rest of the stuff. Everything was in order, but where was the panic button?

"Are you going to be good for me, Jamie?" she called out to her nephew, who was hiding under the sofa. His head popped out when he heard his name. "We're going to have an adventure," she said brightly. "I'm Aunt Meg, the same as usual, but you get to pretend your name is Remington, just for today. Won't that be fun?"

"Remington?" Joannie interrupted. "But that's the name you gave— Oh, I get it. Jamie's supposed to be Sabina's made-up kid. Come on, Meg, that will never work."

"Why not?"

"Because he talks." One hand on her hip, Joannie regarded her sister with pity. "And he's in a very uncooperative phase right now. He knows his name and his address, and his new game is to shout it really loud over and over until you want to smack him.''

Once again on cue, Jamie started to holler out, "Jamie Jacobson, Jamie Jacobson, Jamie Jacobson, 321 Flat—''

"Your masquerade would be over in five minutes,'' Joannie said dryly.

"Can't he pretend to have a different name? He knows how to pretend, doesn't he?''

"Meg,'' Joannie whispered fiercely, as if she didn't want her children to hear, "that would be *lying*.''

"More like pretending,'' Meg suggested.

Joannie wasn't convinced. "Jamie is in a phase where he is just starting to experiment with lies. So we are trying to teach him that lying is a very bad idea. What will he think if Aunt Meg and Mommy pressure him into lying today, but tomorrow we go back to the regular rules? That's how you create screwed-up kids.''

"Okay, okay.'' It was bad enough that she was making a history of lying through her teeth; teaching that skill to her poor, impressionable nephew was beyond the pale. "Forget the whole thing. I didn't want to go anyway.''

"You're giving in?''

Meg flopped into a chair. "What else can I do?''

"Come on. Don't give up.'' Her sister smiled. "How often do you get to go to fancy houses in Connecticut and hang out with gorgeous men?''

"Never.''

"Exactly. So this is your chance.'' She smiled devilishly. "And you can also check up on him and Sabina. Throw a few wrenches in the works.''

"That's what you told me to do at the Rainbow Room and look how that turned out,'' Meg said gloomily.

"You loved it!''

"No, I didn't." But her sister knew her too well. "Okay, I at least liked it a little."

"You loved it!" Joannie's eyes were dancing. "And you loved Alex Thornhill. So go on, go to Connecticut. Have a thrill."

Meg got the distinct impression that Joannie was enjoying these adventures vicariously. She made a mental note to remind her sister that it was a lot more fun to hear about these madcap escapades than it was to carry them off. "What about the baby I'm supposed to take with me?" she asked, trying to bring a little reality back to the situation.

"Well, you know, you could take MaryMeg," Joannie offered. "She doesn't talk much beyond mama and dada and that kind of thing, and she wouldn't technically be lying since she can't say anything."

Meg hardly thought it was her place to point it out, but... "She's a girl."

"Unless your Mr. Thornhill changes her diapers, I don't think he'll know the difference."

"But she looks like a girl," Meg persisted.

"That's because you know she's a girl. To anyone else, she'll pass. Trust me. Unless I dress her in pink with lots of bows and lace, people are always asking me how old my little boy is." Joannie took back the bag, grabbed both kids and motioned Meg to bring her groceries. "Look, we'll swing by my place and get some of her stuff. We'll change her clothes and spruce her up, and she'll make a great little Remington. This is a much better idea, Meg."

"Maybe it is. I just can't believe you're going along with it."

"Why not?" Hitching MaryMeg up on her hip, Joannie grinned. "How often does my kid get to pretend to be rich and famous? Maybe after this we can get her into commercials.''

Meg had the feeling she had just opened Pandora's box. With a sledgehammer.

Chapter Five

Yes, it's true—two is company and three is a crowd.
But don't let that dampen your spirits. After all,
two's company, three's a crowd, and four is positively a party...

—*The Sabina Charles No-Fuss Guide to
Entertaining*

The house in Connecticut was spectacular. As she pulled
her rusty little Toyota to a stop in the circular drive, Meg
felt her mouth drop open.

"When they said country estate, they weren't kidding," she murmured.

The house itself was one of those half-timbered Tudor
beauties, sprawled on a large, leafy lot on a private drive.
Tennis courts and a swimming pool were visible off to
one side.

Homey and comfortable despite its size, it was the kind
of place rich people called a cottage and the rest of the
world called a mansion. Gazing at it, even in the haze of
a late-summer afternoon, Meg expected it to be decorated for Christmas.

"There ought to be snow," she said to herself. "A roaring fireplace inside, evergreen boughs strung all around, with an English sheepdog on the hearth, romping with the kids."

Wealth, privilege and comfort—that was the overwhelming message here. And Meg felt like she fit in about as well as a gorilla at a cotillion. In her jeans and tennies, she certainly didn't look as if she ought to be walking in the front door. Was there a servants' entrance for plebeians like her? And if she didn't use it, would the butler and the upstairs maid beat her away with brooms?

Of course, she always had had a fanciful imagination. Still, she gingerly unloaded MaryMeg from her car seat, wishing she had a sword and a shield to protect her darling niece from all the big, bad rich people.

Joannie had dressed MaryMeg in a really cute little sailor suit left over from when Jamie was a baby, but Meg had no illusions that it would pass for a pampered rich baby's outfit. And the toys she'd brought with her...well, there was no silver rattle from Tiffany's, no stuffed bunny from France.

With children of his own, Alex would surely take one look at MaryMeg and know that she was no blue blood. And that was just too bad. If her niece wasn't good enough, then Sabina could jolly well explain it away.

Squaring her shoulders, Meg marched up to the door, all ready to ring the bell. But as soon as she touched it, loud, somber peals resounded from inside. "Yikes," she cried, snatching her hand away, covering MaryMeg's ears. That was one scary doorbell.

The big wooden door, complete with brass knocker, swung open immediately.

"Finally!" Sabina announced. Perfect in peach linen pants and a matching sleeveless vest, every hair in place, she reached for the baby. "It's my darling Remington."

As Meg reluctantly handed over her niece, Sabina backed up, ushering her inside. And there he was, lying in wait—Alex Thornhill, Lord of the Manor, ready to greet and intimidate the new arrivals.

He looked just as gorgeous as ever. Damn the man anyway. Meg had only seen him in suits before this, but he looked just as scrumptious in a black T-shirt in some expensive silk knit, worn with gray linen trousers. It wasn't fair that someone as dreamy as Alex Thornhill was enough of a dimwit to go after Sabina.

But then, Alex Thornhill was used to doing whatever he felt like. Lord of the Manor, indeed.

Standing there in the front hall, not two steps inside the Lord of the Manor's manor, Meg raised her chin and stared back at him, giving as good as she got. Although it was difficult to remain icy calm when her brain kept reminding her of how it had felt to dance in his arms, she wanted him to know she was no pushover.

"Hello, Meg. Sabina didn't tell me you'd be the one bringing the baby," he said ever so casually. "I thought the nanny was driving him out. Unless you're the nanny, too." He lifted one dark eyebrow. "Is that yet another facet of your job?"

"No. Remington's nanny is a city girl. She doesn't drive," she returned, trying to stay just as cool as he was. She thought she did pretty well, considering she was making it all up as she went along.

"Mommy has missed you, darling," Sabina cooed, squeezing the baby, who took a good look at her stand-in mom and immediately began to scream bloody murder. Her little face took on an appalling shade of red, and her bottom lip stuck out far enough to catch a few of the tears springing from her eyes.

"Aw, sweetie," Meg soothed, taking her back before the poor thing leapt into the air to get away. While Sabina awkwardly tried to dab at the wet spot where the baby had dribbled on her vest, MaryMeg began to calm down as soon as she hit her aunt's arms. Meg ventured, "It was a long drive. I guess she got attached to me."

Alex looked very confused. "She? Do you mean Remington?"

"*He,* of course," she said hastily. "I tend to call all babies *she* when I'm not thinking."

"I see."

The look he gave her was a bit dubious, but Meg didn't think he really thought anything was up. No, most likely he just thought Meg was an even bigger looney-tune than he had before. *No harm in that, right?* she asked herself. *Who cares what he thinks of me?*

"Where are the other things I asked you to bring?" Sabina inquired in a strained sort of voice.

"Other things? Oh, the *other* things." Apparently, she wasn't supposed to mention that she had come laden with gourmet groceries. But the jig was going to be up when the bags came trooping in right under Alex's nose. She shrugged. "They're still in the car. Can you send someone out to get them?" She looked around the front hall expectantly. "The footman or someone?"

"I don't keep servants here," Alex informed her dryly. "But I'll be happy to bring in whatever you need."

"Oh no, I don't think—" Sabina began.

"That way, Sabina can give you a quick tour of the house, and by the time I've unloaded your car, you'll be ready to get back on the road." Alex stuck a hand in his pants pocket, leaning against the doorway into the living room as he bestowed a sardonic smile on Meg. "We wouldn't want to keep you."

"Back on the road?" Meg echoed. She shot a warning glance at Sabina. "Without the baby?"

"I know you're busy, Meg." Sabina gritted her teeth and grabbed for MaryMeg again. But the little girl let out a yelp the minute she touched her and Sabina backed off. "Now that you've so kindly brought out my darling Remy, you're free to leave. I know you won't want to be stuck out here with us, right?"

"But then I'll have to make another trip to come back in a few hours and get darling Remy," Meg said meaningfully.

Offhand, Alex offered, "There's no reason for you to make another trip. We'll just bring the baby back with us tomorrow."

"Oh, no. I wouldn't think of it." Keeping a secure arm around her niece, Meg sent Sabina a very dark look. "As you know, Sabina, darling Remy will only sleep in his own bed, so staying here overnight is out of the question. Besides, I didn't bring any of his overnight things. I think we should stick to the original plan, don't you? I'll take the baby back home in a few hours." Grimly, she added, "It's so much neater that way."

"The original plan was for Sabina and Remington to spend the weekend," Alex interjected. "I think we ought to stick to that."

"But Sabina didn't tell me that was the original plan."

"I must've forgotten," she said vaguely.

"Uh-huh." In other words, Sabina had deliberately lied because she knew Meg would never leave the baby for an overnight stay. And then she thought it would be too late to argue once the child was out here. It was just like Sabina to omit important details when she was being manipulative. "Remington isn't staying," Meg said dangerously.

"Don't you think that's for his mother to decide?" This time, it was Alex who reached for the baby. And damn her fickle little hide, MaryMeg immediately began to clamor to go to him.

As Meg reluctantly released her grip, he steered the baby over in his direction, awkwardly bouncing her a bit in the air. But MaryMeg didn't fuss at all. Instead, she cozied right up to him and began to make little cooing noises, wrapping her tiny fingers around his ear and drooling on him. What a flirt! Apparently, Alex Thornhill had a way with girls of all ages, even when the girl in question was masquerading as a boy in a sailor suit.

Meg just shook her head.

"I, uh, think he likes me," Alex said doubtfully.

"Since you and Remington are bonding so well, why don't we let Meg bring in the packages?" Sabina suggested, giving Alex a glowing look of tremulous maternal pride that was right off the Thanksgiving episode of "Hope Springs Eternal." "Meg dear, you can drive the car around the back and bring the things in through the kitchen."

"And Sabina *dear,* you can meet me in the kitchen."

Since MaryMeg seemed to be enjoying herself so thoroughly, Meg consented to retreat to the car. "I knew I'd end up coming in the servants' entrance sooner or later," she muttered.

Sabina was waiting with the door open when Meg hauled in the first sack of groceries and the diaper bag.

"This is dreadful," Sabina announced, holding up the bag with two fingers. "I would never pick anything in this terrible fabric to carry my baby's accoutrements. What are these creatures on the bag?"

"Sesame Street. Where've you been for the last twenty years?" Meg shook her head. "It doesn't matter anyway, because she is not your baby and I didn't buy a new diaper bag before I came out, okay?"

"She? You brought me a baby *girl?*" Sabina asked, aghast.

"She was the only one available." Setting the groceries on the expansive counter, Meg shook her head. "I can't believe I brought you anybody. You lied to me, Sabina! You said it was for a few hours and now I'm supposed to leave her overnight. I can't do that. Joannie was really good about loaning her, but she's going to freak if it's overnight."

"I didn't lie," Sabina said coolly. "I just shaded the truth a little."

"Is there a difference?"

"Oh, come on, Miss Holier-than-thou." Pacing down the middle of the big country kitchen, Sabina crossed her arms over her chest. She was positively cranky and Meg had never seen her like this. Without her Zen-like glow of serenity, Sabina's face seemed to sag, and there were fine wrinkles creasing her forehead. "As if this whole thing weren't your idea! As if you haven't been lying all along to keep it afloat. As if it's not just as important to you as it is to me that nobody find out what's really going on."

"But I told you not to get anywhere near that man. I told you what you were risking," Meg protested. "All you had to do was stay away from him and we were safe."

"But he wouldn't stay away from *me!*" Sabina began to rub her temples. "Besides, I like him," she said stubbornly. "And it's very good for my career to be seen around with someone like him. Do you realize I made all the soap mags this week, with pictures of him and me at the Rainbow Room? I haven't made those magazines in months."

"In the scale of things, how important is that?"

"It's important to me," Sabina shot back. "And really, Meg, it seems like a much better strategy to me this way. Instead of hiding out from him and creating all kinds of suspicions, I go out with him as if I have nothing to hide." Smiling to herself, she added, "Once he's in love with me, he'll have no desire to blow any whistles."

In a weird way, it almost made sense. Leaving the groceries aside for the moment, Meg groaned. When Sabina made sense, they were all in trouble.

Besides, she disliked this plan even more than the last one. Alex Thornhill, falling in love with Sabina—it was disgusting.

"It will never work," she muttered.

"Oh, yes it will," Sabina persisted. "It will work just fine. As long as he doesn't find out that Remington is a girl, as long as you stop acting so bizarre every time you're around him, as long as you give us some time alone so that I have a chance to *fascinate* him, everything will be fine."

The house of cards just kept climbing to the sky, taller and taller, as the lies they told reached dizzying heights.

And when she thought of leaving them alone so Sabina could "fascinate" him, she felt ill. Was that because it was really a bad idea, or because she couldn't stomach the idea of him with someone else?

Oh, heavens. The man was so far out of her league he might as well have lived on Mars. What right did she have to object to Sabina's plan?

"So you see, don't you, Meg, that you'll have to stop thrusting yourself in between us that way?" Sabina asked in a sulky tone. "It's made him very suspicious. He already told me he thought you were too pushy for a mere assistant. And now he's bound to wonder why you're the one making all the decisions about the baby and whether it stays or goes. I *am* supposed to be its mother, remember?"

Meg felt stung. So he thought she was too pushy and he'd complained about her to Sabina? The rat. Even though she had no intention of giving in, there was no point continuing their argument. "Look, we can't settle this right now. One of us had better get in there and get that baby away from him before he takes it into his mind to change its diaper or something." She frowned. "And it's going to have to be me, because MaryMeg has obviously taken a serious dislike to you."

"I don't understand that," Sabina mused. "I was such a good mother on 'Hope Springs Eternal.'"

Meg stopped, a stalk of celery in midair. "Sabina, that was scripted. We're working without a net here."

"I suppose."

"Okay, fine." Pushing Sabina in the direction of the back door, Meg ordered, "You finish putting the food away and I'll go get the baby. Then I can feed her and start your dinner while you..." She gritted her teeth. "While you fascinate him."

"Right."

With a deep breath, Meg swung open the door into the hall. Time to face the lion in his lair. She resolved not to be remotely pushy, not to give him an excuse to badmouth her or to be suspicious of her role in Sabina's life. No, she would be sweetness and light, the definition of charm itself. She would grab the baby and get the heck out of there, before she had a chance to regret handing him over to Sabina on a silver platter.

Not that he was hers to hand over. So why was she feeling so possessive?

"Hello?" she called out.

"In here."

Following the sound of his voice, Meg found herself back in the front of the house. As large as it was, it didn't seem to have a whole lot of rooms. But the ones it did have were quite spacious and very well-appointed. In fact, with its high ceilings and dark wood trim, and the rooms done up in warm, country colors, it came very close to her first guesses about the place, even if it wasn't Christmas and there was no English sheepdog.

As Meg entered the living room, off to one side of the main hall, she saw Alex, sitting on a dark plaid sofa that flanked the stone fireplace, dandling MaryMeg on his knee. She hadn't expected to interrupt such an idyllic scene.

"He likes me," Alex declared, inclining his head at the baby.

He seemed so thrilled, Meg couldn't help smiling. Maybe he was remembering when his girls were little. Or maybe he just liked babies. Whatever the reason, there was something really appealing about a big-honcho business tycoon making goo-goo noises at a laughing baby.

"And where are your kids this weekend?" she asked, half hoping they were here, too, and she'd get a chance to indulge her curiosity, a chance to see for herself what kind of child had sprung from those loins.

"Oh, uh, back in the city. They got a new nanny this week," he said, with sort of a strange light in his eyes.

"Oh?" She thought she'd give him an opening to elaborate, but he didn't, just went back to beaming at MaryMeg, who was doing great so far in her role as Baby

Remington Charles. Maybe she could do commercials. As long as Sabina wasn't around, anyway.

"They're easy to handle at this age, aren't they?" he said suddenly. "It's only when they get a little older..."

"What?"

He sighed, and she thought for a moment she saw doubt and a kind of regret flicker over his elegant features. "Nothing," he said finally. "It's nothing."

Meg gave him a speculative look. "You know, if you'll forgive me for saying so, you seem different out here."

"How so?" he asked, sending her a speculative look of his own.

"Less...hard." Bad choice of word. "More real," she said quickly. "I guess the country air does that."

"You seem different, too."

Now that was a surprise. She was trying to be less controlling, of course, but she'd hardly had time to get that plan off the ground yet. And she wouldn't have guessed he'd notice if she had suddenly done a Dr. Jekyll and Mr. Hyde. Not with Sabina, the object of his affections, around.

But Sabina was more than the object of his affections. She was also Meg's boss, and the one person who stood between her and unemployment.

It seemed like a good time to make amends, to allay Alex's suspicions and pretend to be a good little assistant who wanted nothing more than the best for her boss. No ulterior motives. No hidden agenda. Just an overzealous employee who had overstepped her bounds.

Slowly, Meg wove around the sofa and sat down next to him. MaryMeg immediately turned her way, holding out one plump little fist, gibbering something that sounded a lot like 'mama.'

"I think he's trying to say your name," Alex said brightly. "Is that Auntie Meg, Remington?"

"Mama," gurgled "Remington."

Meg smiled weakly, taking the baby into her lap and juggling her around until MaryMeg faced Alex again. Maybe if she wasn't looking at her auntie Meg, the baby wouldn't be confused by the family resemblance.

Family resemblance?

Struck with sudden panic, Meg surreptitiously examined the baby. Did MaryMeg look anything like her, in the nose or the eyes, maybe? Was there some dead give-away staring Alex in the face?

"Are you all right?" Alex asked. "You looked a little funny there for a second."

"Oh, no, no problem. I'm fine." After that brief anxiety attack and a thorough once-over, she relaxed a bit. There was no resemblance, at least not as far as she could tell. MaryMeg, like all the other Kaczmarowski babies, looked more like a Kewpie doll than anyone in the family.

Returning to her original purpose, Meg began quickly. "I wanted to apologize for the other night. Sabina told me that you thought my behavior was less than professional." She paused. She didn't quite know how to go on. "I wasn't trying to jump your bones" definitely wasn't right, but she had to say something. "I do want to assure you that what you thought—that I was trying to, uh, whatever—was not true."

"I guess I already knew that."

Reaching out to offer his finger to the baby to chew on, he gazed thoughtfully at Meg. Sapphire, she decided. Instead of clear mountain streams, his eyes were the color of sapphires.

She swallowed past a dry throat. She knew she shouldn't be swooning into his eyes, daydreaming about the color, but it was so damned hard to keep a coherent thought in her head when he was around.

"I should also apologize," he said softly. "I behaved badly myself."

"It wasn't... unpleasant," she allowed. In fact, dancing with him had been about the most pleasant thing she could imagine.

"I made certain assumptions based on the fact that you seem to keep turning up at inopportune moments." He smiled. "And here you are again."

"Here I am again." Well, that neatly underlined the dilemma, didn't it? *Two's company, three's a crowd.*

Meg stood up, hoisting MaryMeg onto her hip. Here she was, gabbing away, falling under the spell of those fabulous blue eyes, when she was supposed to be taking the baby away and giving Sabina an opening to entice him.

"It's time for, uh, Remington's dinner," she managed to say. "I told Sabina I'd be right back with him. I'm going to feed him, to give you two some time to be alone."

"Oh, that isn't necess—" he began, but she swept out of the room before he could finish.

Outside the door, she took a deep breath. Definitely a good idea to be out of there, away from that cozy living room with its cozy fireplace and its even cozier owner, before she was tempted to stay.

"YOU DID WHAT?"

"I called your sister Joannie," Sabina repeated patiently. "Her number was in the book in your purse. I told her we needed the baby overnight and she said fine."

"I don't believe you," Meg responded. She twisted the lid off the jar of strained carrots and turned back to continue this discussion.

Already edging toward the door, Sabina offered her usual tranquil smile. "Call her yourself. She said it was no problem." And she waltzed out, presumably to find Alex and be enchanting.

Meg could hardly argue; there was no one to argue with. "Well, sweetie," she told her niece as she propped her up in the car seat that doubled as a baby chair, "I'm not leaving. I don't care what they do to me, I'm not leaving till you do. And we'll just call your mommy and see what she has to say, because we don't trust Sabina as far as we can throw her, do we?"

Meg fed MaryMeg from the jars of baby food without a whole lot of problem—like most of the Kaczmarowskis, she was a good eater—and then tried to dial Joannie. No answer.

She must've run out for a minute. Meg hoped Joannie didn't call her husband the cop and tell him MaryMeg was being held prisoner by a couple of crazed writers at a posh estate in Connecticut. He'd have the whole force out there in no time.

As she started to pull things out of the fridge for the main meal, she tried Joannie's number again. Still no answer. "Where can she be?"

Meanwhile, MaryMeg sat there in her chair, wide-eyed, chewing on her carrot-mushy fist, watching everything her aunt did. First she preheated the oven for the beef Wellington and the fancy potato casserole, both pre-made in handy foil pans, and then scrounged around for a pot for the vegetables, after which she spent several minutes scrubbing carrots.

"Look, kiddo, the big people are going to eat the same thing you did. Carrots, isn't that fun?" She wiped her hands on her jeans as she stuck the beef and potato pans on top of the oven, waiting for the temperature to rise. "Now you may ask yourself, as I am asking myself, what is Auntie Meg going to eat, while those two devour the romantic and delicious candlelight dinner that Auntie Meg is doing all the work for? And you may ask yourself, why is Auntie Meg doing all this work? Is any job worth this hassle?"

After getting the carrots under way on the stove, she began to chop celery rather enthusiastically, even though she really didn't need that much celery for the salad she had planned. But she was enjoying this chopping thing. Bam, bam, bam. The celery was decimated, and pretty much unusable. "Oh well," she said gaily. "Too bad for poor Mr. Celery."

Just as she tossed the green mushy mess in the trash, Sabina came running back in. "Is the baby's dinner supposed to take this long? He's getting suspicious."

"She's done. You can take her if you want." Meg pointed her knife at the stove, where the foil pans were sitting. "I'm working on your dinner."

"Oh, okay."

"Don't you at least want to know what you're having, in case he asks what *you're* making?" Meg demanded.

"I hadn't thought of that." Sabina chewed her lip, making a dent in her perfect peach lipstick, another aberration Meg had never witnessed. All these imperfections in Sabina's facade were getting scary. "Right now I'm trying to figure out how to tell him he can't help bathe the baby."

"He absolutely cannot. That's one sure way to find out Remington is a girl!"

"I know. But he's very enthusiastic about this whole baby thing." Sabina ran a shaky hand through her hair. "Couldn't you have brought a crankier baby so Alex wouldn't be so enamored of it?"

"She's pretty cranky when she's around you," Meg noted. Indeed, MaryMeg was gazing at Sabina and her little face was already taking on a redder hue.

Sabina reached out far enough to scoot the carrier around, where MaryMeg couldn't see her. "But Alex loves him, er, her. No, him."

Meg ignored the gender confusion. "I haven't gotten through to Joannie yet," she said sternly. "So I don't really think we ought to be scheduling bath time if the baby is going home."

"So, is it time for Remington's bath?" Alex asked brightly, sticking his head around the kitchen door.

Meg quickly slid over by the stove, blocking his view of the prefab dinner pans. At the exact moment Meg declared, "Remington has a rash, no bath tonight," Sabina announced, "Remington bathes in the morning now. Silly me—I forgot!"

As they looked at each other, Alex glanced back and forth between them.

"He bathes in the morning because of the rash," Meg tried.

"Yes, that's right," Sabina chimed in.

And then someone knocked, loudly, on the back door.

"Saved by the bell," Meg whispered under her breath, even though it was a knock, not a bell. Out loud, she said, "I wonder who that could be. Are you going to get that, Alex?"

"No, wait." Sabina grabbed him, pushing him back toward the hallway where he came in. "I think Alex should go, um, upstairs for a minute. I'll get the door."

"Upstairs?" he echoed. "But why?"

"You can draw the baby's bath," Sabina said suddenly.

"But the baby bathes in the morning," the other two chorused.

"Oh, what the heck? Let's be wild and give him his bath tonight."

Meg raised her eyebrows, wondering if Sabina had lost her mind. Alex looked pretty doubtful himself, but he allowed himself to be shooed up the stairs. Meanwhile, the knocking continued, and it was even louder now.

"What was that all about?" Meg demanded.

"Will you please open the door?"

"Me?" She was really starting to question whether cool, calm Sabina had completely lost her grip. Better not to argue at this point. Backing over there slowly, Meg swung open the door.

And then she stepped back. Her sister Joannie was standing on the back steps.

"Hi," she said cheerfully.

Meg's mouth dropped open. "What are you doing here?"

"We came to the back door, just like Miss Charles said." She peered inside. "Nice kitchen."

"And who's that behind you?" Meg asked. "Darla?"

Darla, second youngest of the Kaczmarowski sisters, stepped closer, toting a baby carrier much like the one MaryMeg was strapped into back on the kitchen counter. "Hi, Meg. Yeah, it's me." She lifted the carrier. "We brought Zach to switch for MaryMeg."

"Zach?" Zach was Darla's baby, born about two months before MaryMeg. But what was he doing here? What were any of them doing here?

"Take the baby," Sabina ordered, coming up from behind, lugging MaryMeg in her carrier.

"I don't understand," was all Meg could get out.

"It's all arranged," Sabina said fiercely. She handed MaryMeg over to Joannie.

"MaryMeg can't stay overnight, so we brought Zach to take her place," Joannie said helpfully, chucking her baby under the chin. Her expression clouded. "Meg! She has carrots all over her. Couldn't you at least have cleaned her up?"

Meg was so stunned she couldn't move. "I would've. I didn't know you were coming. I—wait just a second. Are you trying to tell me that we're switching babies in midscam?"

Chapter Six

It's tough to demand perfection when you are trying to run a household, especially if you divide your chores among husband, wife and children. One or more of those parties are bound to shirk their duty and lump it all back on Mom, whose biology, they will tell you, is geared to scrubbing toilets and scouring pans. *Au contraire!* No one's biology is that horrific. And no matter what games your household partners play, do not give in! Organization, patience and the willingness to hold out for a job well-done will ultimately make your household a happier, cleaner, brighter place to be, and make Mom a happier, cleaner, brighter person to be with...

—*The Sabina Charles No-Fuss Guide to a Happy Home*

"I can't believe my baby is getting Sabina Charles for a baby-sitter," Darla said happily. Handing her son off to Meg, she confided to Sabina, "I used to watch you all the time as Serenity. You were so wonderful."

Hastily smoothing her hair, the former soap star recovered a bit of her dignity. "Yes, I know. Thank you."

"My other three are staying with Mom and Dad tonight, so Ron and I can have a night to ourselves. We really appreciate this, Miss Charles," Darla went on.

"Darla—" Meg began, but her sisters were too busy trying to peer into the house to notice.

"Can we see inside, Meg? Maybe a little tour?" Joannie asked eagerly.

"I don't think so," Sabina rushed to say. She eased the sisters back and tried to shut the door at the same time.

"Darla—" Meg tried.

"You'd better get back on the road before it gets too late for your romantic evening with your husband," Sabina put in.

"Oh, okay," Darla murmured, clamping an arm on Joannie and dragging her back a step. "Guess we should get on our way. Nice to meet you, Serenity…I mean, Miss Charles."

"Darla? Joannie?"

"See you tomorrow, Meg!" Joannie called out as they retreated down the steps and into Darla's battered station wagon.

"You can't leave me with Zach," Meg cried. Yes, he had the same basic coloring as MaryMeg and, yes, he was a boy. But… She glanced down into the carrier. "He's bigger. He has a lot more hair! He has teeth!"

At the last minute, just before they were about to pull away, Darla stopped and got out of the car. She came running back to the door.

"I almost forgot," she said breathlessly. She thrust a big quilted bag at Meg. "Zach's stuff. Have fun!"

And then her sisters were really gone. They had switched babies on her and then abandoned her.

She was stuck in Connecticut with a flake and a rake. And a new Remington who didn't look a thing like the last Remington.

She glanced down at Zach, around whom a very definite odor clung.

"I think that baby needs a linen change," Sabina ventured.

All Meg said was, "I want to go home."

MEG MANAGED TO CHANGE and clean the baby, hand him off to Sabina to bathe and then run downstairs to put the foil pans in the by-now-very-well-preheated oven.

Sabina came racing back downstairs within about a second and a half. "I don't know how to do this," she squealed, holding out poor Zach, who was wearing nothing but a diaper. "I made up an excuse for Alex so I could come down and get you. I left him in the bathroom, waiting. Here, take the baby. You need to get it started."

"The bath?" Still holding a wooden spoon, she took Zach in one arm. "You need me to start that? What is there to giving a baby a bath?"

"That's easy for you to say." Sabina looked ready to burst into tears. "I've never done it before."

Sabina was beginning to look as if she'd been through World War III. There were water splotches all over the front of her pretty linen pantsuit and flour dusted across her nose.

Of course, the flour she had dashed there herself, on purpose, to make it look as if she had slaved over dinner. Meg tried to tell her there was no flour involved in the preparations, but Sabina went and found some in a bin and tossed it on her face anyway.

And then, while Sabina crashed a few pans around and sliced a carrot that didn't need to be sliced, Meg raced upstairs and into the master bathroom, galloping Zach, a.k.a. Remington II, on her hip.

"Hello," she said with false brightness, slamming to a halt inside the door.

Alex was pacing back and forth, impatiently waiting. He glanced up when she entered, peered at the baby and then came over closer to examine Zach a bit more closely.

"Is something wrong?" *Of course something is wrong,* she told herself. *It's a different baby!*

She steeled herself for the inevitable, all ready to be thrown out on the street with her nephew and her boss.

"This isn't..." he began.

Meg held her breath.

"A rash." He glanced up. "Didn't you say Remington had a rash?"

"A rash?" They had told so many lies by now, what was one little rash? The important thing was that Alex hadn't noticed the baby switch. She had no idea how he could've missed it, but she wasn't going to quibble. "What a relief. It must be better. The rash, I mean."

"Uh-huh. You know, he looks very different without his clothes," Alex observed. He reached out a finger, catching Zach's little fist. "Isn't that funny? Without his clothes, he looks bigger."

"Everyone says that," Meg said with a hearty laugh. "Trick of the eye."

"Really? How odd. His hair looks different, too. And I think I see a tooth. I didn't notice a tooth before."

"Well, you know, they get them constantly. It's probably new since the last time you looked." She smoothed Zach's hair down to make it look as if he had less of it.

"You know babies. Changing every minute. You really have to keep an eye on the little devils."

She filled the sink with lukewarm water, peeled off Zach's diaper, thanked her lucky stars he was actually a boy and she hadn't taken the wrong baby after all, and then gingerly set him in the water.

"Okay, here we go," she said, pulling Alex forward to be the designated baby bather.

He leaned in behind her, very intent on the task at hand, and she tried very hard not to notice how nice he smelled, how long and strong his tanned forearms were as he reached around her. Meg closed her eyes and bit her lip, taking a few deep breaths before she could go on.

Feeling almost light-headed, she instructed, "Hold him with one hand, and then you can kind of splash water over him with the other. I'll, uh, get a washcloth."

"Ah," Alex said as she showed him how to wash the baby. If she was entranced by watching him, he was clearly entranced by this baby-bathing experience. His jaw was set, his eyes never left Remington II and he concentrated completely on the task at hand. Surely he must've had plenty of opportunities to partake of the wonders of baby bathing with his own girls. So why was this so exciting?

"Bubbo, bubbo, bubbo," Zach cried suddenly, slapping his chubby hands in the water.

"What's that all about?"

Meg shrugged. "Just having fun, I think."

"Bubbo, bubbo, bubbo!" Zach tried again.

"I think he wants bubbles," Alex said triumphantly, as if he'd just discovered the secret to nuclear fusion. He looked around, keeping one hand where it was, support-ing the baby. "Do you see any bubble bath around?"

Caught between him and the sink, Meg had no desire to look for bubbles. Gazing up at him, with his beautiful eyes holding her, she had a desire, all right. She had a desire to close her eyes, to lay her head on Alex's shoulder, to nibble on his earlobe, to pull his wet arms all the way around her...

"Are we having fun?" Sabina asked. She arranged herself negligently against the doorframe. "Did you manage to get things under way without me?"

Meg jumped back, away from Alex. She slipped in a puddle on the floor, reached out to steady herself, wobbled and found herself brought up short, right against Alex.

He grabbed her. Still holding the baby, he managed to reach out with the other arm and haul her backside up against his front before she fell. *Right* up against his front. Well, she'd wanted to be closer, hadn't she? It felt as if she'd got her wish.

It felt... very intriguing.

Meg wasn't moving, not until she had to. She got the distinct impression that moving was only going to make things worse. A lot worse.

So she stayed where she was, locked in his hard embrace, feeling his breath, ragged and uneven behind her.

"Are you okay?" he whispered.

"I—"

But she didn't have a chance to answer. Sabina snapped, "How clumsy of you, Meg. You've gotten Alex all wet."

"Oops." She disengaged herself awkwardly, looking him up and down. All wet. Water looked very good on the man, no two ways about it, dripping from his elegant chin, plastering his dark T-shirt to his chest. "Sorry," she offered.

"Meg dear, why don't you pop down and make sure nothing's burning." Sabina's voice was testy. "I have dinner well under way now, so you ought to be able to look after things while Alex and I finish this."

"Yeah. Sure."

Sabina smiled serenely, making it clear whose turf was whose, and who the interloper was here. Meg had no choice but to vacate.

As she left, Sabina was chuckling over the baby and bath time went on as before.

Meg skulked away, stung that Alex didn't seem to care who his bathing partner was. Sabina, Meg, whoever... The man had no scruples whatever. He was positively a *cad*.

Back in the kitchen, she found herself getting crankier by the minute.

She told herself that she should've been thrilled by the simple fact that this crazy scheme hadn't blown up in their faces yet, but it didn't help. Slamming dishes and cutlery down in the dining room, lighting candles, opening wine, getting everything out of the oven on time, surviving Sabina's forays to keep the illusion alive as well as her lectures on the importance of intruders keeping their paws off Alex if Sabina was going to charm and confuse him, *and* managing to work in five or six trips up and down the stairs to hover around and make sure no one was mistreating Zach... Meg was exhausted.

By the time Alex and Sabina sat down to their candle-lit dinner, Meg wanted nothing more than to crawl into bed and never think about dinner or babies again.

And she especially didn't want to think about Alex, cozied up to Sabina over candles and beef Wellington.

"Men are pigs," she told Zach somberly as she put him in his jammies. "I suppose that's not very nice, since you will yourself be a man someday, but I hope you'll know better than to act all charming and sweet to two women at the same time.''

Remington II didn't answer; he just blew tiny bubbles with his own spit. Talented child.

"Bubbo, bubbo," he gurgled.

As he entertained himself, she tucked him into a lovely brass crib, overflowing with lovely white embroidered linens. Alex had obviously assumed Sabina would want to sleep in the same room as her child, and so, thinking ahead, he'd had a crib sent down and set up in the room intended for Sabina.

Poor Zach. This arrangement meant that he had to share with Sabina. But, like his mother, the implacable Darla, Zach tended to be extremely good-natured. Which was lucky for all of them and the continued success of tonight's charade, even if Sabina was no help whatever.

Speaking of which, Meg wondered how the paragon of womanly virtue was going to accomplish her nightly beauty rituals here in the middle of Connecticut without any of her special equipment. No facial sauna, no peach nectar to bathe in, no masseur, no oil treatments or yards of plastic wrap.

Knowing Sabina, it was all probably tucked away in her six pieces of matching luggage. Because Sabina didn't go anywhere without the whole ball of wax.

God forbid anyone should see her without benefit of creams, ointments, waxes, oils, foundations, sprays, powders and brushes.

A natural beauty, indeed.

Just as Meg was wondering where all the paraphernalia was kept, she heard footsteps coming down the hall. The natural beauty herself burst in the door announcing, "I have to get some sleep," as she began rooting through her luggage.

"Where's Alex?"

"Cleaning up," Sabina mumbled. "Truly the perfect man, don't you think? But I couldn't take it anymore. I had to lie down."

Was that a twitch under one eye? Her beautiful boss really was a mess, Meg decided, giving her a critical once-over. She had changed out of the wet, messy clothes at some point, so that wasn't the problem. No, it was Sabina herself who was crumbling under the pressure.

"You left him by himself?" Meg inquired. "I thought you were supposed to be *enchanting* him."

"Oh, I enchanted him just fine." Sabina fell dramatically onto the bed, clenching a slinky peach nightgown in one hand. "But I insist on a full twelve hours of sleep, you know. I can't keep myself centered with a minute less."

"I guess that means you two won't be engaging in any more...*enchantment* tonight," Meg put in delicately.

Sabina opened one eye. "Is that your way of asking if we're sleeping together, Meg dear? How quaint. Do you really think Alex would have set up all this baby bedding in my room if he had hanky-panky in mind? Do you really think I would've allowed you to stay this evening if *I* had hanky-panky in mind?"

"Allowed me to stay? And here I thought it was a command performance. I thought I was the one doing all the work."

"Don't be tiresome," Sabina grumbled. "Turn out the light on your way out, will you?"

It looked as though beauty rituals were going to have to wait till morning. Eyes firmly closed, Sabina had started to do her Zen breathing, still clutching her night-gown.

Even Zach looked ready to zone out—his eyes were closed and he was sucking his thumb, with one ear of his rabbit clasped securely in his other little fist.

"Are you okay, sweetie?" she asked him, bending over to give him a good-night kiss.

He seemed fine and, reluctantly, Meg left the dark bedroom. She had been a good aunt, she told herself, and Zach would survive one night in a gorgeous crib in a strange bedroom. Plus, she promised herself to sneak back in and check on him every once in a while.

The house was quiet as she backed into the hall and she considered toddling off to bed herself. But, darn it anyway, there was something in her that couldn't countenance the idea of sleeping upstairs when there was still a big mess downstairs.

When she'd left to come up to put Zach to bed, the kitchen was littered with pans and dishes, and Sabina and Alex were piling up more dishes in the dining room as they finished off coffee and the buttery Polish cake known as a poppy seed hedgehog, provided by her mother. Meg wished she'd eavesdropped when they got to the dessert, since she would've bet her life savings that neither of them had ever seen a cake shaped like a hedgehog, but somehow she'd missed the excitement.

Nonetheless, she knew there was a mess down there. Surely neither Alex nor Sabina would tackle it—they were both helpless with responsible tasks like that. And her mother's voice, supported by the combined volume of all six sisters, intoned in her ear, "Never leave a dirty kitchen overnight. You'll get bugs."

"They're his bugs," she said out loud. "What do I care if Alex Thornhill gets bugs in his kitchen?"

But she just couldn't do it.

Besides, nobody had bothered to tell her where she was supposed to sleep.

Resolute, Meg took the back stairs down to the kitchen. She would clean the kitchen within an inch of its life, she would show Alex that somebody in this outfit was competent and reliable, and she would find a place to sleep, even if it meant knocking on the Lord of the Manor's bedroom door and asking for directions.

Hmm. Knocking on Alex's bedroom door. She could just imagine. Smiling to herself, Meg shivered.

Wearing nothing but a silk robe in some dark, dangerous color, Alex would answer her knock, wrenching open the door. His immaculate hair would be tousled just a little and his blue eyes would be warm and soft, a bit sleepy. And the robe would gap open halfway down his chest as he hastily tossed it on and tied the belt.

He'd open that door, he'd reach for her and she'd fall right in...

"Meg, you are out of your mind. Stop it," she told herself firmly as she stomped down the stairs.

She was going to have to stop this rampant imagination of hers before it got her into real trouble. "It has already gotten me into trouble, what with two Remingtons and a rash, five Welsh corgis, Sabina supposedly whipping up beef Wellington and hedgehogs... Oh my God," she broke off as she got a gander at the kitchen.

All the lights were on, making the big country kitchen look very warm and cozy. Shiny brass pots hung over the center island; earthy brown and red bricks lined one wall. It was a *House & Garden* kitchen.

And it was spotless.

There was no evidence at all of the big brouhaha that had gone on here tonight. As she stood there, rooted to the last step of the servants' stairs into the kitchen, Alex swung in from the hall, a dish towel draped over his shoulder and a pair of coffee cups and saucers balanced in one hand.

Catching sight of her, he slowed but didn't stop. "Hello, Meg. I was hoping you'd show up sooner or later," he said in a mysterious sort of voice.

I was hoping you'd show up sooner or later. What did that mean? She wasn't sure she wanted to know.

Very cautiously, she took the last step down into the kitchen. At the sight of him, her mind had jolted back to that mental image of him in the dark silk robe, reaching for her. "Hoping?" she echoed.

He gave her a sardonic smile. "Or maybe *anticipating* is a better word. The way you keep lurking around in the shadows, I knew I'd see you before long."

"Sabina and the baby are asleep," she explained, trying not to sound defensive. *Lurking in the shadows?* She hardly thought she was lurking. "I was, uh, going to clean up. But I guess you already did that."

He turned away. "I don't like leaving a mess," he remarked, and then he opened the dishwasher and began to stick the coffee cups in.

"I don't, either." Meg chewed her lip. "And you've really done a beautiful job, except . . ."

"Except?"

She couldn't help it. She rushed over and grabbed the last cup out of his hand. "Fine china doesn't go in the dishwasher. You have to do it by hand. Plus you've got all the silverware mixed together. And look at how the pans are all jumbled."

Alex looked at her, looked down into the dishwasher and then back at her. "Does it really matter?"

"Well, no, except . . ." She turned away from his maddening gaze and began to rearrange everything inside the dishwasher. "I'm just a perfectionist, that's all."

"About coffee cups?" he asked dryly.

"Well, if you want to know the truth, about most everything." She shut the door and switched the machine on, and then began to wash the cups and saucers by hand in the sink. A little tensely, she said, "And when I know how something should be done, it's really hard to just let it be done wrong. My mother always said that it's easy to accept less than perfection when you're trying to run a household, but you can't give in. Organization," she declared, "patience and the willingness to hold out for a job well-done will ultimately make your household a happier, cleaner, brighter place to be."

"That sounds familiar." Reaching over, he plucked the last saucer out of her wet fingers. And then slowly, carefully, with soft, rhythmic strokes, he dried the dish with the towel on his shoulder. Meg watched the whole thing, wide-eyed, wondering how he did that. How did he make wiping a saucer look so...erotic? "Very familiar," he whispered.

"R-really?" she managed to say. But her gaze was glued to that silly saucer and his long, elegant fingers manipulating the towel, brushing, rubbing it well past merely dry and into the well-loved stage.

"Those words definitely sound familiar," he mused.

His blue eyes were fixed on her mouth. What was wrong with her mouth? Her lips felt suddenly dry. She wanted to lick them, but she couldn't, not under his watchful eye.

Very deliberately, she ignored him. "Okay, the kitchen is perfect," she whispered. "Are you ready for bed?"

Alex smiled lazily. "Are you?"

It was a completely innocuous exchange, so why was her stomach doing flip-flops? He stood there, so tall, so overwhelming, so amazingly gorgeous, and suddenly washing a coffee cup together was more intimate than anything she could imagine. Dancing, bathing a baby, doing a dish . . . there were traps everywhere she turned.

"I don't know where," she said awkwardly, wishing she could somehow move to the other side of the center island without having to push her way past Alex to get there. This way, smashed into the sink by the sheer force of Alex's personality, she had nowhere to run. This was the second time tonight he had boxed her into a sink. Was he just pushy? Or did he have a thing for sinks?

"Don't know where?" he prompted. "Where to what?"

"To sleep." She gave in and licked her lip and he watched the whole thing. Damn the man, anyway. Why was licking her lip such a vulnerable act? "Nobody told me where I should sleep."

"My apologies." Alex leaned in a little closer, gazing at her lip intently. "If you recall, I didn't know you'd be staying when you first got here."

"I, uh, didn't, either," she murmured. "Things just sort of fell out that way."

"Uh-huh." Reaching out his hand, Alex bent even nearer. Meg held her breath. Narrowing his eyes, studying her, he skimmed his thumb, just the tip, along the bottom edge of her lip. Unable to think of a way out, she tried not to move, not to make it worse, not to make it better. "Hmm," he said softly. "There's something on your lip."

"Oh, really?" she breathed.

"Uh-huh. Since you're such a perfectionist, I decided you'd want me to brush it away."

"Right." But she couldn't have cared less whether there was anything on her lip. All she knew was that Alex was very close, with his thumb resting on the corner of her mouth, his hand cradling her jaw, so close she could feel his warm breath on her cheek. And it wasn't close enough. Not nearly.

She had to tighten her hands into fists to keep from tangling her fingers into his dark, sleek hair, to keep from throwing herself at him, begging him to ravish her right there on the kitchen counter.

Your job, your boss, your pride, she told herself frantically, trying to summon up any kind of roadblock.

But it didn't seem to help. Damn it—she still wanted him to kiss her more than she'd ever wanted anything in her life.

And he did. He dropped the tiniest possible kiss, right there, next to the corner of her mouth.

Meg couldn't breathe, couldn't even see. She felt warm, woozy, somewhere approaching the passing-out-at-his-feet stage.

"Do you really think this is a good idea?" she murmured, arching her neck, letting herself relax into his big, hard body even as she pretended she was resisting.

"Why not?" And he kissed her again, on the neck this time, lingering just a bit longer.

"But Sabina. What about—"

"Ah, yes. Sabina." With a sigh of regret, he broke away. Meg languished there by the sink, suddenly bereft. Why in the world had she brought up Sabina?

Because it was the right thing to do.

She made haste to convince herself, arguing it out mentally. For one thing, she reminded herself, he was a heel if he was romancing them both. For all she knew, he'd pulled the same sweet, sexy routine with her boss over coffee and the hedgehog.

And for another thing, Sabina was right. They were much better off and much closer to saving their jobs if he was falling head over heels for Miss Perfect.

"Want to move this to the den?" he asked softly.

Meg glanced up, still engrossed in her thoughts. "But I thought we were going to bed."

His lips curved into a dangerous smile. "And I thought you just decided that wasn't a good idea."

"I meant the kiss," she explained quickly. "I didn't say anything about..." She swallowed. She wasn't going to say "bed" again, not if she could help it. "You know."

"Going to bed."

"Right. That."

"You have to go sometime, Meg." His smile deepened in one corner, giving Alex a hint of a dimple. *Good Lord.* What else was he going to pull out of his arsenal? Lazily, he added, "Plenty of bedrooms and just two of us."

"And Sabina. And Remington."

"You said they were asleep."

"They are."

"So what's the problem?"

"I have no idea..." She caught herself. "Look, I'm not used to this kind of game. I thought you were interested in Sabina. This is very confusing."

"Confusing—that's the word for it." He drew back slightly. "Sorry. I kept seeing you popping up here and there all night. Every time I turned around, there you were. It was a bit hard to concentrate."

"I just wanted to be sure everything was going all right." Okay, so she'd made a nuisance of herself, but she'd had to make sure Zach was okay, that Sabina didn't drop anything damaging into the conversation, that Alex didn't get suspicious.

"I kept waiting, wondering when you'd pop up again." Negligently, he reached out a finger to stroke gently down her bare arm. Meg shivered. "All that waiting and wondering. Well, it's no surprise I feel a little keyed up."

Keyed up? Was that an oblique way of saying he was as stirred up and downright *aroused* as she was?

"So how about a movie?" he asked.

Meg felt her jaw drop. "A movie?"

"Insomnia," Alex explained. Again, the tip of his finger traced the curve of her arm, up to the inside of her elbow, down to her wrist. "I have trouble falling asleep."

She was ready to jump out of her skin, or at least jump in with all sorts of suggestions. It was in her nature to find solutions. And solutions kept her brain busy, not thinking about his hand, still resting on her arm.

"Have you tried warm milk? White noise, like a fan or an air conditioner?"

But Alex was past that. "It works better to sit up late and watch old movies on television." He smiled, looping a hand around her wrist. They both knew her pulse was pumping down there, even as she pretended not to be affected by his touch. "No, you definitely don't seem sleepy, Meg. I thought maybe you'd like to join me."

I would love to join you... She kept her mouth shut.

He lifted his elegant shoulders in a shrug. "Everyone else is asleep. I've got nothing to do. You've got nothing to do. So why don't we do nothing together?"

"I think I should get some sleep. Immediately."

"Aw, come on. Keep me company." He tugged at her wrist. "What have you got to lose?"

It was the stupidest thing she'd ever agreed to in her life. But he was right. She wasn't sleepy in the least. Keyed up— that was one way to put it.

And when Alex Thornhill and the chance to watch an old movie beckoned, how could she resist?

"I happen to really like old movies," she said stubbornly under her breath. And she followed him to the den.

It was a smaller, wood-paneled room, decorated in the same expensively casual style as the rest of the place. Alex sat on one of the love seats and pulled her down next to him. He propped his long legs up on the dark wood of the coffee table, switching on the TV with a remote control. Meg hovered over on her side of the small sofa, trying to decide whether to sit or flee.

Channels flipped past so fast she couldn't distinguish professional wrestling from "Dick Van Dyke" reruns. "Stop a second. How can you tell what's on?"

"I can tell," he said, continuing to zap around with carefree abandon.

Without thinking, Meg grabbed the remote control. "You went right past *Casablanca*. Oh, too bad. It's almost over."

"I don't watch anything in black and white," he said, trying vainly to get the remote back.

Meg held it safely out of his range, sending him a dirty look. "You said you liked old movies. How can you like old movies if you pass up black and white?"

"I like old movies in color."

"That's ridiculous." She pointed the remote at the screen and slowly checked out the channels. "Oh, wow. *Notorious*. I love this one." She edged back into the cushions. "It's just starting."

"Black and white," he said gloomily.

"Cary Grant," she returned with a great deal of enthusiasm. "He is so gorgeous in this movie. There's this fabulous kiss later, maybe ten minutes in."

"Oh, really?" Alex perked up and started to pay more attention. But that only lasted a minute or two. "I don't know. This is pretty boring."

"It is not boring. It's just story setup," Meg said intently. "See? Ingrid Bergman is kind of a bad girl—she's the notorious one—and Cary is coming on to her, because he's a spy. Ooh. Here comes the kiss. Not for a minute, but when he gets the phone call."

"He's a spy?"

"Uh-huh. Didn't you get that? Weren't you paying attention?" She glanced over. Had he moved closer? The love seat wasn't that big to start out with and he was practically on top of her. The fabric of his pants rubbed her jeans, from knee to hip, and his hand, resting so casually there on his leg, brushed her every time she breathed. Meg swallowed. Her leg felt as if it were on fire.

"How about some popcorn?" she asked brightly, furnishing herself an excuse to jump up and get out of there.

But he held her back. "No popcorn. The dinner you made was plenty, thanks."

Her brain was so fried by the fact that he was touching her again, and sitting so very close, that she almost didn't catch the significance. Sabina was supposed to have made the dinner. "*I* made?"

Alex's voice dropped lower, softer. "Did you really think I wouldn't notice?" he whispered.

"I, uh..." She had no idea what she thought. Who could think at a time like this? On the screen, Cary and Ingrid were wrapped in the world's longest kiss and offscreen, Meg couldn't stop staring at Alex's narrow, wicked lips. "Well, I didn't do much," she mumbled.

"Just helped out a little. Sabina was anxious—she wanted everything to be just right, since it was like a first date and everything, and since she was coming from Atlanta, there was no time for her to—"

"Shut up."

Meg blinked. "Shut up?"

"Shut up." And then he grabbed her and kissed her thoroughly.

His warm, hard mouth covered hers, stifling any further arguments as he pushed her back into the sofa cushions, sliding his long, strong body on top of her.

The whole thing—the kiss, his mouth, the flat-out assault on her senses—was overpowering and breathtaking, shocking and incredible.

Meg kissed him back. He had a terrific mouth and it was doing all kinds of crazy things to her nervous system. Little sparks seemed to be shooting down her arms and up from her toes.

She sighed. She let herself slip down under him a little further. *Wow.*

She had been kissed before, but never like this, with such single-minded, ruthless intensity. She had been attracted to men before, but never like this, with such mind-numbing, reckless hunger. This was just...amazing.

"Wow," she breathed, wrapping her arms around his neck, plastering herself against his chest, lifting herself up to keep the kiss coming. "Wow."

Alex pulled back just an inch or two. She figured he'd had to come up for air and she lay back into the sofa pillows, dizzily catching her own breath while she waited for him to launch a second round.

But he didn't.

He leaned in very close, and his eyes were a moody, mysterious blue when he said, very deliberately, "When exactly were you planning to tell me that you're the one who writes the books?"

Chapter Seven

Within any relationship, honesty is truly the best policy. Yes, it is always tempting to shade the truth. Unfortunately, half-truths, even well-intentioned, seem to grow by leaps and bounds, multiplying faster and faster, until the little white lies have taken on a veritable life of their own. And when the ax falls, as it always does, when you must face the crazy quilt of stories you've stitched together, this fact stands clear: you will be very sorry you ever lied in the first place...

—*The Sabina Charles No-Fuss Guide to Modern Marriage*

He waited for her answer. None came. So he asked again. "Well, Meg? When were you planning to tell me? Or were you just going to keep rolling along, letting me make an ass of myself?"

"I don't know what you mean," she whispered.

"Of course you do." She had escaped him before, but this time, wedged firmly under his body, she had nowhere to run to. And he was enjoying it immensely, in a sadistic sort of way.

He'd been playing cat and mouse with her ever since she ventured down to the kitchen, but he had her good and cornered now. He wasn't sure himself if the romantic interlude was part of his original plan to trap her or just a momentary diversion, but it hardly mattered at the moment. She was going to admit to the truth, the whole truth, or he wasn't going to let her out of this den alive.

"Time to come clean, Meg," he told her, in a very commanding tone. He held her down and stared her right in the eye. "I knew from the beginning there was something fishy about you."

"Me? Fishy? That's the silliest thing I ever heard." She turned her head to one side, refusing to look at him.

But he persisted, angry and annoyed that she and Sabina had ever thought they could fool him. Of all the ridiculous stunts.

"That's what you've been trying to hide, isn't it? That Sabina is a first-class fake, that she can't even tie her own shoelaces and you're the real *No-Fuss* expert."

Her face was flushed, but he couldn't tell if that was from their tumble on the couch or from the fact that she'd been found out at last.

"Tell the truth, Meg," he ordered. "I know that's tough for you, but it's high time."

Quietly, she lifted her chin. "You've made a big mistake."

"I don't think so."

"Well, I know so."

With grim determination, she struggled under him, trying to sit up, to push herself free. But he liked her where he had her and he had no intention of letting her go. Although the little wiggle she was doing was just about enough to undo him completely.

"Stop wiggling," he said tersely. "Sit still."

"Let me up!"

But he only leaned in closer. He didn't have a whole lot of practice acting menacing outside the boardroom, but he thought he was doing nicely. "No. You're not going anywhere until you tell me the truth about Sabina."

"You already," she managed between clenched teeth, "know the truth."

Now that was more like it. He relaxed, settling back on his haunches. "So you admit she's a fake and you wrote the books?"

"No way!" Taking her opportunity, Meg scooted out so fast he almost fell off the love seat. With one arm outstretched to fend him off, she nursed her bruised dignity. "Of course Sabina writes the books," she said angrily. "How could I do it? I don't even have a college education."

"Neither did Shakespeare," he remarked.

"Oh, please. How could I write those books?" She swung her arm in a wide, emphatic gesture. "Look at me, Alex. Take a good look. I am a very plain and simple person who has never been married, never owned a home, never even hosted a party without a keg of beer somewhere on the premises. You are looking at someone who didn't even go to her own prom! How would I write books about how to entertain society people, or keep your relationships afloat, or decorate your house to look like a million bucks?"

"This self-deprecating act doesn't become you."

Nonetheless, she had a point. Although he didn't think there was anything wrong with the way Meg dressed or behaved, he had to admit that she wasn't exactly a role model for elegance and style, either. In fact, in her worn jeans and T-shirt, still damp from too many run-ins with various sinks, with tousled hair and no makeup, she looked more like the kid next door than a woman who lectured the world on how to keep it all together.

But he still didn't believe her. There were just too many irregularities. Like Baby Remington, for one.

"What about the baby?" he demanded.

A palpable hit. Meg went very still. Very cautiously, in a voice that sounded a bit too innocent to be believable, she asked, "The baby? What about the baby?"

Alex let out a huff. "Sabina couldn't even give him a bath," he scoffed. "Some parenting expert."

"Oh, the bath!" Her eyes held him. "Is that all?"

"Isn't that enough?" he demanded.

"Oh, sure. Of course. I mean, yes."

"So you're admitting she was faking it?"

"The bath?"

This was getting ridiculous. "Yes, the damn bath!"

Meg smiled weakly. "She wasn't exactly faking it. It's just that . . . she was busy, so I helped out."

"She didn't know what she was doing—it was patently clear." He was starting to get really angry again, the way he'd felt when the light dawned over dinner and he'd seen through their scheme. "Anyone who doesn't know how to give her own child a bath doesn't know enough to write a book," he said firmly. "Some parenting skills!"

"Then I guess you're right out of the parenting sweepstakes, because you didn't know, either," Meg pointed out.

"That's different. I'm a—"

"A guy, right?" Her tone grew a bit saucier. "You're a guy, so it's okay for you to be inept and uncoordinated."

"We're not talking about me," he said with a certain edge. "I already know I'm a rotten father, okay?"

"You think you're a rotten father?" she asked with sudden sympathy. "Oh, Alex, you don't really think that, do you? That's a terrible thing to say about yourself!"

But he waved away her change of subject, doing his utmost to project Off Limits signs with every heartbeat. "We're talking about Sabina, not me. We're talking about the fact that she could not bathe her own child without instructions."

She paused, as if she were waiting for him to go on.

"Well?" he said. "Isn't that enough?"

Meg rolled her eyes. "That's it? You're basing your whole theory that Sabina is a fake on one botched baby bath? You *kissed* me and held me prisoner on a love seat because of *that?*"

He wished she would stick to the subject at hand and quit confusing him with all these tangents. But maybe that was the idea. Meg had always been very confusing. Whether she was dancing or arguing or washing dishes, she had a way of veering off in strange directions and dragging him along for the ride.

"Well?" she prompted. "I'd like to hear what the whole love seat thing…" Here she had the grace to blush, but she pressed onward. That was Meg, hell-bent for leather no matter how much she embarrassed herself. It was kind of endearing, actually. She crossed her arms over her chest. "I'd like to know what that thing in the love seat was all about."

He lifted one eyebrow. "That thing in the love seat? Is that what we're calling it these days?"

Well, if he were honest, she had a reason to give him grief on that account. His conduct had been less than honorable. But, damn it, he had thoroughly enjoyed that kiss and he knew Meg had, too. "Don't tell me you weren't having a good time," he said sternly. "I know better."

Her cheeks grew pinker, but she didn't answer. And he didn't feel bad at all about "that thing in the love seat." It wasn't his fault if the only way to get her to admit the truth was to hold her down and kiss some sense into her. Was it?

"Let's get back to Sabina, shall we?" Meg said fiercely, changing tactics madly, right before his eyes. "Did it ever occur to you that Sabina, like you, is a working parent?"

"What's that supposed to excuse?"

She ignored him and went right on. "So, yes, she has let some of the day-to-day stuff slide. That baby—her baby, I mean—Remington has a nanny, remember? The nanny does the bathing and so maybe Sabina is a little rusty. What does that prove?"

"She's supposed to be a child care expert," he maintained.

"Yeah, well, she knows the big stuff. It's the little stuff that she isn't so hot at." Shrugging, Meg added, "I really don't think she ever said in her books she was a bathing whiz."

"All right, I'll give you the bath then," he said magnanimously, plenty tired of that subject, anyway. "But what about dinner?"

"What about it?"

"*You* made it. We already established that, remember?"

"We did not establish that! I tried to explain and you told me to shut up," Meg reminded him.

"I kissed you," he returned.

"You told me to shut up and *then* you kissed me."

He smiled. No argument there. "I apologize. For both."

Meg shot him a strange glance and he had the feeling she wasn't sure exactly what he was apologizing for. He wasn't sure himself.

"Forget about that for right now, okay? The point here is that *you* made dinner, didn't you?" Alex shook his head, remembering. "I took one look at that dessert thing and I knew there was no way it came from Sabina. You, however, are a perfect match. I don't know anyone else who would offer a dessert in the shape of a porcupine. Or was it a pinecone? What the hell was it, anyway?"

"A hedgehog," she said awkwardly. "A poppy seed hedgehog. I knew I never should've served that stupid thing."

He almost laughed. If he hadn't been so irritated by the whole thing with Sabina, he would have. Trying to stop his lips from curving into a smile, he asked, "What in God's name is a poppy seed hedgehog?"

"My mother made it, okay? It's something they sell in the bakery, for kids' parties and things."

"What bakery?"

"My parents have a bakery. In Brooklyn."

Alex wondered if his face looked as confused as he felt. "Your parents have a bakery in Brooklyn?"

"Uh-huh." She managed a smile. "It's small, but their stuff is really good. My sister Anne-Marie and her husband Bobby work there, too. Of course, when my parents retire and Anne-Marie and Bobby take over, the bakery will go down the tubes pronto, but right now—"

He should have learned his lesson not to let Meg get started on the subject of her family. Yet another sister? How many of them were there? "Meg," he said kindly, interrupting when she paused for breath, "I'm sure your parents' bakery is just wonderful, but the bottom line is that Sabina is supposed to be a gourmet cook, but you made dinner, even if your mother did contribute the hedgehog."

"Oh, right." There was a short pause. Meg avoided his eyes. "Well, you know, the fact that Sabina has written several cookbooks means she has a skill for collecting recipes, not necessarily for cooking."

"I believe she has been on more than one talk show, claiming she tried every one of those recipes herself." And he had the dossier of interviews to prove it.

"And I'm sure she did. She can cook," Meg argued. "Of course she can cook! I think she went to the Cordon Bleu in Paris or something. But she just didn't happen to *want* to cook on this particular occasion. This was different. She'd just got back from Atlanta and she didn't have time to shop or anything, plus she was running around taking care of, um, Remington, as well as trying to impress you, so—"

"So she called in the cavalry."

Meg laughed. "I'm hardly anybody's idea of the cavalry. But even if I did pitch in a little, I don't see why that makes you assume, out of the blue, that Sabina didn't write her own books." She began to chew on the edge of one of those fabulous red fingernails, the red fingernails that he kept imagining raking down his... Alex swallowed.

"It's kind of a logical leap," she said, and he jerked himself back to reality, away from her fingernails.

He was getting nowhere, even though he was still convinced he was right. But Meg was a stubborn little thing and she was clearly not going to give in until he absolutely forced her. Maybe he should have interrogated Sabina instead.

Nah. For one thing, he wasn't sure he could stomach five more minutes in her inane and vapid company. And for another, he had a feeling she'd just smile and tell him whatever he wanted to hear, no matter how idiotic her stories became.

"All right. Let's put aside the fact that she doesn't know the first thing about child care or cooking." He took Meg's shoulders in his hands and turned her to face him head-on. "But I've got you dead to rights on this next one. When we were cleaning up the kitchen and you didn't like the way I loaded the dishwasher, what did you say to me?"

"I don't know." She bit her lip and looked pensive. "Something about being a perfectionist."

"You said it's easy to accept less than perfection when you're trying to run a household, but you can't give in. 'Organization, patience and the willingness to hold out for a job well-done will ultimately make your household a happier, cleaner, brighter place to be.'"

Her jaw dropped. "How can you remember that, word for word?"

"Photographic memory," he said impatiently. "Who cares how I remember?"

"Oh God," Meg mumbled. "Just my luck. He has a photographic memory."

"Forget it, okay?" He shook his head. "The point is, I remember. And when you said it, I recognized it. It's in one of the books." Triumphantly, he pounded the last nail in her coffin. "I thumbed through the *No-Fuss Guide to a Happy Home* a few days ago. Those exact words are in that book."

"It's just something my mother used to say—"

"*Your* mother. What's she doing in Sabina's book?" He searched her eyes. "You see? You can't answer that."

"Of course I can." She shook off his hands. "I do have some input, you know. I'm her assistant. So I probably added it to the book because it fit, or she heard me say it and she took it. But I certainly don't write the books." Primly, she said, "That would be fraud."

"No, Meg, that would be ghostwriting." Cynically, he added, "Happens all the time."

"For fiction, maybe. Or celebrity autobiographies." Meg stood up and began to pace back and forth rapidly. "But for the kind of books Sabina does, well, it would be *wrong*. It would be like Heloise admitting that she's never had a hint of her own, or Bob Vila saying he doesn't know a hammer from a crescent wrench."

He rose, going after her. "Meg—"

"No, Alex, this is serious. You've..." She swallowed and then went on. "You've impugned Sabina's integrity. And mine, too."

He couldn't help the smile on that one. She suddenly sounded like a different person with a different vocabulary, like a character from "Murder, She Wrote." Or maybe a person who could manufacture a fancy enough vocabulary to write a pile of *No-Fuss* books. His smile faded.

But Meg wasn't finished. Launching into another phase of her argument, she said, "It's like the people who buy the books are buying *Sabina*—her image, her reputation, the whole package. They look at her and they see what they would like to be. And that's why they trust her advice on entertaining and cooking and dressing and etiquette, because she's a walking advertisement for living the perfect life. If she had a ghostwriter, people wouldn't trust the advice, would they?"

"Just because they trust her doesn't mean she's trustworthy."

"It isn't me," she said stubbornly. "You're really way off base."

He shrugged, not sure he believed her and not sure he didn't.

The problem wasn't that he found it difficult to believe in Sabina; it was that he found it impossible *not* to believe in Meg.

With those wide, soft eyes and that spark of spirit, she seemed so honest, as if lies would stick out on her like a sore thumb. Like a poppy seed hedgehog.

Meg might be a little odd, with her funny fingernails and her red cowboy boots, but the simple truth was that he actually liked her. A lot. She had an honesty, a freshness, a vulnerability he wasn't sure he'd ever encountered before. She kept throwing him curveballs. And Lord knew he could use the batting practice.

"Oh God," he said out loud. "I don't need this."

"Need what?"

He shoved his hands into his pockets. "I don't need . . ." But he couldn't say it. *I don't need* you.

Standing there, waiting for his answer, looking about as apprehensive as a defendant in the dock, Meg was just so darn adorable. He looked at her and he wanted to push her back down into the sofa and spend the next few days doing nothing but holding her and kissing her and reassuring her that he believed her.

Which was, of course, impossible. Even if Sabina was a fake, even if she did not have the expertise to clean up his life and solve his problems, it didn't mean he could recklessly pursue someone like Meg.

She had hit the dilemma on the head when she'd toted up the reasons she couldn't be the one who wrote the books; unfortunately, those were exactly the same reasons she wasn't remotely the kind of woman he needed to find.

She was funny and fresh, but not exactly mom material, not for the peaceful, organized household he envisioned, at any rate. And certainly not corporate wife material.

Unpolished, sarcastic, feisty, vulnerable. She wouldn't last five minutes in his cutthroat world.

"You believe me, don't you?" she asked, giving him the full benefit of her warm brown gaze.

He wanted to hold her, but instead he took her by her shoulders, telling her gently, "I know you want to be loyal to Sabina and that's very sweet. Really. But you don't have to keep it up with me."

She twisted away, looking anxious and confused.

"Listen, Meg, it doesn't matter much whether I believe you or not," he went on. "Even if Sabina really *can* manage to muddle through and write those books, she's still a fraud. She's marketing herself as an authentic expert and she's not, Meg. We both know that." With more of an edge, he added, "The woman is a total incompetent."

All he'd seen her do credibly was bat her eyelashes. He pitied Remington, who was a very cute little boy. But the poor kid didn't have a chance.

"That's really not fair—" Meg began, but he interrupted.

"What's not fair is that she doesn't know how to do any of the things she says she does. She's pretending to the world that she can handle a lot of things that are way beyond her. You said yourself that people rely on her advice." Alex shook his head firmly. "Advice that isn't worth the paper it's printed on."

How could he ever have believed Sabina could solve his problems? He had based his whole cockamamy theory of how to finally, blessedly, control his daughters on Sabina's expertise. What a joke. Why, she was no more an expert than *he* was.

"She's made a fool of me," he said under his breath, turning his back on Meg. "And Alex Thornhill is nobody's fool."

"Alex—"

"Since she does, after all, work for my company," he said sharply, "I'm beginning to think it is my corporate duty to dispose of the matter of her supposed expertise once and for all."

Meg caught her breath. "You mean tell the people at Daybreak Books that she's an amateur?"

"More like tell the people at Daybreak Books that she's an all-out fake and they ought to find themselves a real expert to market."

"Oh my God." She sat down on the love seat with a thump. "You're going to fire her. Us, I mean. Out the door, down the tubes, back to Brooklyn."

"Sabina's not from Brooklyn." That much he was sure of.

"But I am!"

"You could work for anyone. Why do you—"

"Alex, you can't," she said abruptly, grabbing the front of his shirt and tugging him down to her level. "This is so unfair. You don't know what she's really like. I mean, you saw her half-dead from jet lag, not acting like herself."

Meg was upset, that was for sure, and he had enough decency to be sorry that she was upset, but he still wasn't convinced he shouldn't blow the whistle on Sabina. "That's just not the way we do business at Dateline/Dynasty," he insisted. "Our hallmark has always been quality and integrity. That's not Sabina."

"But I think you're judging her unfairly." More strongly, she said, "I think you should give her another chance."

"Another chance?" He had no idea why he should. "What kind of chance?"

"You obviously liked something about her or you wouldn't have pursued her the way you did, calling all the time, piling up all that research."

"Yes, but that was before—"

"I know, but see, what if you were right in the first place?"

If he were right in the first place, he would have been rushing Sabina to the altar by now, happily contemplating the stability and peace she had in store for his household. Instead, he was worse off than when he started. He now faced the prospect of returning home to nanny number thirty-seven, undoubtedly packing her bags even as they spoke, with all the problems of two motherless children once more tossed in his lap.

It was galling. It was depressing. And it was Sabina Charles's fault.

"You shouldn't let one weekend deter you," Meg persuaded. "I mean, I was calling you Mr. Bulldozer," she told him, as if that were some kind of compliment. "I can't believe you'd give up that easily."

"Meg, I don't know what you're trying to do here."

"I'm trying to fix things between you and Sabina," she said sharply, still clasping handfuls of his shirt, rocking him back and forth with her exuberance. "It should be pretty darned obvious!"

"Fix things, as in fix us up?" he asked slowly.

Now he was even more bewildered. He thought he'd made it clear he was no longer interested in Sabina and might be interested in Meg, not in the same way, not long-term, but in some capacity, at least for right now. What else was the wrestling on the love seat about?

He narrowed his eyes. Did Meg throw herself onto the couch that enthusiastically with any guy who came along?

And if not, if she really was as attracted to him as he was to her, in a very intriguing and individual way, then why the hell was she trying to throw him back at Sabina?

"You want me with Sabina now?"

"Kind of. I guess." She bit her lip. "Yes. Yes, I do."

"But if you're so gung ho to match me up with Sabina," he said warily, "why were you trying so hard to keep me away from her in the beginning?"

"I was overprotective," she offered anxiously. She released his shirt and stood up, pacing again, as he fell back onto the love seat. "I was wrong. Besides, she told me that she really likes you. And she's my boss. And I like her. You said it yourself—I'm loyal to a fault. I want what she wants."

Then why were you necking with me in the wee hours of the morning? This had to be the oddest employee-employer relationship he'd ever seen. "What is really going on here?" he asked.

"I—I don't know what you mean."

He eyed Meg for a long moment. "You are telling me the truth now, aren't you, Meg?"

"Yes, of course."

"Because I won't tolerate being lied to, not by you."

"I wouldn't lie to you, Alex."

She was holding out pretty well, but he thought he knew a way to call this bluff. "If you want me to give her another chance, if that's what you *really* want, Meg, I might be willing to reconsider."

She held her head high. "Great."

He'd assumed she would say no when push came to shove, that she would pick him over Sabina. He was wrong. Yet again. It was getting to be a habit.

As he glowered at her, Meg said quickly, "You won't regret this, Alex. I swear." Half wringing her hands, dancing on one foot, she leaned over and planted a delicate kiss on his cheek. And then she bolted from the room.

Alex groaned and fell back into the cushions of the love seat. He wouldn't regret it, huh? By agreeing to this scheme, he'd let Meg escape.

Considering that fact, he regretted his decision already.

MEG TIPTOED PAST THE CRIB where Zach was peacefully snoozing, his worn stuffed rabbit in his arms. She blew him a kiss but kept on going. When she stood next to the big four-poster bed, she bent down far enough to give Sabina a good shake. "Wake up, will you? This is a crisis," she whispered.

"Mmmph" was all that greeted her.

"He almost had us," she hissed, pounding on the bed to emphasize her words. "He figured it out, almost all of it. Thank God I talked him out of it, but he knows, Sabina. He knows!"

"Mmmph?"

"Are you awake? Did you hear me? He *knows!*"

"Wha—"

"Are you awake?"

"Yes, yes, yes. Be quiet!"

"Completely awake? Because this is important."

"It better be," Sabina mumbled, her eyes still shut. "You know that nothing is supposed to interrupt my sleep. If you don't get the proper amount of sleep, your face shows it. Look at the Rolling Stones. All those lines and wrinkles, and I know it's because they didn't get enough sleep—"

"Okay, okay." She'd heard that speech before, but the Rolling Stones were the least of her problems at the moment. "Listen to me—are you listening?—*he knows*. And he isn't a happy camper, either. In fact, he seems really ticked off that you aren't good at babies or cooking. I mean, I figured it would be a scandal if anyone, especially him, found out you didn't write the books, but I didn't expect him to take it so personally."

"What?" Sabina shot up in the bed, losing any hint of her well-practiced tranquillity, staring wide-eyed at Meg. "He knows you wrote the books? You told him?"

"No, I didn't tell him. I lied through my teeth. What do you think, I'm crazy?"

"How does he know?"

"He figured it out," she said grimly. "I told you he would. I told you ten minutes with the two of you alone together and he would."

"But I was so charming," Sabina insisted, clearly crestfallen. "I know things were frantic, what with the baby and the running around, but I centered myself, I did my mantra, I found my peaceful space."

And you threw flour on your face. Meg refrained from mentioning that.

"And then," the *No-Fuss* queen continued, "over dinner, I gave him the scene where Slake first fell in love

with Serenity. Word for word. He should've fallen in love
with me. It was all there in the writing!''

''You did a scene from 'Hope Springs Eternal'?'' Even
Meg was aghast at that one.

''Of course. We had the best writers in the business,''
Sabina told her earnestly. ''Why shouldn't I use their
words when I'm playing a similar scene in real life?''

*Because real life isn't a soap opera—sometimes it just
feels that way.*

''Forget about that for right now, okay? We have to do
something about Alex, and fast.''

''But if he knows, what can we do?'' Her eyes took on
a strange light. ''We could get something on him and
blackmail him into being quiet. Serenity would never
blackmail anyone, of course, but she has been blackmailed herself. And there was that one time, with her evil
twin—she blackmailed half the town, and I played her,
too, of course.''

''Forget Serenity and her evil twin. We're not black-
mailing him.''

Meg shook her head. How had they descended to this?
When she'd started working for Sabina, she'd thought
her boss was so reasonable, so sweet. Only now the
world's favorite expert on living a charmed life had de-
veloped a split personality and seemed to be having a lot
of difficulty telling fantasy from reality. And somehow
it fell to Meg to yank her back into the real world.

''Look, Sabina, he doesn't know for sure, okay? I kept
lying long enough that I sidetracked him.'' She shrugged.
''I think he may even have believed me.''

''So he knew, but you convinced him he was wrong?''
Sabina asked slowly. ''Is that right?''

''So far. I bought us some time, at least.'' She paused.
''And I bought you another chance.''

"At what?"

"At captivating him, of course." Over in the crib, she heard Zach stirring and she lowered her volume, if not her intensity. "Look, I pulled your fat out of the fire tonight. I did what I had to to get him off our backs. But now it's your turn to do some fat pulling."

"Huh?"

"Forget it," she said impatiently. "Our only chance is for him to fall for you—hook, line and sinker."

"But he should've done that tonight. I gave him all my best lines."

"Maybe you should concentrate on making *yourself* sound interesting and smart and forget about Serenity," Meg suggested quickly. "Here's the plan, okay? You go out to dinner with him and this time you stick to the.game plan. No Serenity. Stick with *Sabina*. You know how to be the quintessential Sabina Charles—you've done it a hundred times on TV and radio and no one has ever suspected a thing."

"Well, that's true enough."

"So go out with him and be convincing. Be seductive. Forget the chitchat—go for sex appeal."

Even she couldn't believe what she was saying. She kept telling herself it was her only chance to save her job, but she was having trouble working up any enthusiasm, even so. And she knew darned well it was no longer just her livelihood on the line. At this point, she would have given the whole wretched thing up gladly.

But she couldn't. Because now her pride was involved. Now the truth was the one thing she couldn't face.

The bottom line was not very pretty—Alex had furnished her with a chance to come clean and she had lied again.

Now, even if she found the courage to fess up and throw herself on his mercy, he would never speak to her again. *Alex Thornhill is nobody's fool.* Wasn't that what he'd said?

Yet she'd lied to him anyway. She had looked him right in those fabulous blue eyes and known she couldn't tell him the truth. She just couldn't.

And there was no going back now.

Feeling positively wretched, she forced herself to go on. "Have you got all that, Sabina? No cooking, no babies," she ordered. "Nothing but the two of you. Moonlight, music, love and romance..."

The Rainbow Room. Alex's arms. But she blocked the images out as best she could.

"Yes, yes, Meg. I'm sure I can handle it. Go away now. If I don't get my sleep, I won't be able to do anything." Sabina slipped back down into her bed and Meg could hear her beginning her mantra.

As she backed away from the bed, Meg tried not to feel too apprehensive. She had made her choice.

Instead of confessing and throwing herself on Alex Thornhill's mercy, she had chosen to brazen it out. She had chosen her pride over any ethics she might have.

She had chosen her pride over any more snuggling in love seats with Alex Thornhill. Bad bargain.

So he was going to go out with Sabina, and if the perfect *No-Fuss* package did her job properly, Alex would be smitten before they got past the appetizers.

Meg took a deep breath. Was there even a chance this would work?

And would she be able to stand it if it did?

Chapter Eight

Curiosity is vastly underrated, what with the dire predictions about expiring felines and all that sort of nonsense. Don't believe the warnings for a moment—charge full steam ahead! As it happens, curiosity can be a healthy and energizing force in your professional life and it can help you make lots of new friends on the personal front...

—*The Sabina Charles No-Fuss Guide to Life after Divorce*

The clock struck nine and Meg jumped.

Tonight was the night. The Big Date. Would Sabina be a dream? Or would she be a dud?

Meg had been climbing the walls ever since her boss had left more than an hour ago. She wanted desperately to know how it was going and she wished, for one insane moment, that they'd thought to wire Sabina before she left.

"Gee, I could've whispered hints in her ear if the conversation bogged down," she muttered to herself. "Me and Cyrano."

Although it actually sounded more like a stunt on "I Love Lucy," where Lucy and Ethel concoct a plan....

"My life has turned into a sitcom," she moaned, throwing herself into a pretty peach club chair across the room from her desk.

In keeping with the farcical atmosphere, Meg had hidden out like a total coward when Alex dropped by to pick up Sabina. Although she'd been eavesdropping like mad, she hadn't wanted to actually face Alex. Not when one look at him would conjure up heady memories of that kiss, that outrageous, fantastic kiss.

When one look at him would have her crying in her beer that she'd let him go.

"Now, Meg," she told herself sternly, "you really have to get yourself in hand here. He was never yours to let go. What are you, nuts? He's Mr. Suave, Mr. Eligible Bachelor, Mr. High Society. And you're nobody!"

The truth wasn't pleasant, but she kept giving it to herself, anyway. "So he gave you a thrill in the love seat," she said out loud. "It was probably just some tactic he was pulling. Those corporate guys are very tricky. They don't call them sharks for nothing. So just because you don't know why he kissed you doesn't mean he didn't have some reason that had absolutely nothing to do with really being attracted to you or wanting—"

"Meg, are you talking to yourself in there?" Sabina called out from the hall.

Meg glanced down at her Mickey Mouse watch. Sabina wasn't due home for hours. Was the date that much of a disaster? And why was she so immediately, incredibly happy to think it was?

"Why are you back so early?" she asked quickly.

"Why are you here so late?"

She wasn't about to admit she'd been waiting up for Sabina like a mother hen with an absent chick. "I was working late," she said instead. "The galleys are here on the updated *Dress to Impress* book and I had to look at them right away."

"Oh. Okay." Without further question, Sabina floated toward the stairs, as if she were planning to retire.

"Where are you going?" Meg demanded. "What happened between you and Alex?"

Sabina shrugged, lifting the shoulders of her elegant peach dinner suit in an eloquent gesture.

"We had a lovely time," she murmured. "He took me to the Four Seasons Grill, where, of course, everyone who is anyone meets to eavesdrop. I saw Freddy, who played Slake on 'Hope.' He gave me the eye, I'll tell you. And I also saw Maurice and Belinda from Daybreak Books, and they were quite impressed when they saw who my escort was. I told you that dating him was a good career move, because, of course, everyone who is anyone—"

"Okay, okay. But what happened?" Good career move? They were hovering on the edge of professional disaster and Sabina was rattling on about nonsense.

"Well, unfortunately, we never got past the appetizers." Sabina's eyes clouded. "And it was going so well."

Meg was past the antsy point and well into fear. "So what happened?" she tried again.

"Halfway through dinner, he got a call from his housekeeper to come home right away because his daughter needed him." Sabina sighed extravagantly. "I didn't even know he had a daughter."

"Two. Sydney and Lolly," Meg said automatically. "Eight and six. Blond like their mother."

Sabina shot her a very odd glance. "You're certainly up on the details."

Meg ignored her. "Which one was it? Is she okay? Not sick or anything?"

"Oh, I don't know." Sabina waved a careless hand. "Something about some curtains on fire or something. Nothing major."

"That's terrible," Meg murmured. "I hope she's okay. I hope Alex is okay."

Losing his wife and now perhaps nursing his motherless child through a fire-related injury. What a horrible thought. She wondered if she should call the hospitals or at least phone Alex, just to make sure everything was okay.

"Sabina, you do think his daughter was all right, don't you? He didn't say anything about any injuries from the fire?"

"I don't know. It sounded to me as if everything was fine." She shrugged again. "Except the nanny was quitting, so he had to go home right away."

Meg still felt that she ought to check, just to be sure. Odd that the nanny was quitting in the middle of the evening, though. And hadn't Alex said she was new, too?

"So what about you and Alex?" she asked anxiously. "Everything went okay as far as it went? He believed you? And he didn't say anything about spilling the beans to the people from Daybreak?" The people from Daybreak, who just happened to be sitting right there, eating in the same restaurant.

"No, no, everything was fine. I was..." Sabina smiled with all her customary self-possession and serenity. "I was quite charming, quite flirtatious and romantic. I added a sort of sparkle in my eyes, you know, just to entice him."

"Sounds terrific," Meg muttered. If there was any real personality hiding under all the layers of Sabina's artifice, she had clearly lost it years ago.

Meg just shook her head. She had only herself to blame for how bereft this made her feel. If Sabina was enough of a goon to method act her way through a simple dinner and if Alex was enough of a goon to buy it— well, it was all Meg's idea, wasn't it?

Meanwhile, there was still the issue of this mysterious fire and Alex's children. What a bizarre thing to happen during the middle of a date.

"He said we should reschedule the dinner," Sabina said vaguely, "after he finds a new housekeeper."

"When will that be?"

"I don't know." Her expression grew murky once more. "I hope it isn't going to be too long. I really think I've hit on just the right mix of things to keep him interested. A little Serenity, a little of her evil twin and then a dash of Murphy Brown, just for spice. He is awfully good-looking and I really enjoyed walking into the Four Seasons on his arm. I wonder where he'll take me next," she mused. "Le Cirque? Lutèce? You know, I wonder if Alex can get into the front room at Mortimer's."

Meg barely heard the names of New York's finest restaurants pass by her. She was still muddling through the problem of Alex's children and their burning curtains.

Why would their nanny quit because of an accident like that? And why would someone like Alex be turning over household help so rapidly? Very curious.

And Meg was nothing if not curious.

So what if Alex was off-limits? So what if she was trying to push him together with Sabina? One tiny favor that happened to assuage her curiosity as well as help the matchmaking scheme wouldn't hurt anything, would it?

"Look, Sabina, I might be able to help," she said suddenly. "I might be able to baby-sit."

"Baby-sit? For Alex's children?"

"Sure," she said casually. "Why not?"

Why not, indeed? Why not get a firsthand look at his swank Fifth Avenue apartment? Why not get a look at his children? She couldn't help it—she was still dying to know what kind of offspring someone like Alex would produce. Besides, she liked kids. She had several nieces in the five-to-ten range and they were her favorites— young enough to color and play dolls, yet not old enough to get fussy about boys.

She wasn't sure what it said for her social life that she truly enjoyed the company of seven-year-olds, but there it was.

"Really?" Sabina asked. "You're sure?"

"Sure." She was getting surer by the minute. She could see his place, meet his kids and keep an eye on the date with Sabina all in one fell swoop. Meg smiled. She liked things much better when she was in control.

"Okay," Sabina agreed easily, pulling off her earring as she strolled toward the phone. "I'll call him right away."

ALEX STIFLED A YAWN. Good heavens. They'd barely been served their entrées and already he was hoping he'd be rescued by a phone call that his condo was under siege.

He knew he shouldn't have chosen a French restaurant. For one thing, he didn't like the food. Where was a simple, perfectly cooked steak when you needed it? Instead, he was stuck with something whose name he couldn't remember, photographic memory be damned. Paupiette of something, whatever a paupiette was.

Sabina was happier with her food, although he hadn't the vaguest idea what she was eating, either. It didn't matter. She seemed more inclined to wave it around on her fork than eat it.

She was also doing her best to offer scintillating conversation and he had to give her credit for that, although he could swear he'd heard at least one of her anecdotes told by somebody else on a talk show. Candice Bergen on "The Tonight Show," perhaps? Had Sabina appropriated someone else's anecdote the way she had other people's work product?

But then, he had a suspicious mind.

"Lovely restaurant," she murmured. "Do you come here often?"

"No, actually, I don't believe I've ever been here. My secretary recommended it."

"My compliments," Sabina said, lifting her wineglass and speaking breathlessly, with a bit of girlishness, "to your secretary."

And then she winked at him.

Alex blinked. Yes, she had definitely winked at him. And now she was artfully licking her bottom lip with the tip of her tongue. What did she think this was? A dinner date or a seduction scene?

When he had first hit upon the brilliant idea of bringing the great Sabina Charles into his life, he had contemplated seducing her, if necessary, to bring peace to his home front. But he had abandoned that idea long ago.

Apparently Sabina had not.

Feeling a bit queasy, although that could have been the fault of the paupiette, he fiddled with his napkin. How extraordinary to be out to dinner with a beautiful woman who was obviously—very obviously—making a move on him and then to feel absolutely incapable of responding.

For the sake of politeness, he should have at least managed some measure of flirtation in response. But he couldn't.

No, he couldn't. And it wasn't as if she turned him off or repulsed him. It was just that she bored him silly.

She was giving him the eye and he felt *bored*. In fact, he couldn't even concentrate on what new coquettish words she was whispering at him over the table. Something about seafood as an aphrodisiac. Was he eating seafood? He had no idea.

Whenever he didn't force himself to concentrate completely, his mind began to play tricks on him. It was as if there were a small candle burning in there, keeping alive the bizarre idea, the peculiar hope, that maybe Meg would turn up when he least expected it and inject some life into these dreary proceedings.

He kept catching himself looking over his shoulder, secretly expecting her to be hiding behind a waiter, lurking around the edge of a plush banquette. Damn the woman, anyway.

She'd made a habit of popping up when he didn't want her. So why couldn't she try it when he did?

"WELL, AREN'T WE having fun?"

Trying to put on a brave face, Meg sat very gingerly on the skinny red sofa, which felt as if it might collapse if you looked at it funny.

Of course, the couch had it head and shoulders, or perhaps arms and legs, over that spindly looking white chair. Meg knew Louis XVI when she saw it; after all, she'd written a book on home decor, which had included illustrations of famous styles. She'd never actually known anyone who owned a Chippendale table or a

Hepplewhite chair, however, and she'd never imagined that she would.

Very chichi. The whole place looked like a museum if you asked her, but that was apparently how rich folks lived. Or this kind of rich person, anyway.

Sabina's town house was very pretty and elegant, but at least the stuff in it was new. Alex appeared to go for something more like you'd find in those funky little back rooms at the Metropolitan Museum.

In her opinion, this place was nowhere to raise a family. How were kids supposed to roughhouse in a museum? And these girls couldn't even go outside to blow off steam, since they lived on the twelfth floor and there was no one to take them past the barrage of doormen and elevator guys. They could stare out the terrace at Central Park but never actually go there. Wasn't that jolly?

Not that Alex's daughters showed any sign of roughhousing or blowing off steam. So far, they'd sat very nicely on the rickety living room chairs, hands clasped in their laps, staring openly at Meg. They both wore very nifty little dresses in tiny French country prints, both had bows in their hair, both had shiny patent leather Mary Janes with white anklets, and both were immaculate.

Upscale, urban princesses. Not the kind of kids she was used to.

But Meg refused to be intimidated by two solemn little girls, no matter how well dressed. "So," she said conversationally, "where do you go to school?"

"We don't," the older one returned. That would be Sydney, the more immaculate of the two.

"You don't? Why not?"

"We were kicked out."

That raised her eyebrows. "Kicked out? What did you do, smoke in the bathroom?"

It was intended as a joke, but the Thornhill girls exchanged quick glances, as if getting their stories straight before responding.

Sydney regarded Meg gravely. "How many do you want to know?" she asked finally.

"How many what?"

"How many *reasons*," Lolly supplied impatiently. "How many schools do you want to know, because it's kind of a lot."

"A lot?" Meg wasn't getting this. "A lot of schools?"

Sydney nodded. "There was Breckenridge, where we set the wastebasket on fire. And Cluny, where we put the spiders in Madame LeBeau's desk. She was screaming and jumping around, 'member, Loll? That was so funny. And Ramsey, where Lolly spit strawberry milkshake all over Talbot Kittredge. Although maybe it was that we let all the frogs go from the science room that did it at Ramsey—"

"You guys are kidding, right?"

They shook their heads from side to side vigorously.

But Meg still wasn't buying it. "Oh, come on. You didn't do all that."

"Oh, *well*," Sydney announced in a very disparaging tone, "we thought you really wanted to know. But if you don't..."

"Uh-huh." Meg was taking all of this with a grain of salt. There was no way these pretty little angels had set fires and liberated frogs. Well, maybe the frogs. But fires... Fires. The subject of fires had come up recently. "Why did your last nanny leave?"

"The last one?" Sydney chewed her lip. "I dunno. Do you 'member, Loll?"

"Was that the one with the clothes we threw out the window?"

"Uh-uh. That was two or three ago."

"Shoes on fire?"

"No, dumbo," Sydney shot back, swinging her legs in her chair. "That was way long ago. Oh, wait, I know. This one was by accident. Lolly washed her doll's hair with toothpaste—"

"I did not!"

"Did, too," Sydney insisted. "You were going, 'Eek, eek, Barbie got a perm,' and running all over the house. And then you ran right into Mrs. What's-her-name, right into her big fat butt and she fell over."

"She fell over like an elephant. She almost squashed me," Lolly confirmed.

"And she had a cigarette in her hand, which was bad, because our nannies are not supposed to smoke, but she did anyway and when she fell, she grabbed the curtain with her same hand that had the cigarette and it went on fire." Sydney lifted her chin. "So it was not our fault that the curtain went on fire."

Meg just sat there with her mouth open. *Oh my God. Alex's daughters are demonic.* Because even if they hadn't done the things they said they had, making up the stories was pretty scary in itself. "Does your father know about this?" she asked in a very thin voice.

"Well, kind of." Lolly tipped her head to one side. And she looked so sweet and cute. "He always has to talk to the firemen. So he knows."

"But, you guys, that's terrible!" Meg knew she sounded like a real Pollyanna, but she couldn't help it. What was she supposed to do, run from the room screaming? "Why do you do these things?"

"Well, at the schools we did it because we didn't like it there," Sydney explained matter-of-factly as Lolly nodded. "And with the nannies and stuff, we did it because we didn't like them. They were stupid and mean and they told us to sit in our room and be quiet. It was dumb. So we got them to go away."

Meg's general theory on children was that they were bound to be a little wild now and again, that you were just firm and compassionate and they would come around to doing things your way sooner or later. But with these two... Well, their crimes were out of her league.

There was her cousin Bruce, the scandal of the family. He had a penchant for trouble, too, and he got kicked out of St. Vincent Xavier for setting fire to the trash can in the boys' rest room. He'd straightened out eventually, hadn't he? What did they do to him? Reform school?

With her sisters and cousins growing up, with her sisters' kids and cousins' kids now, Meg's game plan was very simple. If you let them play hard enough, they were usually too tired to misbehave too badly.

But she wasn't at all sure that would work with incorrigibles like these.

"Okay," she said abruptly, "let's talk turkey."

"Gobble, gobble," Lolly said, giggling at her own joke, wobbling unsteadily on her chair.

"That means, let's be honest with each other, okay?"

They glanced at each other, seemed to consider and then nodded in unison. Maybe honesty was a novelty.

"How many schools are we talking about, that you've been kicked out of?"

Lolly screwed up her face and looked at the ceiling, as if the answer were up there. "'Bout a million."

"Six," Sydney allowed. "Six or seven or eight."

Ouch. Well, it could have been worse. "And how many nannies?"

"Just nannies, or do housekeepers and opera girls count?" Sydney asked seriously.

"And one buttle guy, too," Lolly added.

"It's not buttle, dumbo, it's butler."

"Buttle, buttle, buttle!"

Now this kind of nonsense she was used to. "How many?" Meg prompted.

"Hmm. I think Daddy said ninety-eight." Sydney looked at her sister for guidance. "Is that what you think, Loll?"

"Daddy knows 'zactly. Hunnert and fifty-eight, that's what I think."

Meg felt this information was less than reliable. She wasn't sure there were one hundred and fifty-eight nannies in all of New York. "Whatever it is, it's a lot, huh?"

Two pretty blond heads bobbed up and down.

"Okay, well, tonight you're with me and I'm really tough. Not mean, just tough." Establish firmness up front, she thought. That seemed like a good idea. Although surely someone in all those schools and all those nannies had thought of it. "I want a pact that while you're with me, you won't set anything on fire, throw anything off the balcony or out the windows or anything else you know is really, really bad. If you get the urge, you come to me and you say, 'Meg, I'm itching to spit milkshake at someone,' or, 'I really, really want to set something on fire,' and then we'll find something else to do, okay?"

They considered, although they weren't really going for it yet.

"Because you see, you guys, if you really act up, then I have to call the cops."

Lolly giggled again. "We knows lots of them. They come when you call 911."

Forget the cop thing. But that was okay. Instead of negative reinforcement, she firmly believed in offering something positive. "If you are really good and behave really well..." They both rolled their eyes as if they'd heard this one a million times. But Meg was stubborn. "If you're good, we can have a lot of fun. We can play games or dolls or whatever you want. But only if you're good."

Sydney sat up straighter, sending Meg a pained expression. "Yeah, we know. You want me and Lolly to go play quietly in our rooms. And if we're quiet for the whole night, then we can go to FAO Schwartz and get any toy we want."

"No way. I'm not giving you any toys. You have plenty of toys," she said. Even a quick glance around the room made that clear. "I mean all three of us can do whatever you want. You know, play Twister or hokeypokey or something." She narrowed her eyes. "I said we could have *fun.* What fun is it if you go play in your rooms by yourselves?"

"I dunno." Sydney looked at Lolly, who shook her head. "They always tell us that."

"And besides, we don't have Twister," Lolly said loudly.

"Okay, well, would you rather go out, then? I'm sure we could have fun outside, get some fresh air, that kind of thing."

"Where?"

"Where do you want to go?" Having fun here was like pulling teeth.

"We go to the toy store a lot," Lolly volunteered.

"Also the movies and the theater and the museums," Sydney said in a very bored voice. "And we saw *Cats* and we saw *Beauty and the Beast* and we saw *Nutcracker.* We go shopping, too. On Madison Avenue where all the stores are."

Not the stores Meg knew, but she was hardly surprised.

Lolly piped up with, "Mommy only buyed us certain
kinds and that's where they are, so that's where we go."

Apparently Puff, the paragon of high-society wifely
virtue, was every bit as chic as her husband. Although
Meg had heard there were people who sent their children
away to boarding school at the age of six months, people whose children wore clothes only from Madison Avenue boutiques, she had never known any personally.
Until now.

And these two and their personality disorders were not
exactly a walking advertisement.

"Well," Meg said dryly, "what with the stores and the
theater and the museums, your social life sounds a lot
more exciting than mine."

They shrugged. "Mommy took us lots," Lolly announced. "But since Mommy is gone, we mostly stay
home, or the nannies take us if we're quiet."

"This quiet thing keeps coming up. Quiet doesn't
sound like too much fun." Meg feared she was beginning to sound positively hearty, like some bizarre latter-
day Mary Poppins, with her spoonful of sugar and all
that. But maybe these kids didn't need any more obtuse
adults telling them what to do. Maybe what they needed
was a peer group. You could always trust other kids to
keep one of their own in line. "Maybe you have some
friends you want to come and visit? That might be fun."

Again, they exchanged glances. "We don't have any
friends," Sydney said politely.

"Not from school?"

"We don't go to school."

"Oh, right. I forgot." Scrambling for solutions, Meg
only knew one way out. She would turn the matter over

to a higher authority. She would ask her mother. "Listen, would you like to make some new friends?"

"Maybe," Sydney said slowly.

"All right." She put on a bright smile. "Let's go to Brooklyn."

Again, it was the older of the two who did the talking. "What's that?"

"That's where I used to live. I have lots of nieces and nephews and half of them are usually hanging out at my mom's house, because they like to play together. You can play with them. It will be fun." She just hoped it wasn't a complete and utter disaster.

Sydney tipped her head to one side. "Maybe we could go there."

Meg ticked off everything she could think of on her fingers. "If you come, you have to stick by me on the subway. Do what I tell you. Behave or we have to come home and then sit around and be bored again. Okay?"

Lolly leaned up to whisper in her sister's ear, after which Sydney whispered back even more heatedly. After a conference that lasted several minutes, Sydney stood tall. "Okay. We want to come."

"And you'll do what I tell you?"

Sydney shrugged. "Sure."

But as Meg took their hands and rang for the elevator, she hoped she wasn't doing something very stupid. Letting the baby lions out of the cage without even bothering to bring a whip did not seem like a terrific idea.

She eyed them suspiciously, wondering exactly who was in charge here. Maybe she ought to frisk them for matches before they left.

"DESSERT, SIR?"

Alex woke up. "Hmm? Oh, no, nothing for me." He

had been miles away, wondering what Meg was doing, envisioning some idyllic scene at his house. Maybe Meg and the girls were playing Chutes and Ladders or making cookies together.

Okay, so it was farfetched. But it was still possible. He remembered his own mother rolling out the dough for sugar cookies in the big steamy kitchen, letting him decorate a few extras of his own. Meg and his kids making cookies . . .

He smiled.

"So you like the idea?" Sabina asked.

"Very much," he murmured. He sat up. "Hmm? What idea?"

"My idea to offer my jewelry line to your shopping network as an exclusive," she said with a bit of a huff. "Do you mean you haven't been listening to me for the past fifteen minutes?"

"I'm sorry. My mind must have—"

"I have never been so insulted in my life," she snapped. "I don't care if you are the vice president. I don't care if you are going to tell my publisher to pull the plug on the *No-Fuss* books. I don't care if your shopping network *is* the best place to sell my makeup and jewelry lines. I don't like you!"

"I'm sorry, Sabina."

"I'm leaving," she announced, gathering up her beaded peach purse as she rose. She raised a hand to her forehead, closed her eyes and took several deep breaths. And then she smiled, with all the empty-headed calm he had come to expect from her. "So nice to have shared this evening with you. Thank you."

As he watched her glide smoothly through the diners, aiming for the door with her head held high, he had to admit it. He was relieved. Down to his socks.

"Waiter," he called. "Check, please."

He knew all the objections to starting something with Meg; he knew them by heart. But suddenly he didn't care. He wanted to see her and to be with her and he had no more time to waste on pale substitutes.

He got out of there as fast as he could, hailing the nearest cab and not bothering to wait to call his limo. He still had that rosy image of Meg and his daughters, dropping spoonfuls of dough on cookie sheets. He wanted to get home.

But as he opened the front door, no cozy domestic scene greeted him.

There were no homey odors wafting out from the kitchen and no charming pictures of tranquillity. Instead, the living room was a mess of scattered papers and rumpled cushions and the Louis XVI chair was sitting on its side.

And then he heard shouts and thumps coming from the back of the apartment, as if someone were fighting.

"Oh, no." He felt palpable disappointment. He'd known in his heart that Meg wouldn't be any different, that she, like so many others before her, would go down in flames when confronted by his darling daughters. But he'd had such hopes.

Wondering what he was going to do this time, he raced down the hall toward the source of the commotion. The noise was coming from his own bedroom. What were they doing in there?

As he wrenched open the door, Meg and Sydney stopped where they were, both whirling to meet his gaze. But Lolly was giggling too hard to notice there was a newcomer and she spun around full circle, bringing a huge pillow with her, thwacking Meg soundly on the rump.

Meg jumped at the impact but then caught the girl, holding her still. "Lolly, um, your daddy's home," she announced brightly.

Both girls dangled their pillows awkwardly. He noticed that Sydney's pillow was leaking feathers out one end.

Meg said, "This isn't what it looks like."

Alex surveyed the room, from the thoroughly rumpled bedclothes to the liberal number of feathers dusting the floor and floating in the air. "What it looks like is a pillow fight."

Meg set Lolly back on the ground. "Well, that's what it was."

"We went to Boogertown," Lolly said cheerfully.

"Brooklyn," Sydney corrected, yanking her sister's arm. "Not Boogertown."

"On the subway," Lolly added, paying no attention to the restraint. "We went to Boogertown on the subway."

"You took my children to Brooklyn on the subway at night?"

"It wasn't that late," Meg protested. "I've been riding back and forth to Brooklyn on the subway my whole life." A little more firmly, she added, "And we had fun, didn't we?"

His daughters nodded with enthusiasm.

"Well, this isn't what I expected," Alex commented as he bent over to pick up a green marble bust of Alexander the Great that had either fallen or been knocked off its pillar. Its nose was chipped. Alex frowned down at it.

Puff had done the master bedroom in green and gold, with a few objets d'art like this one. He had never cared for it particularly, although it was impressive in an arty sort of way. It didn't improve it any to lose half its nose.

Mostly he was just off-balance and confused. Okay, so they weren't throwing anyone out the windows. But a pillow fight? Did they have to do something so noisy and boisterous? He wanted his daughters to be nice, polite young ladies again, not hooligans.

"And why did you pick my room for this?" he asked, directing the question at all three of them.

"We tried the front room, but it was boring because things kept knocking over. And your bed is the bounciest," Sydney said solemnly. "Meg said we could jump."

"Your pillows are bigger," Lolly chimed in. "They knock people over better."

Meg shrugged. "It seemed like a good idea at the time. Sorry about your, um, whoever that guy is."

"Alexander the Great."

Meg lost some of her contrite act as her lips curved into a mischievous smile. "You have a bust of Alexander the Great in your bedroom? Why, Alex, that's kind of kinky. Is there supposed to be some kind of message in that?"

"No," he said shortly, refusing to rise to the bait. He didn't appreciate her using words like *kinky* in front of his children, either. "Okay, girls, fun's over for tonight. Time for bed."

He was absolutely shocked when they chorused, "Okay. 'Bye, Meg!" and scampered off, just like kids on TV.

Lolly stuck her golden curls back around the doorframe. "Hey, Meg, can we go to Boogertown again?"

Behind her, Sydney corrected, "Brooklyn, you dumbo!"

"Uh, we'll have to ask your dad," Meg managed to reply.

As soon as the girls were safely out of earshot, before he even had a chance to open his mouth, Meg said quickly, "I know you were kind of shocked because it was so noisy, but we only had a few complaints from the neighbors and we did have fun."

There went the co-op. "A *few* complaints from the neighbors?"

"What a bunch of fuddy-duddies. I mean, jeez, you'd think they were never kids themselves." Lamely, she added, "I was trying to let the kids play hard enough that they would be too tired to misbehave. It's kind of this theory that I have."

"Interesting theory."

"I think it worked," she said hopefully. "You know, they were really good in Brooklyn. Better than I thought they'd be after I heard about all the schools they've been kicked out of and the nannies they've set on fire. Jeesh. That had me worried. But my ma said no, they're normal, just not getting enough exercise. I think sometimes a peer group helps. Like they'll be awful to adults, but they don't want all the other kids to dislike them. Or maybe just because things are so rambunctious at my house that they didn't stand out. But they made friends right away and we really had a—"

"Meg, could you please be quiet for a minute?"

She stopped in midbarrage. "Okay." After a moment, she asked, "Why?"

"Because there's something I have to tell you."

"Uh-oh. Is this about Sabina? Because if she didn't prove to you that she really *is* Sabina, I'll be—"

"Meg, listen to me," he interrupted. "I had a terrible time with Sabina. I don't care who she is."

Meg looked up, meeting his eyes. "You don't care?"

"No." He took a few steps in her direction. "I'm just not interested in Sabina."

"No?" she asked, and he came up right beside her.

"No," he whispered, taking her in his arms. "I'm interested in you."

Chapter Nine

When buying antiques, there are times when caution is definitely called for. The old adage that something that seems too good to be true *is* too good to be true should be stitched on a sampler and hung in the parlor just to remind us.

But sometimes, every once in a while, you simply have to trust yourself and go for an item you really want, even if you can't be sure it is authentic. If you know the risk and take the plunge anyway, you might just find the risk was worth taking. Who knows? You might enjoy the piece so much you simply don't care if it is authentic...

—*The Sabina Charles No-Fuss Guide to*
Collectibles

I'm interested in you.

Could she believe what she was hearing?

She didn't have a chance to figure it out. Before she could even react, Alex pulled her closer, lowered his lips to hers and kissed the pants off her without further ado.

Oh God. He was such a great kisser. As his arms tightened around her, pressing her up against him, she couldn't help but kiss him back, could she?

But this was too weird for words. She had been so sure he was mad about the pillow fight and the noise and the mess.

If this was how he showed anger, she wouldn't mind seeing him mad all the time.

His mouth was warm and liquid, so right as he delved deeper. Hastily, hungrily, he moved his caresses to her ear and the curve of her jaw.

"Oh." She sighed, relaxing, melting in spite of her better judgment.

Alex nibbled her neck, and that whole side of her body seemed to tingle and burn, all at the same time. Had she lost her mind?

"Wait a second here," Meg managed to say, dizzily backing away from his overwhelming embrace.

She swallowed. She breathed. She tried to jump start her brain. Every time he put his arms around her, her mind took a holiday. She had never experienced this sort of automatic pilot before, where her body seemed to operate independently of her common sense.

"Why wait?" Alex murmured, reaching for her again. "Don't worry, Meg," he whispered. "I won't say anything about Sabina. I promise. I just don't care about that anymore."

That was wonderful to hear. A tiny bubble of hope floated free inside her. *He's not going to rat on Sabina. My job is safe. Maybe I can have him and the job....*

She needed to think. Could this be?

"Wait," she said again, even huskier this time.

"Mmm," he murmured, taking her arms, fastening them around his neck. His hands slid over her curves, roaming free. "I don't want to wait. I'm enjoying *not* waiting right now."

"So am I." She sighed, almost giving in. She let herself touch the sleek softness of his hair, let herself angle in a little closer as he dropped kisses around the curve of her ear and into her hair. How could she resist him?

But she steeled herself. There was one more thing that had to be dealt with. She'd been telling herself all along that a woman like her had no chance whatever with a guy like him. And she still couldn't really believe this was happening.

"Alex, listen," she said with as much conviction as she could muster while he was nuzzling her like that, "I would like to believe you, that you're really interested in me, but . . . but you were awfully fired up about Sabina there for a while. We're not exactly the same type. So what do you want with me?"

"What I want from you is *you*," he assured her, and his voice was sweet and sexy, as gentle and as persistent as his hands, tugging her closer, wrapping her in his embrace.

Maybe he was serious.

"But you went after her big-time," she tried, even as she closed her eyes and enjoyed the heady feel of his lips descending on the curve of her neck, the sensation of his hand edging closer, almost but not quite touching the underside of her breast. She tried not to moan. But she couldn't breathe. Her body felt so hot, so steamy. Everything inside her was tight, edgy, waiting.

And where was his hand? *Oh God.* She was lost.

"Yes, I did go after Sabina. But that has nothing to do with us, with now. Just a momentary lapse in judgment, I guess."

Even through the haze of desire, she heard what he said.

"And while it's also true that, thus far in my life, you have not been exactly what you might call my *type*," he said roughly, angling a hand to the curve of her bottom, pulling her so close she could feel every muscle in that long, hard body, "I'm discovering you are exactly the type I need now, at this moment."

And then he kissed her again, hard and greedy and sure.

Gasping for breath, she broke away, grabbing on to him for support even as her mind raced a million miles an hour.

How could she buy into this? But how could she hold out when he did things like that?

Okay, so she knew she was being foolish to the max. There was no way this could ever work.

He dropped a kiss next to the corner of her mouth.

Maybe it could work for a little while.

And then a small, perfect kiss in the other corner.

Maybe until they both woke up and smelled the coffee.

Maybe it wouldn't be so terrible to let herself fall for Alex Thornhill and his sweet words and his blue eyes and his fabulous kisses.

His hard, hot mouth covered hers.

Just for a little while...

She had never been kissed like this, as if both their lives depended on it. It was stunning, breathless, mind-numbing.

"There's something about you," he murmured, breathing warm words in her ear. "Something fresh and alive. Something different. I like you, Meg. I honestly like you. More than any woman I've ever met."

And then he smiled, flashing perfect white teeth in that sexy, generous mouth, bathing her in warmth and charm.

Meg had to hold on tighter if she didn't want to ooze into a puddle right there, with him breathing on her and smiling like that, feeding her outrageous compliments. Had he really said there was something fresh and alive and different about *her?*

She had to admit she did feel ridiculously alive at the moment, as if there were tiny fireworks being set off everywhere his fingers touched, everywhere his lips brushed, everywhere...

"Wow." She sighed, tightening her arms around his neck, giving him free rein to keep doing whatever he was doing to make her feel this way. His breath tickled her. His embrace tantalized her. All in all, Alex was driving her crazy.

"Oh, yeah. Meg, I definitely like you."

"Well, you know, I kind of like you, too," she allowed.

Alex smiled, even more devilish than the last time. Still stroking her arms, her cheeks, her hair, never losing the connection of the kiss, he nudged her backward toward the big, rumpled bed.

"We shouldn't," she tried to protest, even as she fell back. "Your kids are just down the hall."

"The door is closed. And we won't do anything dangerous," he promised, climbing in after her, looping a hand around the back of her neck, drawing her back to him. "Just a few kisses. I just need to—" his gaze was smoky and hot "—hold you a little. Just a little."

He nipped at her lips, barely grazing her.

She let out a little moan of suppressed desire that she couldn't believe came from her very own lips. It sounded positively wanton.

Apparently Alex thought so, too. Without further ado, he pulled her underneath him on the soft bed, blasting her with a ferocious, soul-deep kiss that left them both shaking.

"Nothing dangerous, huh?" she gasped.

From the doorway, a small voice piped up, "Are you guys playing Twister?"

She felt Alex go perfectly still on top of her.

Slowly, Meg lifted her head and turned toward the hall, where Lolly's curious little face appeared, poking through the small crack where the door hung open. Her eyes were round and blue, exactly the same shade as her father's.

"Twister? Uh, not exactly," Meg said weakly.

Neatly setting her to one side of the bed, Alex got up and moved toward the door. "I'll just put Lolly back to bed," he said firmly.

Meg knew when fate was presenting a golden opportunity. "And I'll just say good-night." As he ushered Lolly down the hall, Meg scrambled off the bed and headed for the door.

"Good night, Meg!" Lolly shouted as tonight's babysitter disappeared down the hall.

"Meg, don't—"

But she had to get out of there before she sank into Alex's bed and never escaped.

From way down the hall she heard him vow, "I'll call you tomorrow. Meg? This isn't over."

Those words were the last thing she heard as she closed his front door. Wide-eyed and dazed, she leaned back against the cool door for just a second.

The great and powerful Alex Thornhill had just told her he liked her, he was interested in her and that he would call her.

Life had suddenly become a lot more complicated than she had ever imagined.

"LOOK, HERE'S THE THING," she explained to her sister. Propping her feet up on the coffee table, Meg balanced the phone on her shoulder. "I know this is so unbelievable as to be downright scary, but Alex Thornhill asked me out."

"Why is that so unbelievable?" Joannie inquired. "I could tell you had the hots for the guy."

"Okay, yeah, fine. But what I have the hots for is not exactly what usually has the hots for me, you know?"

"Oh, please." Meg could hear the lecture coming before Joannie said another word. "Is this going to be that 'poor little me, I never went to prom' stuff again? Because, Meg, I've been telling you for years, it's just because all the stupid guys at P.S. 84 were intimidated by you. You talk a lot, you're really smart and they were, like, bulldozed. But this Alex guy is obviously more your speed, that's all."

Meg laughed in her sister's ear. "Joannie, time-out while you buy a clue, okay? You want to talk about whose speed Alex is? Let's just say he's cruising the autobahn in his Porsche while I'm tooling the Jersey Turnpike in a '73 Pinto."

There was a short pause. "So buy a new car."

"Well, that's what I'm thinking of doing," she said a little defensively.

Again, silence filled the line. After a moment, Joannie said tentatively, "Meg, don't take this the wrong way, but I was only kidding. I don't think a new car will help you impress Alex Thornhill."

"I'm not really going to buy a car." Exasperated, Meg shook her head. "I meant it as a metaphor. I think that's what I meant it as, anyway. Metaphor, simile, something like that. Sometimes I really wish I'd gone to college."

"You don't learn that stuff in college. I think that's sixth-grade English class." Joannie waited, although Meg could hear the annoyance seeping over the wire. Finally, her sister demanded, "Are you going to explain what you're talking about, or am I going to sit here waiting for another English lesson?"

"What I meant was, well, I was thinking of a new look, maybe a cool outfit or something. After last night, when he and I sort of, you know, hit it off..." That was a bizarre way to describe last night, but nothing better came to mind and Meg charged ahead. "Alex called this morning, first thing, which I thought was so nice of him, because then I didn't have to wait all day, sweating it out, wondering if he was really going to—"

"Meg, you're a goner," her sister groaned. "Marry the guy and get it over with, will you?"

She ignored the comment. If her family had had their way, she would have married the first guy who ever took her out. They thought if somebody winked at her, it was tantamount to a marriage proposal. "This is not that serious, okay? We haven't even had one date."

"I have feelings about these things," Joannie maintained. "I could tell by the way you said his name the first time you met him. I think this is the one."

"Oh, he's definitely the one," Meg said with a lovestruck sigh before she had time to hold it back. She scrambled to sit up straighter. She confided, "I'm just not sure I'm *his* one, if you know what I mean."

"Aw, Meggie, will you get a grip? You shouldn't go out with him at all if you're going to be this weird about it."

"I'm not being weird, I'm just being…" Insecure. But who wouldn't be when faced with the likes of gorgeous Alex Thornhill and his wardrobe and his apartment and his dead wife, whom he had so much as said was perfect in every way? "You know, it's kind of odd. He never talks about Puff. He said she was perfect, I think, that night at the Rainbow Room, and I know she was blond because the kids are. But that's it. I've never even seen a picture. And I've been in his bedroom. Wouldn't you think there would be a picture there?"

"You've been in his bedroom?"

"Don't get your undies in a bundle. It was just a pillow fight with the kids. They wanted to jump on his bed," Meg explained, conveniently leaving out the tangle in his sheets after the kids toddled off to bed.

Well, nothing had happened, had it? Yes, she told Joannie everything, but that was one incident she preferred to keep quiet for the time being. After she knew whether anything would come of it, *then* maybe she'd tell Joannie the whole story. Maybe.

"No pictures of Puff, huh? Well, y'know, he's probably still dealing with it. Sometimes it feels even worse when you have to talk about it. And grief like that— something that big—takes time. You know, he probably loved her so much that he just can't bear to talk about her." Joannie's theory made sense, even if it wasn't something Meg wanted to hear. Joannie breathed a heartfelt sigh. "It's kind of romantic, don't you think?"

"All in all, I guess I'd rather he got over it."

"Meg!"

"I don't mean to sound heartless or anything, but it's been two years." Okay, so she sounded heartless. Meg sighed. She did have a great deal of sympathy for Alex and his children, having lost the center of their family.

Really she did. It was just that... "He needs to give up this image of Puff as the paragon of wifely virtues so that he can move on and take care of his kids. They're hurting and he's not doing anything."

"So maybe that's where you come in?"

"Surrogate mom? Replacing the perfect Puff? I don't think so." Meg frowned. They both knew that was way out of the realm of possibility.

"Don't worry about it, Meg. I'm sure he's not comparing the two of you or anything."

Ouch. That was one notion she didn't need planted in her fertile brain. Comparing her to Puff... although at least it gave her an idea. "Sorry, Joan, gotta go," she said abruptly.

"What? Where are you going? You haven't told me anything about this date with Mr. Wonderful or anything," Joannie wailed. "Where is he taking you? He took Sabina someplace really fancy, right? So he better take you someplace just as good," she said loyally.

"Okay, okay. Here's the scoop—Alex was going to have a few people over for drinks before this benefit they're all going to. My first date, and it's a test." More to herself than to her sister, Meg added, "We can't just go to a movie or something. No, *I* have to meet a whole pile of society people."

"Wow," Joannie murmured. "A big fancy party at his place. That sounds cool."

"It sounds scary if you ask me." Meg closed her eyes. "And like a real dim bulb, I offered to do the arrangements."

"Throw a party like that? You volunteered?"

"Not really a party, just drinks and hors d'oeuvres at his apartment. And I thought, I've called the caterers for Sabina before, so what's the big deal? I can call the ca-

terers for Alex." Meg knew she was trying to convince
herself more than her sister. "I used Sabina's favorite
caterer—you wouldn't believe what they charge, but
they've done Rockefellers and Trumps and Kennedys, so
I figured they were safe. Their special hors d'oeuvres are
wild mushroom polenta squares."

"Jeesh. Whatever that is, it sounds fabulous. See,
you're coping just fine. Your party will be a big hit."

"God, I hope so. I just don't know." Yes, she felt sure
she had handled everything so far with aplomb. But that
was only the beginning. The idea of standing in the
wings, planning a small cocktail party for a slice of the
social elite, was actually not all that daunting. But when
she considered actually attending the party, things got a
lot scarier. "The problem is that I don't have anything to
wear. And that's why I called you originally."

"A dress?"

"Or whatever. Something really special."

The Kaczmarowski sisters had been borrowing one
another's clothes since they were in Buster Browns. Now
that they were adults and all wore roughly the same size,
it was like having one big communal wardrobe.

Living in Manhattan, Meg didn't get to participate in
the wholesale fashion exchange as often as she used to,
but she still loaned and borrowed when something important came up.

"Hmm," Joannie said, musing. "I sure don't have
anything. Well, Anne-Marie has that black lace number
she wore to her high school reunion. Very va-va-va-
voom."

"Too slutty."

"Okay. How about Rhonda? She got that pink thing
with the lace collar when she sold Mary Kay."

"Pink? Too prissy."

"Darla's gold jumpsuit?"

"Too disco."

"Kim's red halter?"

"I wore it to the Rainbow Room."

"Jeez, Meg, I just don't know."

"I'm thinking," she began, then paused. This was heresy in the Kaczmarowski household, but she was going to do it anyway. "I'm thinking of buying something new, of going to a really chichi store and paying full price."

"You're kidding," Joannie said with a hush. "Full price?"

"No, I'm serious. If Alex's kids can buy their clothes on Madison Avenue, why shouldn't I?" Meg gathered courage. "If I want to fit in, I need to look right. Not just look nice, but classy and expensive."

"Meg, I don't know..."

"You don't think I can look classy and expensive?" she asked with a certain edge.

Well, she wasn't all that positive herself, but she'd hoped Joannie would be sure enough for both of them.

"Come on, that's not what I meant." After a long pause, Joannie said in a very honest and forthright tone, "I just think you should be yourself, that's all. I think he likes *you,* and trying to act like somebody you're not is not going to do anybody any good."

"I'll be me," Meg argued. "Just a classier and more expensive version."

Her sister sighed. "I suppose there's no harm in that."

"I'm going to knock his socks off," she promised. "I've got three days before the party. That's plenty of time to get a makeover and buy a new outfit. But first—"

She broke off, aware Joannie would object to what she had just decided to do.

"But first what?"

"Oh, nothing. Listen, Joannie, I really do have to go this time. Later, okay?"

But after she hung up, she completed the thought she hadn't wanted to share with her sister.

Out loud, she said, "I'm going to get a makeover and buy a new outfit, but first I'm going to do a little research."

Curious as always, not to mention a whiz at research, Meg knew exactly what she was going to do.

"I'll bet you a nickel Puff Thornhill was all over the society pages a few years ago. Let's just see what she looked like. And maybe then I'll know what I have to do to fit in at Alex's party."

She couldn't try to be like Puff, of course. But maybe just a hint would be nice. . . .

SHE SHOULDN'T have looked.

Puff was perfect. Smiling as she stood arm in arm with Yo-Yo Ma at some gala event she'd chaired, arching a fine eyebrow at some bon mot uttered by Gore Vidal, inclining her head at Alex in a picture announcing their wedding, Puff was cool and glamorous, with an impeccable air of privilege and assurance.

Her clothes were simple and chic, all in shades of cream and pale yellow. Her hair was a sleek blond chignon in one photo, a crisp pageboy in another. Her gaze was poised and calm.

And she looked enough like Sabina Charles to be her sister.

"Well, we've figured out the source of that attraction, haven't we?" Meg grumbled. "No wonder he picked her picture off the back of a book."

But it wasn't just the pictures. She'd also assembled a résumé of sorts for Alex's departed wife.

Puff, née Pamela, Lovell Thornhill; father, one-time ambassador to Luxembourg; attended the Nightingale-Bamford School for Girls and then Bryn Mawr, just like her mother and her sister. Worked briefly as a fashion buyer for Saks before marrying media exec Alexander Roger Thornhill in June 1984. Two children: Sydney Alexandra, born 1987, and Ann Lovell, called Lolly, born 1989.

Even the dry details of her résumé seemed perfect for Alex, what with the ambassador father and the chic schools—even a chic profession for a limited time.

Alex had married a beautiful blond fashion buyer who'd attended Bryn Mawr. And when she was gone, he'd looked around and, lo and behold, just happened to pick a beautiful blond TV star-author who'd attended Swarthmore, which Meg seemed to recall was just down the road a piece from Bryn Mawr.

Puff and Sabina, two of a kind.

Meg frowned as she stuffed the clippings into a desk drawer. Ever since she'd found the first one, she'd been staring at the damn things. She had suspected she wouldn't be a thing like Puff, and that much was true. But she hadn't realized there would be a Sabina connection. How truly depressing.

"But I'm not going to think about that right now," she said sternly, beginning to untie the belt on her robe.

Instead, she had to get dressed for this terrifying party. She'd been at Alex's apartment most of the day, making sure everything was ready.

The catering service had it all well in hand, though, and Meg had left several hours ago to come home and get ready. Instead, she'd spent half her time staring moodily at articles about Puff.

"Forget Puff," she ordered herself. "Forget the ambassador and Bryn Mawr." Time to be the new Meg.

She had a brand-new outfit, and it couldn't have been more elegant. With sedate pumps and pearls, the ice pink dinner suit was going to look perfectly, well, *perfect*. A Fifth Avenue stylist had blown her hair back into a straighter, more dignified do, and she'd gotten the same makeup Maria Shriver used—the saleslady had promised. She'd even clipped her nails down to a more respectable length and glossed them in a pale pink shade of polish.

Finished finally, Meg surveyed herself in her mirror. All in all, a very odd package.

"I shouldn't have done this," she said slowly. Yes, she looked classy enough to go work at the Junior League. But she felt like a real jerk. The suit's severe lines weren't all that comfortable, the shoes were hideous, and she'd never worn pearls before in her life.

But the main problem was that the clothes and the hair went only skin-deep. Underneath, it was the same old Meg, itching to get out. Idly, she wondered if there was still time to get to Brooklyn and borrow Darla's gold metallic jumpsuit.

But her time was up. Alex would arrive momentarily to pick her up, but that didn't mean she felt completely prepared when the knock came.

"Meg?" Alex called out from the hallway outside her apartment. He knocked again. "Are you ready?"

Inside, she began to quaver. What if he didn't like this version of the new Meg? "Just a minute," she told him. "Be right there."

But she couldn't hold out forever. With one last desperate look at her conservative silhouette, she went to get the door.

"Hi there," he said breezily, kissing her on the cheek, offering flowers. "Great to see you."

"Great to see you, too. You look fabulous." She knew her voice sounded like a gushy schoolgirl's, but it really was a treat to look at him. Every time she was away, she forgot how gorgeous he was. And in a dark suit with a white shirt—banded collar, no tie—he looked even more debonair, even more devastating.

"Pink roses. How nice. They go with my outfit." She'd never cared that much for roses, especially pink, but at least they weren't peach. She thanked her lucky stars for that. "They're beautiful, Alex. Just beautiful."

Not as beautiful as Alex, of course, but then, few things were. It was a daunting prospect.

She waited, wondering if he would notice how different she looked. But he seemed a bit anxious himself, which was very unlike Alex. Maybe he, too, was worried she wouldn't fit in with his hoity-toity crowd.

"Do I look okay?" she asked, braving a spin in front of him.

"You look wonderful." He seemed surprised she would ask. "It's a little subdued for you, but very pretty. You always look wonderful."

"Well, thanks for saying that, but I just wanted to be sure." She laughed self-consciously. "I wouldn't want to embarrass you in front of your friends."

"Embarrass me? Don't be absurd." Alex kissed her cheek again. "Besides, these people are no big deal.

They're not really even friends, to be perfectly honest, just people associated with the benefit. It was one of Puff's favorite charities, so I've kept up the connection."

"Yo-Yo Ma? Gore Vidal?"

He gave her a very strange look. "No, of course not. Just a few acquaintances, Puff's sister—"

"Puff's sister?" Meg began to pace, worrying out loud. "Oh God. Relatives. Does she look like Puff? I've seen pictures of Puff. All your kids do is talk about Puff. All you do is talk about Puff."

Alex sent her a bewildered glance. "I never talk about Puff."

"Your silence speaks volumes."

"Meg, what is wrong with you?" He narrowed his eyes. "Are you feeling all right?"

"I'm fine. I think." Okay, so she wasn't fine. She was actually dripping with nerves and outright fear.

But who wouldn't be, in her shoes? Instead of Cinderella's slippers, she was slogging around in matronly pink pumps. Meanwhile, she had to go pretend to be confident and charming in a sea of people who instinctively knew which fork to use, how to juggle hors d'oeuvres and a drink without spilling either and what to call the Sultan of Brunei without causing an international incident.

All this mental effort was only making things worse.

"I'm just not sure I belong at this party," she tried to explain.

"Well, they aren't the most fun crowd in the world, but you said you wanted to come." He lifted one dark eyebrow. "Didn't you?"

"Yes, but . . ." Meg wrung her hands. She couldn't remember ever in her life literally wringing her hands. Her first pearls and her first hand-wringing, all in one night.

"I did want to come. I wanted to see if I had any business dating you, if there was any way I could ever fit into your world."

"What?"

She waited for Alex to say something else, but he didn't. He was standing back a bit, really looking at her for the first time. Undoubtedly appalled and horrified. Undoubtedly deciding that she was too neurotic for words and he never should have asked her out in the first place.

Probably sorry that he hadn't stuck with Sabina. She might be a flake, but she also dressed up well.

"Meg, I—"

"Don't say anything," she interrupted. "Don't say anything, okay? I'll be fine. Really, I swear."

"Just be yourself, Meg," he said kindly, in a tone that did absolutely nothing for her self-confidence.

It was the same lousy advice she'd gotten from Joannie. Had these people never heard of the benefits of pretending to be something you weren't?

And how could she be herself now that she'd strapped herself into somebody else's outfit and somebody else's fingernails?

Chapter Ten

Feeling a little nervous about choosing a dress for a party or special occasion? Here are some suggestions:

1. If you're in doubt about color, remember, black is always a fabulous choice.

2. Choose something comfortable, something easy to get out of when nature calls, something that fits you now, not something you're absolutely sure you can lose a few pounds to get into later.

3. Most important, pick something that fits your personality. It's no fun masquerading as Princess Di all night if your personality is really closer to a trashy rock star. Of course, if your personality is close to a trashy rock star, you are unlikely to heed anyone's fashion advice, anyway. And if your personality is nothing like a trashy rock star but you find yourself gravitating toward that wardrobe, you are probably more in need of the *No-Fuss Guide to Finding a Good Therapist* . . .

—*The Sabina Charles No-Fuss Guide to Dressing to Impress*

"Come on." He opened the door, ushering her out. "We have to get back. I left the girls alone with the caterers and there's no telling what trouble they've gotten into."

"No new nanny yet?" Blessedly letting her mind drift from her own appearance, Meg mused, "I just don't understand why you have such trouble keeping nannies. Okay, I know their track record isn't great, but underneath they're great kids. And I'd think nanny services would be knocking down your door trying to get in."

"They used to," Alex muttered.

All the way down in the elevator, Meg pondered whether she should venture into another area she had promised herself to stay away from.

First she'd mentioned Puff, and then let slip her own neurotic doubts about being good enough to hobnob with Alex's friends. And now she was contemplating handing out advice about how to raise his children.

Very dangerous turf. But she couldn't hold back the words that were just dying to get out.

As he led her into his limo, she finally came out with it. "Look, Alex, I don't mean to tell you how to handle your girls, but—"

He glanced over at her. "But what?"

"It's just that I really don't think anything is wrong with Sydney and Lolly." Except for a few fires and loose frogs and spiders, of course. "I mean, I know they miss their mother and that's obviously why they keep getting into trouble, but the thing is..."

"Yes, Meg, I'm waiting," he said in a forbidding tone.

Ignoring the chill, she barged right along. "I don't think there's anything wrong with them that a little attention from you wouldn't fix."

"Attention from me?" Both eyebrows rose in an expression of utter disbelief.

"Yeah, like taking them to the zoo or to the park to throw a football around," she suggested.

Charming visions of all the possibilities filled her mind, rosy pictures of pink-cheeked, windblown little girls romping with their adorable father and a big dog—that mythical English sheepdog again.

If only Alex would just loosen up and get the poor kids out of the apartment.

"Football?" he echoed. "They're girls."

"Who have a lot of energy they need to blow off somewhere."

"But, Meg, I can't be playing football with them. I have a job," he said darkly. "I work twelve- to fourteen-hour days. I travel a lot. I have major responsibilities. Child care is not something I can be involved with on a day-to-day basis."

"Well, there's your problem in a nutshell," she said with all the blithe assurance of someone who had already written a bunch of books telling other people what to do. "Your job is your first priority when your family should be."

"I want my family to run smoothly so that I can focus on my job," he noted. "And my job to run smoothly so that I can provide every advantage for my family."

"But what they need is not more advantages," Meg cried. "What they need is *you!*"

Stubbornly, Alex declared, "I've worked very hard to get where I am. Yet you sound as if you're suggesting I drop out and start acting like 'Father Knows Best' all of a sudden."

"What's wrong with that?"

He cast her a dire look. "It's not me."

"Maybe it should be."

Alex held up a warning hand. "I couldn't, even if I wanted to." He shook his dark head with conviction. "I couldn't. Besides, things worked perfectly well the way they were before, before Puff..."

Meg squeezed his arm. "I'm sorry. I know things are tough with her not here."

And I should never have brought this up. Two painful subjects rolled into one. But didn't he see what a mistake he was making?

"But you have to be flexible now," she said kindly. "For the girls' sake, you have to adjust. Like Dustin Hoffman in *Kramer versus Kramer*. Or that movie with Diane Keaton. They were suddenly totally responsible for their kids, so they had to change and reprioritize their lives."

"Meg," he said carefully. "My life is not a movie."

She had heard this sort of deadly calm, irrefutable tone before, back before the *No-Fuss* books, when the editor at Daybreak had said, "We don't care what you're proposing. Without Sabina Charles, there is no book." When her high school principal said, "I don't want to hear one more word out of you about auto mechanics. Girls take home ec!"

Meg didn't deal well with that kind of tone.

"I want things to go back the way they were," he continued. "It was reasonable and easy and it worked. Puff took care of the apartment and the house in Connecticut and the children. And I took care of what I do best—establishing a position of strength for all of us."

"What you need—"

"What I need is not to turn into some sensitive, diaper-changing Superdad. What I need is a support system, a... a wife."

"A fantasy wife," Meg said under her breath. Some paragon, some Stepford wife who could jump right in and take Puff's place, who could smooth away all of Alex's problems on the home front, who could magically make life easy for him again. In other words, a pipe dream.

"What did you say?"

"Do you think maybe you're being unrealistic?" she inquired.

"It worked before. Why shouldn't it work again?" His lips pressed into a narrow line. "In any event, Meg, I don't think you ought to be dispensing advice on how to balance career and private life, considering the job you've done and some of the stunts you've pulled on behalf of Sabina."

"I've never pulled any stunts!" she shot back. Well, there was the baby switch, but Alex didn't even know about that.

"We'll discuss this later," Alex said ominously as the limo pulled into the garage of his building.

It was not the most auspicious beginning for their first real date.

As they arrived at the apartment, everything was bustling but under control. Although there was still time before things were expected to get under way, the living room furniture had been rearranged to accommodate guests, the string quartet was tuning up over in the corner and the black-jacketed waiters were organizing the trays for the fabulous array of hors d'oeuvres.

Meanwhile, Alex's daughters were watching it all from the sidelines, as good as gold.

"See, I told you they'd be fine," Meg declared as Lolly trailed after one of the waiters, who was setting up trays of champagne flutes. All that glass within Lolly's reach made Meg a bit more anxious than she let on. "She's fine," she repeated to herself.

"Meg, you look funny," Sydney told her, pulling on her sleeve. The little girl gave her a good once-over and frowned. "Your hair is funny. And your fingernail polish, too. It's pink." Her scowl deepened. "I thought you liked red fingernails, Meg. Real long ones!"

She had no sooner uttered her commentary on Meg's manicure than the buzzer from downstairs rang, letting them know they had a guest. Meg experienced a moment of panic—guests already?—but then she realized it would be Joannie, arriving to pick up the girls.

Good. Maybe this would stop the inquisition from Sydney about the change in her nail polish.

Since they had no regular nanny or baby-sitter who could entertain them elsewhere during the party, Sydney and Lolly had been invited to come to the Kaczmarowski household in Brooklyn for the evening. Meg's parents were having a birthday party for Anne-Marie's little girl, Amber, who was seven, so they'd invited Alex's girls, too.

It wasn't a big deal; there were always extra kids around the Kaczmarowski household. Except for the fact that Meg's mother was getting pretty curious about the mysterious Alex Thornhill, whose children kept turning up at her house. Meg had told her parents very little about him, nothing even hinting at a dating situation so far, so they were operating under the assumption that this arrangement was work-related.

Joannie, bless her heart, had offered to drop by and chauffeur the Thornhill girls to the birthday party. And here she was, right on time.

"That will be my sister," Meg explained, buzzing her up.

"I feel kind of odd about this," Alex told her. "Your family is kind enough to baby-sit my children, and I've never even met any of them."

"It's fine. Really," she assured him. "You've met me, of course, and now you'll be seeing my sister Joannie in a few minutes."

He had, of course, met one niece and one nephew, too, and come very close to running into two sisters at the back door in Connecticut, but he didn't know that. And Meg didn't plan to tell him. If he was furious to think Sabina was merely inept, what would he do when the full scale of the deception came out?

Preferring not to think about that, Meg hurried on, "Besides, with seventeen grandkids, plus a bunch of other relatives and their kids and grandkids and whomever else Amber invited, trust me when I tell you they won't notice two more."

"My girls?" he asked dryly. "I think they'll be noticed."

"Because of the clothes, you mean?"

That clearly was *not* what he meant. "What's wrong with their clothes?"

"Well, they're kind of formal." Given what she was wearing herself, Meg had little room to object to the Thornhill girls' frilly dresses and white lace anklets. But that didn't stop her. She had fallen back onto the subject of Alex's daughters, about whom she had formed a whole fleet of theories. And she had no trouble sharing her views. "Kids are supposed to get dirty, you know. Shorts and tennies are more what they wear. But Sydney and Lolly don't own anything grubby like that."

"They don't? Why not?"

"I don't know." Meg was dumbfounded. "You mean you didn't pick out those clothes? Who did?"

"I don't know. Their nannies, I suppose. Or maybe they did themselves."

She had assumed they looked like little princesses all the time because that's what Alex wanted. But this was adding up to even less involvement in their lives than she had supposed, even with her lowest guess. Alex definitely needed some parenting lessons, whether he liked it or not.

But then the doorbell rang, announcing Joannie, and Alex moved to get it. So Meg ran off to round up Lolly and Sydney. Quiet and uncommunicative, the two marched right in front of her in their crisp little pinafores.

"Hey, guys," Meg called down to them. "Why so glum? You had fun at my mom and dad's house before, remember?"

"Yeah, but..." Lolly jutted out her lower lip. Sydney gave her sister a quelling stare.

"But what?" Reaching down, Meg took a hand from each of them, hoping to offer reassurance. "You can tell me. We're pals, remember?"

There was a moment of silence as Sydney snatched her hand away and whispered something to Lolly.

"I'll say it if I want," Lolly snapped. Turning her face up to Meg, she said, "We had fun that time because you came, too. Now we're going all by ourself."

"And Daddy is staying here with *you,*" Sydney added in a very accusatory tone.

Uh-oh. Visions of fires and spiders plaguing her parents' household appeared before Meg's eyes. When the Thornhill girls were feeling cranky and ignored, disasters followed. She had tried to tell Alex what the problem was, but he hadn't wanted to hear.

"Listen to me," she told them both sternly. "I know you want your dad with you. But he's busy tonight." As Sydney began to form an objection, Meg held up a hand. "I know, he's always busy, but this is just for tonight. I promise that tomorrow, if you want, your dad will take you out to the park, just the three of you. But you have to be good tonight."

"The park?" Sydney asked with a very calculating edge. "Tomorrow? Just me and Daddy and Lolly?"

"The park. Tomorrow," Meg promised. "Just you three."

"Are you sure?" Sydney inquired primly.

This child was sometimes a bit too smart and savvy for her own good. But Meg was prepared to bluff. "Yes, I'm sure. He already told me he was planning it. So it's all set. *If* you're good tonight and don't play any tricks on anybody."

She had no authority whatever to negotiate for Alex, but she didn't care. If he refused to take a few minutes on a Saturday to spend with his children, then she had no qualms about bulldozing him into it personally.

"Come along, you guys. My sister is waiting to take you. And cheer up, will you?" She tousled Lolly's hair. "It will be fun."

"What took you so long?" Alex whispered in her ear as she brought the girls to the door.

"A minor problem. I fixed it," she murmured back. "Hi, Joan. How are you? Have you gotten introduced to Alex?"

"Oh, yeah, sure. We've had a nice chat, haven't we?" To Meg, she mouthed, "Wow. He's *gorgeous*."

Meg's gaze flashed to Alex, but he didn't seem to have noticed the assessment.

"Your sister reminds me a lot of you," he remarked, giving Meg a rather dazed smile.

Juggling an antsy Jamie on one side and a sleepy MaryMeg on the other, her sister gave Meg the fish eye. "What's with you, Princess Di?"

Meg knew what she meant, but she asked anyway. "What's that supposed to mean?"

"Meg, I have never seen you dressed like that. It's... weird." Joannie looked her up and down slowly. "Kind of Jackie O, about 1960. All you need is the pillbox hat."

"Wait a min—"

"And her fingernails are pink," said Sydney, as if that were a crime. *"Pink."*

"She looks fabulous," Alex put in. "A little—"

"Subdued. Yeah, I know." Although she had wanted a different look, Meg was getting tired of all this attention to her appearance. What with the argument with Alex about his child care and the fuss with the kids about going to Brooklyn for the night, Meg was already starting to feel frazzled. She was also already sorry she hadn't worn something more comfortable. "Joannie, don't you have to get going?"

"Yeah, sure, Princess Di." Joannie smiled, handing over MaryMeg as she temporarily shifted Jamie to the other side.

Meg held the drowsy baby carefully, praying MaryMeg didn't drool on her expensive dinner suit.

"Are you sure you can handle four kids all by yourself?" Alex asked dubiously.

"Aw, sure. No problem. Anyway, my husband's down in the car waiting. No problem, right, ladies?" After putting Jamie down and taking his hand, Joannie guided the two little Thornhill girls out into the hallway and then she took her own daughter back from Meg's arms. "Okay, everybody, here we go."

"Your daughter is very cute," Alex said politely, watching the exchange. "As a matter of fact, she looks very familiar. Have I seen this baby before, Meg?"

Joannie froze. Guilt was written all over her.

Oh my God. He recognized the baby. "She probably looks like some baby in a commercial or something," Meg said heartily, turning MaryMeg's face around and into Joannie's shoulder before he could get a better look.

Damn it. What kind of goon was she? It hadn't even occurred to her that Alex would remember what the first fake Remington had looked like.

Luckily, this time the baby was dressed in pink ruffles, with a little rosette on an elastic band around her head. It wasn't exactly the Remington sailor-suit look.

"She really does look familiar," Alex mused.

"You know what they say, all babies look alike."

"Right. People say that to me all the time," Joannie agreed.

"Do they?" But he was still gazing intently at Mary-Meg, and Meg began to perspire inside her chilly pink suit. Apparently real glamour girls didn't experience nerves or apprehension or they wouldn't wear outfits like this.

"Better get moving, Joan," she reminded her sister in a singsong voice. "People are going to start getting here any minute."

"Uh…oh, okay." But Joannie didn't move. And Alex was still peering at the baby.

At the end of the hall, the elevator dinged and Meg knew what that meant. Real guests.

"See you, Joannie!" she said, practically shoving her sister out into the hall with the children. " 'Bye, kids! Have fun."

As Joannie herded the kids down the corridor, as Meg almost collapsed with relief that he hadn't quite recognized MaryMeg, a woman in an enormous black hat with a very pretty young man on her arm waltzed down to the Thornhill apartment.

"Alex, darling," the woman breathed, peeking out from under the feathered brim of her hat, "why is everyone standing out in the hall?"

"Just saying goodbye to my daughters," he informed her. "Hello, Fenn. Nice to see you. It's been a long time."

"Yes, it has." She sent him a coy glance and Meg tried to figure out what undercurrents were running here. It was all very odd. Although her escort's hand was firmly plastered just above her skinny bottom, Fenn was giving Alex hungry looks, and he was acting as if he had a rod up his spine.

"Fenn, this is Meg Kaczmarowski, a friend of mine. And, Meg, this is Fenn Fortinbras," Alex said smoothly. "Puff's sister."

Puff's sister? But her nieces—the daughters of her dead sister—had just walked past her and she hadn't even noticed. Nonetheless, Meg put on a smile. She wanted to make a good first impression with Alex's sister-in-law, even if the woman was a cold fish when it came to her nieces.

"Nice to meet you," she offered.

Was she supposed to shake hands? Did rich women do that? Apparently not. Fenn Fortinbras simply swept past her, right into the apartment, leaving her young male companion behind in a cloud of expensive perfume.

Meg raised an eyebrow as she turned, watching Fenn. Ms. Fortinbras's hat was the most striking part of her outfit, but just barely. She was greyhound thin and she was dressed in black, head to toe, which only increased the dramatic effect.

She had a black jacket, cut much longer in the back than the front, almost like a man's tailcoat, with a good deal of chest showing. Beneath it she wore a calf-length straight skirt and lace-up granny boots. The overall impression was Mary Poppins mixed with a scarecrow.

Her hair was swept up under the hat, so Meg couldn't tell what color it was, but all in all, her coloring didn't seem as pale as Puff's in the pictures Meg had seen.

Her date, on the other hand, was quite cute. He looked no more than twenty, with the wholesome, robust good looks of a lacrosse player fresh off the fields at Harvard. Of course, Meg had no idea what a lacrosse player looked like, but she felt sure this boy was it.

"You remember Choate, don't you?" Fenn asked vaguely, waving a hand in the air.

"Campion Choate," the boy said, moving to drape a possessive arm around Fenn. He nuzzled her neck, right there in front of Alex and Meg and everybody.

If she thought it was kind of crude, Meg didn't have a whole lot of opportunity to worry about it, because more guests arrived hard on their heels.

As the musicians and the waiters began to strut their stuff, as drinks and food and music began to flow, Meg met Drew Mortimer, a good-looking, if rather fleshy blond man, introduced by Alex as a longtime friend of Puff's, and his fiancée, LouLou someone, who was young, pale and even thinner than Fenn.

LouLou's outfit was the same basic idea as Fenn's—a high-fashion black getup that hung yards of extra fabric

on her spare frame, except hers was all in lace. She wore
a see-through overdress tossed ever so sloppily over a
short black slip dress, with ornate satin shoes.

Meg found out LouLou's last name when the next pair
arrived. Another painfully thin woman, this one a bit
older, danced in, also wearing black. Her outfit con-
sisted of a big hat pulled way down over her eyes and a
loose satin jacket and chiffon skirt. She bypassed intro-
ductions and headed immediately for Fenn and Campion.

"LouLou von Norbel's mother," Alex muttered.
"Luciana Ludwig von Norbel, called Lucky. She's a de-
signer, maybe you've heard of her? Nasty old harridan.
I didn't realize I'd invited her."

Meg didn't know what to think, except she thought it
was probably a good idea to steer clear of Lucky Luciana if she was that much of a pain. The fact that there
was a stuffed dead bird festooned on her hat should have
been a hint that she wasn't a nice person.

As for the others, well, Meg might have seen a few of
these names in the society pages next to Puff's, but she
wasn't sure. And were they all dressed bizarrely, or was
it just her?

Luciana's rear was brought up by a fay old gentleman
who looked like everyone's idea of a proper British butler. He had a positive twinkle in his eye, although his rosy
cheeks and general high color made Meg wonder whether
the twinkle was due to good nature or premium Scotch.

"John Jasper White," he said with a flourish, pressing a kiss into her palm. "Everyone calls me Jasper."

What with Fenn and Choate and Lucky and LouLou
and now Jasper, Meg's head was spinning. Where did
they get these names?

Nonetheless, Meg smiled back at Jasper—he was the first person who had acted remotely friendly to her—but she wasn't all that cheery inside. Instinctively, she felt she'd dressed all wrong, as if the other skinny waifs in the room were staring at her curves and critiquing her suit. Pink, for goodness' sake. They were all in sophisticated black and she was in *pink*.

"Alex, who is your charming friend?" Luciana asked from his elbow. She turned a critical eye on Meg. "How sweet she looks. Not at all your usual type."

What did that mean? The woman seemed to be implying that Alex's "usual type" was more like a street-walker. Meg bristled as Alex put a restraining hand on her arm. Was he afraid she was going to pop old Luciana one?

"Meg is a friend of mine," Alex put in. "She offered to arrange this little gathering for me."

"Oh, I've got it," Lucky Luciana said suddenly. "She's your secretary! Isn't that delightful—an office romance—a real Cinderella story. You know, old Foxy Bellows married his chambermaid. So...refreshing."

Poisonous Luciana was now all but calling her a servant. Not that there was anything wrong with being a maid. It was just that the nasty old woman was so clearly trying to say, *You are not of my class and I know it.*

Well, Meg had news for Lucky Luciana. She knew it, too. And she didn't care one bit.

So, as Alex explained in icy tones that Meg was not his secretary, Meg lifted her chin, vowed not to feel cowed and slipped away to mingle. Or at least eavesdrop.

Near the flower arrangement on the mantel, skin-and-bones LouLou was telling Jasper and a few of the others a story. Under cover of pretending to examine the flowers, Meg listened in.

"Everyone had such fun at Mimsy's wedding," LouLou drawled. She giggled as she leaned on Drew, her date. "Of course, her dress was ghastly, but Mimsy has such terrible taste that it's become part of the joke to see what she wears."

Jasper murmured, "Ah, yes. And did you see Harriet Marienbad? Poor, dear Harriet. Had a bit too much to drink."

Clearly enjoying his gossipy tale of woe, the man was positively smirking. And Meg had thought he was the nice one in the bunch.

"I thought she was going to fall right into her food, which was, by the way, a disaster," he continued. "Even the hors d'oeuvres were just too dreadful for words. They used Mia Massima to cater it, with those tired old wild mushroom polenta squares, as if we haven't seen those at every cocktail party we've been to in the last three years. I guess Mimsy hasn't heard that *no one* is using Mia Massima anymore."

No one? Meg gulped. Mia Massima was the caterer she'd hired. They were working tonight.

And wild mushroom polenta squares were even now winding their way through the party on silver trays, along with about thirty other appetizers prepared by the caterer in contempt.

Thank goodness no one seemed to have noticed. Yet. Jasper and LouLou were by now on a different topic, dissecting some other poor hostess's mistakes. And then Fenn joined them.

Jasper said slyly, "Fenn, darling. We were just discussing Renalda's party last weekend. I saw your husband there, love. And how is Harry?"

Fenn had a husband named Harry? Then what was she doing with young Campion Choate?

Fenn only smiled. "Harry is, as always, thankfully absent."

The others tittered as Lucky, smirking under her dead bird hat, waltzed up to join the fray. "Fenn, darling, so lovely to see you. I caught the new show at your gallery. So delightful. Where do you find all those adorable young men? They are all so...talented. And I'm sure they are ever so grateful for your, uh, patronage."

Fenn's laughter tinkled, but it sounded forced. "Want to borrow my address book, Lucky? And how is *your* husband? Why, I haven't seen the baron in months. Don't tell me you killed him off and I missed the fun?"

"I don't kill my husbands when they become inconvenient," Luciana sniffed. "Although if I were married to your Harry, I might give it serious thought."

Lurking behind them, trying to look inconspicuous, Meg was frankly horrified. It was one thing for a bunch of snobs to be mean to her, but these people weren't even nice to one another.

From under her huge hat, Fenn inquired sweetly, "Is that an engagement ring, LouLou? Did darling Drew give that to you? What a fortunate girl you are. And I can attest to that personally. Why, just the other night I was telling Drew that very thing."

Yikes. Was Fenn suggesting that she was sleeping with Drew Mortimer, too? She had a husband, a boyfriend, a stable of young artists at some gallery and the slickly handsome Drew on the side? Where did she find time?

If Meg had been worried about her own foibles, she wasn't anymore. Alex's circle of acquaintances—including the paragon Puff's sister—was positively licentious.

"Ah, and there's little Margie, hiding out behind the orchids. Margie?" Fenn called out. "Margie dear, do come and join us."

Meg jumped. Heavens to betsy. The execrable Fenn was talking to *her*. She'd thought she was safe back there with the flowers. Warily, she eyed the circle of snakes. She'd heard what they did to one another; she hoped they'd keep their fangs off her. If they didn't, she wouldn't be responsible for the consequences.

"And where did Alex find you, dear little Margie?" Fenn purred. "You're so different from the women he usually dates."

"It's Meg," she said plainly. "Not Margie. Meg."

She figured the smartest thing to do was politely answer their stupid questions and then get out of there. But she wasn't sure. Smacking a few heads together might be more effective. And more fun, too.

"So where did you meet Alex?" Fenn asked again, leaning in avidly.

"I work for Daybreak Books, which is a subsidiary of Dateline/Dynasty, you know, Alex's company." Meg smiled boldly into the snake pit. She wasn't ashamed of who she was or what she did. "I'm Sabina Charles's assistant."

"Who?" LouLou inquired, looking as vacant as ever.

"Sabina Charles. She's written all the *No-Fuss* books." Underlining her point, Meg added, "They've sold about three billion copies worldwide."

"Oh, I believe I've met her," Lucky said slowly. "A lovely woman. Quite brainless, but then, what can you expect? She writes those dim little books for dim little people. She'd have to be brainless."

"Our demographics tell us that the readers of the Sabina Charles books are really quite well-educated, intelligent people," Meg said testily.

They could call Sabina names all they wanted, but there wasn't a thing wrong with the books. Those books

were Meg's pride and joy and she wasn't going to sit still
while the likes of Lucky von Norbel cut them to rib-
bons. Dim little books for dim little people? Ha!

At her side, Jasper pulled a glass of water off a tray
and handed it to her. "Here, dear. You look parched."

Feeling a bit thirsty, Meg took a sip. "Ye gods!" she
sputtered. It looked like water, but it tasted like Drano.
"What was that?"

He smiled. "Russian vodka, chilled. It's fabulous with
beluga caviar, which unfortunately you aren't serving."
Raising an eyebrow, Jasper sneered down at a small ap-
petizer on his plate. In a heavily dramatic tone, he asked
grandly, "And what is that nasty little thing I spy down
there? Could it be a wild mushroom polenta square? Ah,
woe is me." After a few charming little retching noises,
he announced, "I believe I smell the fetid cuisine of Mia
Massima lurking about the premises."

The others giggled and Meg fumed.

"That man is a menace," she said under her breath.
She was still wheezing from his little trick with the vodka
while he took the opening to insult her caterer.

"Excuse me," she said quickly. Head held high, she
escaped to the kitchen to scare up some water or a soft
drink, anything to rid her throat of the burning sensation.

Busying herself at the island pouring a glass of cranberry juice, she almost didn't notice that someone had
followed her. But as the door slammed, she wheeled
around.

He was blocking any exit, offering her an unctuous
smile as he reclined indolently against the doorframe.

"Drew, isn't it?" she asked uneasily. The one who was
engaged to LouLou but sleeping with Fenn.

"I'm flattered you remembered my name," he said softly, moving in closer. "But I can hardly say I'm surprised. Our eyes met and I knew you felt the electricity."

"I—I never met your eyes." Meg backed up into the center island, but Drew kept coming.

"But of course you did." When he reached a hand around her as if he planned to grab her, she slid quickly to one side. But oily Drew followed her, pinching her bottom as she slapped him away.

"Back off, bucko," she said loudly. She scanned her options, but right now she was trapped by the island, cut off from the door and escape.

"Puff and I were extremely close," he murmured, bending down to whisper in her ear as she twisted away. "I guess you could say Alex and I share our taste in women."

Good grief. The man was all hands. As she tried to elude him, she heard the crash of glass and liquid behind her, and she knew she'd knocked over the cranberry juice. Damn it, anyway. Red liquid was already seeping into the fabric of her expensive pink suit. She was a lot more concerned about the stains on her jacket than she was about the idiotic pass coming from Drew Mortimer.

"Tut-tut, pretty little Meg," he whispered. Had he actually said *tut-tut?* Was he a moron or what? "I'm finding out you're nothing like Puff."

"Yeah, I know." She stomped on his foot and elbowed him hard in the midriff at the same time. It was gratifying to hear the sharp grunt he made on contact. Frowning, Meg shook her dripping red sleeve. "If Puff was anything like the rest of you clowns, I'm beginning to understand why Alex was in the mood for a breath of fresh air."

Drew fingered his ribs gingerly, backing off a few steps. Unfortunately, he was still smack-dab in front of the door, blocking any escape. "Well, you are that. I was hoping you'd be a little friendlier, though." He managed a shifty, coy expression. "I miss Puff and our, uh, *friendship.*"

His implication was more than clear, even if she didn't buy it. "Oh, please," Meg scoffed. "If Puff had Alex, what would she want with you?"

"The same thing her sister does," he said slyly. "Puff and her sister were two of a kind. They married extremely busy men so they'd have plenty of time to keep up their hobbies, if you know what I mean."

"I don't believe you." Perfect Puff, the woman Alex was still mourning, would never have stooped to an affair with a slimeball like this. Meg stalked past him, determined to get to the door, even if she had to remove Drew Mortimer physically.

"Come on, Meg, don't be so hard on me," he cajoled.

But the door was wrenched open from the other side, knocking Drew aside.

And Alex stood there, filling the doorframe, glowering at both of them.

Chapter Eleven

If you're feeling bored and in a rut, never underestimate the power of a change of scenery. Move the furniture! Add a new lamp or a throw for the sofa!

You'll be amazed at the change in your attitude when you change your surroundings...

—*The Sabina Charles No-Fuss Guide to Home Decor*

"Is everything all right here?" Alex asked slowly. "I was beginning to wonder where you were, Meg."

"Everything is fine," she told him. "Now that you're here."

She scooted over and grabbed his arm, cozying up very close. She could tell the sudden enthusiasm took Alex by surprise, but she couldn't help it. She wanted to be away from slimy Drew, and fast.

"Are you sure you're okay?" Alex asked softly. His arm tightened around her and it felt awfully nice. His touch sent the familiar rush of tenderness and heady desire flooding through her veins, reminding her of just how much chemistry they had going for them.

Alex. He was the reason she was here, of course. She had forgotten for a moment exactly what she was doing at this stupid party. The original plan had called for her to come tonight and test the waters, to see whether she could fit into his crowd. At this point, the answer was clear. No way.

But instead of worrying about it, instead of retreating, Meg had pretty much decided to go the opposite direction.

No retreat. Because who cared if she didn't belong here? Instead of trying to fit into this terrible crowd, she fully intended to rescue Alex from their clutches.

"Are you okay?" he asked again.

"Sure, sure, I'm fine." She glanced back over her shoulder to where Drew lay in wait. She whispered, "But you know, Alex, that guy's a real jerk."

"I know."

"You do? Because it's not just him," she confided, warming to her subject. "If this is high society, give me low anytime. Fenn and Lucky Luciana and her anorexic daughter LouLou. And that old turkey Jasper. They're all a bunch of creeps, if you ask me."

"I know," he said gloomily.

"Then why do you hang around with them?"

"Well, I don't, really. I never did." Alex ran a hasty hand through his hair, barely mussing its elegant cut. "I'm afraid I never paid much attention to them—Puff was the social one. I was always busy working and she seemed to enjoy all the balls and benefits, so I let her handle it. But tonight I actually listened to what they were saying. They're awful."

Heavens. If Puff was the one who socialized with the snakes and Alex really didn't know anything about them, then maybe what Drew had said was true. Maybe Puff was as sleazy as the rest of them. In which case, she was clearly no paragon. And no one for Meg to try to emulate.

But it couldn't be true. Could it?

Meg grabbed his lapels. "I'm so glad you agree with me about these people. So can we get out of here, please? I know it's your apartment and it's probably not polite to leave your own party, but—"

"Meg, what is it?"

"This party is a real drag," she said with feeling. "These people, they're not just jerks. They're worse than that."

"What exactly happened here?" he asked, narrowing his eyes.

"You really want to know?" She had no intention of saying anything about Drew's ugly innuendo, but there was plenty to go on without that. "First Fenn called me Margie. Then Jasper slipped me vodka, pretending it was water, and then he made this barfing noise at my hors d'oeuvres. And *then* that horrible Drew guy made a pass at me in the kitchen. He's engaged to LouLou and sleeping with Fenn on the side and he made a pass at *me!*"

Alex went rigid. "Excuse me," he said, removing her hands from his lapels, "while I go choke that lowlife."

Meg grabbed him before he could get by. "That's very sweet, but not necessary. I'm fine. He's just an idiot." Alex's jaw was still clenched quite tightly. "Aw, come on, Alex. You don't want to dirty your hands choking him. He's not worth it."

If he was this upset about a pass at her, what would he do if he knew that Drew was spreading sordid rumors about Puff? According to Mr. Scumbucket, he and Puff were playing horizontal rumba while Alex was at work. Alex thought Puff was perfect; he'd said so on several occasions. So what would he do if he heard the vicious stories? Meg shuddered to think.

Alex turned suddenly, giving her an intent look. "What do you say we blow this place? I didn't want to go to the benefit anyway and I find I can no longer stomach another minute in the company of these people."

"Are you kidding? I'm definitely up for it," Meg told him. "Definitely."

"But first—" With one swift movement, Alex spun her around and stripped off her jacket, which he folded gingerly over his arm. "Your jacket is dripping, dear."

She stood there, feeling conspicuous in just the plain sheath. Actually, the outfit was a lot more comfortable without the jacket. But a lot barer, too.

But Alex wasn't finished. "What are you doing?" Meg asked, but he was reaching for the clasp on her pearls and then hoisting her up high enough to remove her shoes. "My shoes? What are you doing?"

"I've been wanting to do this all night," he muttered, holding the necklace and the pumps in one hand, dragging her along behind him with the other, steering them both around the guests.

"Alex, wait—"

But he was making a steady course for the terrace doors, pulling her along with him.

"Alex—"

But it was too late. He dropped her hand and then, with a flick of his wrist, he tossed her pearls and her jacket off the terrace and into the darkness below. And then he sent her pink pumps overboard, too, one at a time, end over end.

Meg craned her neck to see where they had disappeared to, but all she could make out were the vague outlines of some shrubbery and trees and a very busy street down below. Who'd ever have thought her possessions would end up in the middle of Fifth Avenue?

"I guess you didn't like my outfit," she managed to say.

"I liked it just fine. It wasn't you, that's all."

With a determined smile, he advanced on her.

"Oh, no you don't," she said, backing up. Without her shoes, she was a whole lot shorter than he was and she felt terribly vulnerable all of a sudden. "There's nothing left to take off or I'll be in my underwear."

"That's not such a bad idea, but I can save it for later," he murmured. "In private."

"Alex, stay away—"

But he grabbed her, steadied her and looked her right in the eye. Meg gulped. What next?

"Hold still." As she stood there, rooted to the terrace, with the sultry late-summer breeze wafting over them like a caress, Alex lifted his hands to her cheeks, tipped her face up and...

And then he slid his fingers all the way back into her hair and rumpled it ruthlessly.

"What was that for?" she asked, astonished, brushing back an unruly wave that had fallen over her cheek. But the light breeze sent it right back where it was the moment she let it go.

"You just aren't you with your hair all slicked down." And then he gave her the briefest of kisses on the cheek, before sending a reckless grin her way.

Alex was positively boyish all of a sudden.

"Are you okay?" she asked carefully.

"I'm fine. I'm wonderful." He turned her around, pointing her back in the direction of the apartment. "And I am thrilled I don't have to waste a whole evening being polite to a bunch of snobs and hypocrites."

"This is very unlike you," she murmured, but he was behaving like an irresistible force at the moment and there was very little she could do.

As she hesitated, he slid open the terrace door, leading the way back inside.

"Alex, I'm barefoot," she whispered, cowering behind him. She didn't want to go back in there and face those people in her stocking feet, half-dressed, with no jewelry and tousled hair.

"No problem." As she yelped, he swung her up into his arms and strode through the crowd. The snobs and hypocrites whispered and snickered, but Alex just smiled, carrying Meg smoothly to the door.

She couldn't believe it. Manhattan's elite were watching as Alex Thornhill, eligible bachelor and media magnate, marched through his party with her, plain old Meg Kaczmarowski, clasped securely in his arms.

It was truly bizarre. Tomorrow, every fashionable tongue in town would no doubt be wagging about Alex and his chambermaid, Margie. People like Jasper and LouLou would be dining out on this story for weeks.

Meg stifled a giggle. This was the most delicious entrance or exit she'd ever made. Alex's arms were warm and strong and his smile was bright enough to light up every window at the Plaza Hotel. She could feel the steady beat of his heart through the crisp, cool linen of his shirt and the hard wall of his muscled chest, pressing against the side of her breast.

Tightening her arm around his neck, Meg tried to remember to breathe. Held like this, she wouldn't have cared if he were hauling her through a swamp full of crocodiles.

Although, catching a glimpse of Fenn's calculating expression, Meg decided this was a lot more fun than crocodiles.

On the day she'd first met Alex, she remembered wishing that someday, instead of Sabina, *she* could be the one in the spotlight. It felt very much as if she'd gotten her wish.

When they were clear of the stuffy apartment Alex set her down on the hall carpet. "Where to?"

Meg shook her head. "I don't know." She held up her hands. "Where can I go dressed like this?"

Softly, very softly, he said, "Your place might be nice."

"I—I don't think that would be a good idea." Him, her, the two of them, all alone in her small apartment. She knew how that would end up. At the moment, with the memory of his arms around her still playing havoc with her senses, they would end up that way anyplace they went if she wasn't careful.

"Come on, Meg." He leaned a little closer. "What are you afraid of?"

"You, me, the two of us, all alone in my apartment."

He tipped his head down, brushing his cheek against hers. "What's wrong with that?"

"Nothing." She swallowed around a dry throat. "Nothing at all. Except..."

"Except?"

"I don't know. Don't confuse me." She took his hand, interlocking her fingers with his, gazing up at him. "I feel really good when I'm with you, but when I'm not, I'm just plagued with these doubts."

"Like your doubts that you wouldn't fit in up here in this rarefied air? Hey, kid, don't look now, but you won.'' He grinned. ''I don't fit in, either. Obstacle overcome—I chose you instead of them.''

''Right. I know.'' Minor obstacle overcome. What about all the other ones? She stared down at her shoeless feet. ''But I still feel like I don't really know you all that well and you sure don't know me.''

''I know all I need to know.''

Yeah, right. Like the fact that she'd written all the *No-Fuss* books, even though she'd insisted she hadn't. Like the fact that she'd made up all the stuff about Remington and the Welsh corgis. Like the fact that everything about her and Sabina and their intertwined careers was a lie. He knew none of it.

Why didn't I just tell him the truth when he asked me? Why? Maybe because she had known, deep in her heart, that he wouldn't want her if he knew the truth. Oh, sure, he was willing to accept her as a poor, abused victim of mean old Sabina. Sabina the slave driver, taking advantage of her lackey, Meg. *That* he would buy.

But what about the real truth, the truth that it was all Meg's idea? All Meg's little game from the word go. She had no education and no expertise, and yet she had this great idea to make a living telling other people what to do. So she talked Sabina into being the front. Then she'd blithely made up a cockamamy biography and sold Sabina like a piece of meat, just to get those books sold.

And it worked.

Until Alex Thornhill came into their lives, it worked just fine.

Machiavellian Meg. Who ever would've thought it? Not Alex, obviously.

And yet she couldn't let him get any closer, couldn't contemplate deepening their relationship when things stood this way, with this great gulf of misunderstanding lying between them.

The simple truth was that those books were a fundamental part of her personality. She was proud of her books. Yet she couldn't take credit for what was hers, couldn't share it with Alex, or she would face losing the books forever. And losing Alex, too, when he found out how long she'd been lying.

"Meg, will you please tell me what this is all about? I'm clueless here." He took her by the shoulders, offering a mystified gaze. "I thought we did something really great in there just now. I mean, it was once extremely important to me to be a mover and shaker with that kind of crowd. Yet tonight, I thumbed my nose at all of them. I feel great about that and I thought you did, too. So what gives?"

She blinked, confused. What did he mean about it once being important to him to climb the ranks of society? Hadn't he always been there? She had no idea. She knew where Puff grew up and went to school, but not Alex. About his background, she knew practically nothing.

And she realized, all of a sudden, that she knew just as little about him as he knew about her.

"Wait, I have an idea," he said abruptly. "Whatever the problem is, let's save it for another day, okay? Let's go to Brooklyn." He started down the hall, leaving Meg to trail behind.

"Brooklyn? Why?"

He shrugged, buzzing for the elevator. "You wanted me to spend more time with my kids. They're there, aren't they?"

"Well, yes, but—"

He winked at her. Alex, winking?

"And I can meet your parents, your sisters, the whole clan. Maybe I can fill in a few of those blanks." He pulled her close, shoving her gently into the open elevator. "Who knows, Meg? By the end of this evening, maybe I'll know everything there is to know about you."

Numbly, Meg watched as he pressed the button for the underground garage. "We're really going to Brooklyn?" she asked weakly.

"Yeah. We'll skip the limo tonight. I'll drive."

With her mother and her nosy sister Anne-Marie there to pull out everything from her bronzed baby shoes to her high school graduation picture, he was probably right. By the time the clock struck twelve, Alex was bound to know a whole lot more than he'd bargained for.

AS THEY ARRIVED, hand in hand, Alex stepped back, well into the sidelines. If Meg had felt out of place at the small soiree at his apartment, then he felt equally out of place at the boisterous birthday party at her parents' house.

The celebration was in full swing, spilling out the back of the bakery and into the garden. Chinese lanterns had been strung from the trees, giving the small yard a festive air, although the kids kept trying to knock them down, which became somewhat of a point of contention as people kept yelling back and forth to stop the kids. If his daughters were among them, Alex didn't see them.

Somebody else had set up a boom box, and who got to choose which tape came next was also a cause for controversy. But everybody seemed to be having a wonderful time in spite of all the loud voices and high spirits. Or maybe because of them.

Or maybe it was because of all the fabulous food—all kinds of pastries and cakes were floating by on paper plates and he didn't recognize a one of them as anything he'd ever eaten.

No poppy seed hedgehog, though.

"That's my father," Meg said, pointing, "the one dancing with the little girl balanced on his shoes. She's Amber, the birthday girl. It's kind of a tradition—all the girls get to dance with Grandpa on their birthdays." She grinned at him. "That's how we learn to be such terrific dancers."

"So *your* grandfather is the one who taught you to lead, huh?" he asked lightly, squeezing her hand. It was a nice tradition. Out of his ballpark, but nice. He had grown up without that kind of tradition himself, but then, there had been no extended family around to create them.

"And there's my mother. Oops. She's spotted us. We're dead meat now."

A very perky, slightly plump woman with very dark hair done in a kind of Donna Reed 'do came stomping right over. She was wearing an apron, which made her look even more like Donna Reed.

"This is my ma, Betty Kaczmarowski," Meg introduced in a small voice. He noticed how quickly she moved behind him and the message was clear. *With my mother, you are on your own.*

Alex smiled down at Meg as he extended a hand to her mom. "Mrs. Kaczmarowski, it's very nice to meet you." He hoped he got credit for doing the name perfectly, without even a second's hesitation. He sent a sardonic glance over his shoulder at Meg. "Your daughter has told me so much about you."

"No, really?" Betty blinked at him. "She hasn't told us a thing about you. Walter," she called out loudly, "come on over and meet Meggie's new boyfriend. That's my husband, Walter," she said, patting Alex on the arm as if they were old pals. "I know he'll want to meet you."

Alex sensed Meg cringing behind him.

"Oh, now she's done it," she murmured. "Now they're all making a beeline straight for us."

Before he had a chance to catch his breath, he was inundated with sisters and brothers-in-law and children, all clamoring to be introduced. First it was Meg's father, who was unassuming enough. He just shook Alex's hand and then shuffled back to polka with his grandchildren.

But the sisters were a different story. They all talked at once, they all had husbands and kids to show off and his head was spinning before he got past the second sister.

There was Anne-Marie, who had thin lips and a rather critical expression and asked a million questions about who he was and where he came from; Rhonda—or was it Brenda?—who looked a lot like Meg, and her husband, Eddie, who had a tight T-shirt and huge biceps; Darla, who kept giggling, although what she had to giggle about with four children all under the age of five was beyond him; and Kim, who had very short, spiky hair and was an artist of some sort. Kim also had a very tiny baby who kept wailing, and all the others took turns bouncing it and chuckling at it to make it stop.

The tallest, thinnest sister was Teri, who was married to the dentist. Or was he a child psychologist? Whoever he was, the others obviously considered him quite a catch.

They were all very nice and *very* curious. Within about ten minutes, Alex felt as if he'd been debriefed by the Pentagon. But they did it with such good humor it was hard to feel pressured. And they punctuated their questions with jokes and innuendo, a lot of nudges and winks, as if all their lives were an open book, as if they all adored their husbands and their kids and didn't care who knew it.

After the other party tonight, this bunch was refreshing.

While the others continued to bombard him with questions, Alex noticed a couple of girls who looked about the same age as his staring at him solemnly.

"Hi. Do you know where Sydney and Lolly are?" he asked the girls.

"Over there," they chorused, pointing to a pack of kids trying to knock a fat red lantern out of a tree with a stick. But then they turned back to stare at him again.

"Are you going to marry Aunt Meg?" the bigger one asked loudly.

The smaller of the two stopped chewing on her hair long enough to add, "She's the only one without a husband, you know."

He choked as Meg said, "Go away!" and shooed the kids out of there.

"Meg, I—" he began. He felt he had to say something in the aftermath of that rather frank question, but she stopped him.

"Don't you dare," she warned him. "Not a word."

Meanwhile, he had lost sight of his daughters again as Joannie, the last sister, came up to join the party. He'd already met her, of course, as well as her children, and he still thought that baby looked familiar, but he hadn't met her husband, the cop. Mike, maybe? Whoever he was, he had a lethal handshake. While Alex's hand was being wrenched by Mike, Joannie focused on Meg, demanding, "What happened to you? That's not what you were wearing when I saw you before. And you don't have any shoes!"

This announcement caused a major ruckus as everyone descended at once, desperate to know why half of Meg's outfit, including her shoes, was now missing. And Anne-Marie took off at once to get Meg some shoes from her house.

After a barrage of questions and sly jokes, Meg finally said, "Enough! Enough! Leave me alone! Leave us both alone!" Under her breath, she muttered, "You'd think I'd never brought a guy home before."

"You never have," Darla returned with another giggle.

After sending her sister a quelling stare, Meg dragged Alex inside, where it was quieter. They stood there, face-to-face, in a tiny entryway.

"I knew I shouldn't have brought you here," she said tensely. "You'd think they were starving and you were a rump roast."

"Gee, Meg, no one's ever called me a rump roast before."

She smacked him on the shoulder. "Stop it, okay? Just don't feel sorry for me, whatever you do, because I know they're weird and pushy, but they're family, and you were the one who wanted to come here—"

"Hey, stop it." He pulled her over to his side of the hallway, where he could put his arms around her. "I liked them, okay?"

"Oh, you did not."

"I admit I was a little overwhelmed, but I'm sure I would come to adore them in time."

Meg laughed at his attempt to be diplomatic, but he saw the tension ease from her shoulders and he knew she was relieved he was taking this so well.

"Hey, listen," he said softly, "I think this is great. Really. The relatives and the kids and the noise. It sure isn't how I grew up, but it's great. I can see a lot of you here.''

"Thanks. I think."

She leaned back into him, relaxing, and he wrapped his arms around her, holding her tight. There was something about the feel of Meg in his arms. It just felt *right*. It was the oddest sensation to be filled with this amazing peace, this serenity, when he held on to Meg. Maybe it was what all those people out in the yard felt when they danced on Grandpa's shoes or sampled the newest bakery goods proffered by Grandma.

Family. Meg felt like family to him. Yet he had never known family before—not with his mother, not even with Puff and his daughters—so how did he recognize it?

"That reminds me, Alex," Meg ventured. "You said you didn't grow up this way and I realized I don't know a thing about how you did grow up. Or even where. Are your parents still alive? Do you have brothers and sisters?"

Alex suddenly wished he were not involved with such an inquisitive woman. "Okay," he said finally, "here's the short form. Modest upbringing. Small town in the Midwest. No and no. Got it?"

"No, I don't get it." She twisted around far enough to give him a quizzical look. "Because I don't remember what order I asked the questions in."

He sighed, unwilling to elaborate, just as his daughters came slamming into the house, saving him from further embarrassment.

"Daddy!" Sydney shouted, breathlessly charging into him and almost knocking him over, followed immediately by Lolly.

"Careful." He stepped back far enough to disengage himself from both girls.

Lolly went hopping up the steps the rest of the way into the house, burning with excess energy, but her sister stayed down on the landing, grinning at him.

"Sydney, you're filthy," he said in surprise. "And what happened to your dress?"

He stared down at his daughter, who barely looked like herself. There were smudges of various colors all over her face, as if she'd painted herself with two or three coats of jam plus a layer of dirt. The pocket was torn off her dress and a row of lace hung jaggedly from one edge.

But Sydney was always the immaculate one. Even when she caused trouble she was clean. What had she done?

"Oh," Sydney said softly. As she gazed down at her ripped, dirty dress, her enthusiasm seemed to fade, right before his eyes.

"I didn't mean—" he began, but Meg stepped in.

Putting her arms around Sydney, she said, "Sweetie, that's okay. We can fix it. Were you having fun? It's more important to have fun than to worry about your dress when you're at a party."

Sydney brightened a bit. "Really?"

"Of course." Meg took her hand. "Want to go find Lolly and bring her back?"

"Maybe." The girl glanced over at her father. "Daddy, are you mad at me? Does this mean you aren't going to take us to the park tomorrow?"

"The park?"

"Of course he's not mad," Meg put in quickly. "Of course he's still taking you to the park."

"I am?"

She elbowed him hard. "Yes, you are."

"Okay." With her wide blue eyes still fixed firmly on him, Sydney tripped up the stairs after her sister.

"So what's this about the park?" he asked.

"I haven't had a chance to tell you that yet," Meg returned with dignity. "But I promised. So you have to do it."

"All right. I suppose." He took her hand. "Thanks for helping with Sydney. I didn't mean to—"

"I know you didn't." She ducked her head. "I was just pretty rambunctious myself when I was a kid, so I understand what it's like to be at a party when everyone is all wound up and running around, and the last thing on your mind is whether you're getting dirty." She gazed at him thoughtfully. "Besides, when I met your girls they were so quiet, it was kind of scary. I think it's good for them to blow off a little steam, don't you?"

"I guess it's good for everyone to blow off steam," he said dryly.

But Meg's deep brown eyes darkened even more and she drew her brows together. He sensed another lecture coming.

"Here's a tip, Alex," she said a shade sharply. "You need to spend more time with your daughters, and soon. They're your flesh and blood, but I don't think you really know them at all."

He had never thought that was part of his plan. Involved parenting was for other, more emotional, warm, fuzzy people, people who lived in the suburbs and had sheepdogs and station wagons. The men in his world didn't have time for that kind of thing. Did they?

He kept his silence.

"Alex, this is something you really are going to have to get a grip on. All those nannies and housekeepers—what's wrong with raising your kids *yourself?*"

"I—" he began, but he never got a chance to even think of a response because one of Meg's legion of brothers-in-law slapped open the screen door and grabbed her by the wrist.

"Hey, Meggie, I was afraid you left. Come on outside. They're playing our song."

"Sorry, Eddie, I don't want to—"

"Meg," he said with a laugh. "Me and you always do the 'Beer Barrel Polka.' Don't be a spoilsport."

She gave Alex a rueful look. "Alex, I have to—"

"Go right ahead."

And Meg was swept away by her sweaty, hearty, jovial brother-in-law.

It gave Alex time to consider what she'd just said. Maybe she was right. He'd never thought he was supposed to really *know* his daughters. He was supposed to provide the funds for their dresses and their lessons and their coming-out parties, give them a strong financial and social footing and act the proud but distant patriarch. Wasn't he?

After all, the love and the mushy stuff were Puff's job. Weren't they?

He had no idea. But then, he'd never really known her, either.

He had not had the kind of marriage enjoyed by members of the noisy Kaczmarowski clan. No, he'd had something quieter, more sedate, less intimate, less messy. He and Puff...

Had had nothing. Absolutely nothing. She might as well have been hired help.

It was a terrifying thought.

But the screen door slammed again; this time it was Rhonda. At least he thought it was Rhonda.

"My husband is dancing with Meg, so I need a partner," she said with a giggle. "Come on, Alex. You can't hide out all night."

He allowed himself to be pulled outside, under the lanterns, onto the grass, where they were all whooping and hopping and doing a dance he'd never seen the likes of. At least if he was dancing, he didn't have to think about his sterile life and his lifeless marriage.

Throwing himself into it, he didn't take long to get the hang of this polka thing, since Rhonda was every bit as strong a leader as her sister.

Almost without noticing, he discarded his coat and accepted a beer and started to sweat and laugh like the rest of them. He had tromped on so many toes and danced with so many sisters and kids by now he couldn't keep track.

"Hey, Syd," he called to his own daughter. "Come and dance with me."

"Don't know how," she mumbled. She wheeled around and ran back into the trees with the other kids.

He let her go. This time. But he vowed he would dance with his daughter one of these days. And do a lot of other things, too. Starting tomorrow when they went to the park.

It was as if a weight had been lifted from his shoulders. He had decided. Maybe it wasn't too late to learn new rules, to make amends.

"Change partners!" someone shouted, and Alex found a new woman thrust into his arms. New? Hardly. It was Meg.

He pulled her into his arms and lifted her off the ground, twirling her around till they were both breathless. Meg's skin was moist and hot under his hands and he could smell the fresh scent of her hair mixed with his own sweat.

It was a very heady odor.

His arm tightened around her waist; he dragged her right up against him. He couldn't have said whether it was the result of too many beers or this new emotional freedom he was experimenting with. Whatever the reason, with her parents and everybody watching, he staked his claim right there. The song was just as fast and furious as the last one, but he danced slow, close, hot, telling Meg with every step that he had no intention of letting her go. With her body hard up against his, he bent down, he kissed her, he pressed deeper, looking for the answers only Meg could provide.

"Hey, break it up, you two!" one of the brothers-in-law yelled out. "We got kids here."

A couple of others hooted and laughed and Meg broke away.

Her eyes were wide and uncertain, and he could feel her body trembling. "Wow," she whispered. "When you slow dance, you don't pull any punches."

"Daddy, Daddy, Meg, Meg!" Lolly shouted.

They both blinked, jolted out of their trance. Alex recovered first. "What is it, Lolly?"

"Can we stay over with Nikki and Becky? Please, please, please? They invited me and Sydney and we really, really want to. Please, Daddy?"

"Nikki and Becky are Rhonda's two," Meg explained. "Hey, Rhonda, is it okay if Alex's girls stay over at your place?"

"Yeah, sure." She was hustling her children together even as she spoke. "We're leaving right now, though."

"They have Barbie's Dream House!" Lolly confided. "And Twister. And Amy and Amber are coming, too, so it will be really fun, because there's no b-o-y-s there."

"That sounds great. What does Sydney think?" He scanned the yard till he found her. She was standing next to the one just identified as Nikki and they were arm in arm, spinning in circles. "Sydney? Do you want to go to..." The second name escaped him, but he had a sudden epiphany. "To Nikki and Becky's house?"

She stopped spinning long enough to nod vigorously.

"Okay, then," he said doubtfully. "I guess it's all set." He had no experience with this sort of child swapping, but the kids and the adults seemed to think it was perfectly normal to take extras home with them.

Meg squeezed his hand. "They'll be fine. You can pick them up tomorrow."

"For the park. I know."

And she gave him a smile that lighted up the backyard. Forget the Chinese lanterns. This girl had wattage to spare.

"Come on, Meg, I'll drive you home," he said.

She was quiet in the car, but it didn't bother him. After all that energetic dancing, she was probably worn-out. Besides, this had been an evening of such contrasts, of such discovery, he didn't blame her for being a bit overwhelmed.

So he had good intentions when he walked her up to her apartment door. He really did. He was going to kiss her good-night quickly and then take off.

"Tonight was great," he whispered as she slipped her key in the door. "I haven't had this much fun since... well, maybe never." He smiled. He bent down and gave her a very small kiss. "I almost hate for it to end."

There was a pause before Meg asked, "Does it have to end?"

Alex froze. If he moved, he was afraid he'd break the spell. He lifted one eyebrow. ''Meg, are you inviting me in?''

''Yes.'' Her lips curved into a sexy smile as she leaned backward, pushing open the door with one hip.

And then she pulled him inside.

Chapter Twelve

When you are making the decision whether to become intimate, do not let emotion sway you. There is a proper time and a place for everything, and you will know in your heart as well as in your head whether you have chosen correctly.

Factors to consider include how well you know the other party, whether you feel sure you have been honest with each other and how long you expect this relationship to last. Once you consider those simple facts, your decision should be clear...

—*The Sabina Charles No-Fuss Guide to Sex in the Nineties*

Meg backed up, deftly avoiding the dark lumps of furniture in her living room, determined to drag Alex back to her bedroom and jump on him so fast she wouldn't have time to think about what she was doing.

Frantic, dizzy, she considered pulling him down onto the sofa or even the living room floor, but she quickly abandoned that idea, making her way to her bedroom. No, there was time to get it right.

It had to be right. Because she was going to make love with Alex Thornhill.

And never let it be said that when Meg Kaczmarowski decided she wanted something, she didn't reach out and take it.

It was irrational and probably very foolish. But she couldn't help it. All the way home in the car, one thought had been uppermost in her mind.

There will never be a better time.

She had survived his world and smuggled him out of it. And he had actually enjoyed hers. The kids were taken care of for the night, and she was pretty sure she had made inroads on the issue of Alex accepting his paternal responsibilities. Obstacles overcome; barriers set aside.

And then there was the other side of the coin. Chemistry. She didn't know any other word for this amazing thing happening between them.

She looked at him and she fell apart. One look, and from out of nowhere, she was desperate to touch him, to feel him, to see how fast these crazy, fabulous, impossible feelings could spin inside her.

They had danced under the summer sky and he had held her so close she couldn't breathe. He had kissed her and she had wanted it to last forever.

But she wanted more. She wanted Alex. All of him. Tonight.

Whatever fears she had, whatever truths lay untold, she dashed them ruthlessly aside, as carelessly as she stripped off his jacket and threw it into the living room. And then she took Alex by the hand and tugged him over the threshold to her room, wrapped her arms around his neck and drew him down to her. This time, with a great deal of enthusiasm, she kissed *him*.

"You really do like to lead, don't you?" he whispered, and his lips traced a path over the exposed skin of her shoulder, up the slope of her neck, around the curve of her ear, sweet enough, slow enough to make her shiver in his arms. He pressed a kiss right onto her mouth. "You have the most luscious lips, Meg. I can't get enough of kissing you."

She sucked in a breath.

"But it's time I did a little leading of my own."

And he looped an arm under her knees, sweeping her up into his embrace, hauling her across the room and dropping her into the soft quilts and pillows of her bed.

Dazed and restless, she just sat there for a moment, trembling, drinking him in. Could she really be this lucky?

As always, she was awed by his astonishing good looks. In the shadowy bedroom, he was even more gorgeous, a dramatic slash of dark and light, of great bones and elegant lines, of height and power and devastating intensity.

But there was more, too. There were his fabulous blue eyes, thick-lashed and smoky, trailing over her where she sat on the bed, making her feel beautiful and hot, all at the same time. And his clever hands. One touch and she was his.

He smiled, dangerous in the dark bedroom, and Meg felt the tingles begin from the inside out.

So what was he waiting for?

Scooting over, giving him lots of room, she kicked off the shoes Anne-Marie had loaned her, not sorry at all that all she was wearing was a thin, sleeveless pink dress and her underwear. More might have been decorative, but it also would have gotten in the way.

She held out a hand, offering a tremulous smile. "I love looking at you, but I'd rather you came in here with me."

"Never let it be said that I don't give a lady what she wants." He took her hand, raising it to his lips, but paused a second to stare down at her plain pink fingers. "You know, it's a real shame about your fingernails. I had fantasies about those long, wicked red nails."

Meg swallowed. She knew exactly what he meant. "They'll grow," she ventured.

"I don't think I can wait that long."

Extending her hand, she scratched the edge of his jaw, very lightly, with the nails she had left. "Can you make do till then?"

He raised an eyebrow. "Absolutely. As long as you're sure this is what you want."

Meg nodded. "Absolutely." She took a deep breath, inhaling enough air to ruffle her nerve endings down to her toes. Yet she had never been so sure of anything in her entire life.

He was the one. And this was right.

He slid in beside her, reaching for her hungrily, one hand clasping her hip and the other tangled in the wild waves of her hair. Meg looped her own hands around his shoulders, his wide, strong shoulders, and then thrust them inside his shirt, shoving it aside. Buttons were nothing to her; she simply ripped them away, eager to be rid of the shirt, to feel his hot, slippery skin, to let her fingers play over the sculptured muscles of his chest.

The thin fabric of her dress was scrunched up between them, far enough that she could feel his trousers brushing her bare thigh as he nudged a leg in between hers.

His fingers followed, dancing around the hem of her dress, edging higher, sliding to the inside of her thigh for one tiny, reckless second, making her catch her breath.

She felt woozy, light-headed, but she held on to Alex, held on for dear life as his hand brushed over the curve of her hip and the swell of her round bottom, urging her closer, pushing her into him, letting her feel the whole rock-hard length of him.

She couldn't hold back a soft, shaky moan.

As she clasped her arms around his waist, rocking against him, greedy for more, he slid down the straps of her dress, pausing to dust moist kisses over her shoulders and her throat. And then he cradled her face in his hands and covered her mouth with his, delving inside.

"Meg, you taste so good," he whispered, giving her a brief respite before his lips devoured her again. "Do you know what you do to me?"

But she couldn't find enough air to answer. "I have a pretty good idea," she murmured, going very still as his fingers moved to her back, to the top of her zipper.

He paused, his eyes gazing directly at hers. And he eased the zipper down a fraction of an inch. His fingers teased the newly exposed skin, rubbing slowly, sensuously inside the opening where her dress gapped. Each notch on her spine was offered the same loving, painstaking attention as he worked his way down.

It was the longest moment of her life as he drew the damn zipper down.

Finally, agonizingly, he peeled the dress and then her bra away and Meg watched him, feeling vulnerable, but also powerful.

He drew a deep, shaky breath. He ran his hands over her arms and her back. "You feel wonderful." He nipped her bottom lip. "You are wonderful."

He reached out one finger to tweak the rosy, taut tip of her breast. It was achingly sweet, terrifyingly sexy. Meg could take no more.

She wanted to hurry this, to push him faster, but no matter how desperate her caresses became, he moved so tantalizingly slow.

Didn't he know she was burning up, ready to die right then and there?

There were too many new places to touch, too many corners and curves to ply with kisses and so little time. The passion between them was already escalating so high and she hadn't mapped nearly enough of his long, slim, sweat-slick body.

But he surprised her. Without warning, he fell back into the bed, away from her.

"What—"

He cut her off, angling one arm around her and rolling her over on top of him. Stem to stern, she could feel him now, under her, alive and pulsing. For a long moment, she gazed down at him, so dark and devastating. So delicious.

"It's your call," he offered in a husky whisper.

"My call?"

"Where we go now is up to you."

She was wanton, brazen, and she didn't care. She moved against him, just barely, enjoying the ripple of desire that small motion sent through them both. "I know where I want to go." And she reached for the top button of his pants.

It was all the cue he needed. "Let me."

Faster than she could react, he'd stripped off his pants and hers and pulled her down underneath him. He braced himself above her, just inches away, slamming her with one last fierce, possessive kiss.

"I love you," he whispered, so soft and low she wasn't sure she'd heard right.

And then he slipped inside.

It was beautiful and terrible to feel so much, to want so much. Meg cried out his name, arched into him, told him every way she knew how—with her arms gripping him tight, tighter, with her legs tangled around him, with her mouth, even now whispering his name and kissing his cheek—that she loved him desperately. Her whole body was tuned to his rhythm as he pushed them higher, bringing her so close to the top.

Not without him. She didn't want to...not without him.

"Meg," he moaned right into her ear, and she couldn't hold back. She was splintering, shattering, out of control as he suddenly went rigid, spending himself inside her.

Meg tried to breathe again. But it was too soon. She lay under him, limp and exhausted, as the tremors lessened.

But Alex's embrace remained tight around her.

"Oh my," was all she could manage. "Oh my."

And he laughed out loud.

"It's not polite to laugh," she mumbled, still gasping for breath.

But his lips were curved in that same crooked smile as he dropped a small kiss on the tip of her nose. "You amaze me. God, I love you."

"Is this for real?" she asked, awestruck.

"As real as I know how."

"Oh, Alex." She circled his waist with her arms and squeezed him tight. "I love you, too. Isn't this fantastic?"

"Uh-huh." On one side of his mouth, the smile grew deeper. Delicately, he said, "And if you keep giving me these full-body hugs, it's going to get a lot more fantastic very soon.''

Her cheeks flushed with warmth as she glanced down the front of his body at the very obvious evidence of his renewed desire. ''We have all night,'' she whispered, snuggling in. She gave him a naughty wink. ''I don't mind losing a little sleep.''

HE WAS STILL DOZING peacefully when she awoke. Sprawled like that across her bed, he looked warm and soft and just delectable. He looked . . . vulnerable.

Meg bit her lip. How could she make love with him, how could she tell him that she loved him, without telling him the whole truth about herself?

''You have to tell him the truth,'' she whispered.

But he was so cute and so sweet. And she didn't want to spoil the moment.

After he woke up, after they made love a few more times, maybe after breakfast. Then she'd tell him.

Later. Much later.

With a dreamy smile, Meg tucked herself back against Alex's chest, nestled right over his heartbeat.

Later.

''YOU SLEPT WITH HIM and you haven't told him yet?'' Joannie shrieked, aghast.

''I couldn't,'' she said miserably.

''Meg, he is going to be so ticked off when he finds out, especially since he asked you point-blank and you lied anyway.''

''I know, I know. I was going to tell him this morning,'' she swore, ''but he got up and left right away because he had to pick up his kids to take them to the park. I could hardly say, 'Oh, wait a minute, before you leave,

I forgot to tell you you were right the first time and I did write the books. My mistake. Silly old me.'"

"Oh, *Meg.*" Joannie heaved a big sigh. "You have to tell him."

"I know."

"Immediately," Joannie declared. "Right now. Get dressed, go find him and then just spill it. He loves you. He'll understand."

"Do you really think so?" she asked hopefully.

"I have no idea. But one way or the other, you're going to have to find out."

That was exactly what she was afraid of.

"HELLO?" Alex peeked his head around the screen door. "Anybody home?"

"Come on in," a voice from inside called loudly. "Just leave the kids if you need to get going. I'll be right out."

"I'm not leaving kids—I'm taking them," he said in confusion, picking his way over a jumble of toys and the crumpled remains of a box of animal crackers. A toddler was happily smashing blocks together in one corner, while a baby snoozed in a swing in the other. "Are Sydney and Lolly here?"

"Oh yeah, sure." Darla, one of the younger Kaczmarowski sisters, came running in, clutching another chunky baby on her hip, with several little girls dancing behind her. "Hi, Alex. I wasn't sure what time you'd be coming."

"I would've been earlier, but I thought they were at Rhonda's," he said vaguely. "That's where they went last night, right?"

"Yeah, but, see, Rhonda had to go in to work today, kind of unexpectedly, so she dropped them all over here." She beamed as she gestured at the disheveled living room.

"I run day care, so everybody is always dropping their kids with me. Joannie's here, too. Have you seen her? She's leaving MaryMeg with me while she takes Jamie to the dentist."

"No, I haven't seen her," he replied. "Well, I won't keep you. If you could just get Sydney and Lolly, I'll be on my way."

"Right. Sure." She scanned the room. "I think the bigger kids are out in the backyard. Hang on a sec. Here," she said brightly, handing him the baby, "you take Zach and I'll go see if I can find your girls."

"I don't—" But it was too late. He already had Zach, whether he wanted him or not. Darla was gone.

Lucky for him, Zach didn't seem to mind being handed off to a stranger. As Alex awkwardly held him, the little boy grinned with mischief and began blowing tiny bubbles of drool.

"Bubbo, bubbo," he said brightly.

Cute kid. As a matter of fact... Alex peered closer. He knew this child. And not just because he'd been introduced to a whole pack of them last night, either.

"This is Remington," he said out loud. He looked the little boy over one more time. Definitely the same baby he'd bathed in Connecticut.

"Bubbo, bubbo," the boy confirmed cheerfully.

But he was sure Darla had just called this kid Zach. As his mind raced, Meg's sister Joannie entered, carrying a baby of her own.

"Alex!" she said, her eyes wide. "I, uh, didn't expect to see you here. Have you talked to Meg recently?"

"This morning," he said, distracted by his confusion over Zach. He looked up. "Why?"

"Oh, no reason." She began backing toward the door. "No reason at all."

"Joannie, do you know whose baby this is?" he asked. And then he caught sight of the one she was carrying. And suddenly something went *clunk* inside Alex's brain.

Two babies. One smaller, with less hair. And he knew both of them. He'd held one on his knee and given the other one a bath.

"Oh God," he mumbled. "There never was a Remington, was there?"

Sabina didn't know the first thing about child care because she didn't have a child.

Meg had palmed off two different children as Sabina's baby and he'd never suspected a thing. He was a total and complete idiot.

"Excuse me?" Joannie asked weakly.

Swiftly, he announced, "Tell Darla I changed my mind and I'm going to leave Sydney and Lolly here for a little while. I'll be back." He looked around for someplace to stash Zach so he could just get out of there and *think* for a minute.

"Okay, but—"

"Listen, Alex," Darla said, waltzing back in, "the girls are doing Barbie's wedding in the backyard and they need a few more minutes. Can you wait?"

"No, I don't think so." Without further ado, he hefted Zach back into her arms. "Zach is yours, right?"

"Of course." She gave him a bewildered look. "Why, do you want to baby-sit again?"

"Again?"

"Darla," Joannie interrupted in a warning tone.

"Huh?"

But he already had that piece of information digested, thank you. He was roaming farther afield now, to someone who wrote books about how to control your children, someone whose sister ran day care. "Excuse me,

Darla,'' he began, searching his mind for a good example. "What would you do if your child was throwing a tantrum in a public place?"

She shrugged. "It's no big deal. It happens to everybody. You just have to be patient."

His mind fed him the exact passage: *When it comes to dealing with a misbehaving child, patience is indeed a virtue.*

"I mean, it's hard to do, but you have to hang on and wait them out."

It can also be exceedingly hard to come by.... But you will prevail, never fear.

"And if things really get out of hand," Darla said with a chuckle, "the rule around here is, consult the expert—ask Ma!"

And if things get too far out of hand, never fear to seek outside help from an expert....

The shared wisdom of the Kaczmarowskis was coming back to haunt them all.

"Does that help?" Darla asked kindly.

"Yeah, it helps more than you know." He turned to go but then pulled back, posing another question. "There is one more thing. It's about Meg. Would you say she's a good writer?"

"Writer? Like her handwriting?"

"Yes, her handwriting!" Joannie said suddenly. "She has terrific penmanship."

Joannie was in on it, but the others didn't know. It was as clear as if she'd come right out and said it. "No, actually, I meant her writing skill, as in books and papers and that kind of thing."

Darla was sending some very odd looks to Joannie. "Well, yeah, I suppose Meg is a good writer," she offered, still trying to be helpful. "She wrote all our compositions in high school. Is that what you mean?"

"Shut up," Joannie warned, but it was too late. He already had plenty of ammo.

"I'll be back later to pick up my daughters," he told them. And then he escaped. Behind him, he heard Joannie shout, "Call Meg. Immediately. She has to know he knows."

"Knows what?" Darla demanded.

Knows everything, Alex answered silently. *Finally, I know everything.*

MEG TAPPED ON THE DOOR of his apartment. "Alex? Are you home?" She'd been through half of Central Park, with no sign of him or his kids, so she could only assume he'd come back home. "Alex?"

"He's not here." The door swung open from the inside, revealing Fenn Fortinbras. What was she doing here?

"Hello, Fenn. Where's Alex?"

She glared down her nose at Meg. "I don't know. I came by to get the Louis XVI chair from the living room." Peering around Fenn's skinny frame, Meg could see the rickety gilded chair in question. "It was Puff's," Fenn said haughtily, pushing the chair out into the hall, "and Alex said I could have it back."

"But how did you get in there?"

"I still have a key. She was my sister, you know."

Meg eyed the other woman with a great deal of suspicion. Sneaking in and making off with the furniture was a bit odd. "Does Alex know you have a key?"

"Who cares?" Fenn's gaze raked Meg up and down. "You know, at first I was just mystified. I saw you and I thought, 'What can be going through that poor boy's mind?'"

"This is none of your—"

"Oh, please. Of course it's my business. Alex is still family," she said with a lofty air. "So I thought, perhaps he's out of his mind with grief. And then I remembered." She laughed curtly. "Grief? Over Puff? I hardly think so."

Meg fell back a few steps into the hallway. "I really don't think—"

Fenn kept going as if Meg hadn't even spoken. "But then I hit on the answer. You're good with the kids, right?"

Meg blinked, shocked. "Well, yes, but—"

"Child care," she said with a smirk. "I knew it! Alex is desperate to find someone to take care of his rotten little girls. Nannies and housekeepers have been running in and out of here like water. So he got you instead." She crossed her arms over her skinny chest. "Charming."

"That's ridiculous."

"Oh, come on. Think about it." She smiled with superiority. "It's for your own good if you realize up front that Alex couldn't possibly have love in mind. He certainly didn't with Puff." She sniffed. "God knows, Puff was no prize. Although I'm not sure Alex even knew about her, ahem, proclivities. Cat's away, mice play, all that. But Alex wouldn't have cared if she'd slept with the entire Seventh Fleet."

Meg tried to escape, but she could still hear the venom spewing behind her.

"Alex wanted one thing and one thing only from his wife—a ticket to the big leagues. He had the money, she had the class and the connections. Who cared if they barely knew each other?"

Meg turned. "Barely knew each other? They had children together!"

"Sex doesn't require all that much intimacy," Fenn drawled. "Are you really that naive?"

Throwing her hands up in the air, Meg made tracks for the elevator. "I'm not listening to you."

"I guess you are that naive." Fenn chuckled. "I suppose you think he has to be honest and aboveboard because he's a man of the people. Humble beginnings do not a paragon make."

"Well, neither does a silver spoon!" she said hotly. Any association with Fenn had cured her of that misapprehension. But then it dawned. "Wait a minute. Whose humble beginnings are you talking about? Alex?"

"You mean he didn't tell you? Tsk, tsk." She arched one delicate eyebrow. "Alex grew up in the sticks—middle of nowheresville, baby. Poor as a church mouse. No father, and his mother was some sort of menial servant. Puff was willing to overlook it since he had the bucks, but I never could understand why. And he wanted her for the entrée into society, of course. This time," she said, sending Meg a smug smile, "he's willing to barter his name for a baby-sitter."

Meg's head was spinning. Fenn had painted a picture of a greedy social climber from the wrong side of the tracks. Could that be Alex?

And he wanted her as a . . . baby-sitter?

She knew better than to trust Fenn, but still, it all made a bizarre kind of sense. Not the kind Fenn thought.

But still . . .

IN A WHIRLWIND of thoughts and doubts, Meg hailed a cab and headed for her office at Sabina's town house. She needed a quiet place to think and Sabina's Home of Peach was at least that.

But when she unlocked the front door, she almost got knocked down by Sabina, who was rushing to leave, toting a huge box.

"Where are you going? What is this, moving day?" she asked.

"Alex Thornhill closed us down," Sabina remarked smartly. "Lock, stock and barrel."

She wasn't sure she'd heard correctly. "What?"

Sabina gave Meg a grim stare. "I just got the call from our editor at Daybreak. Per Alex Thornhill, there will be no more *Sabina Charles No-Fuss Guides*. They are kaput."

"But why?"

Sabina shrugged. "The editor was furious. He said Alex called them about an hour ago and said no more *No-Fuss*. He told them I wasn't writing the books and we were all in big trouble."

Weakly, Meg fell back against the door. "He knows."

Sabina rattled on—something about him being a real jerk but, oh well, she had prospects. "There's always 'Hope Springs Eternal,'" she said blithely. "They're talking about bringing me back."

But by then Meg was good and angry. "He promised!" she said fiercely. "He promised he wouldn't say anything, way back when he came back after your date. He promised! How dare he do this now?"

Wheeling on one heel, she stomped off, even more determined to find Alex and give him a piece of her mind.

After her, Sabina called, "Wait, Meg! I didn't tell you the rest of it!"

"I don't care about the rest of it!"

She broke into a run.

Chapter Thirteen

There are frequently minor disagreements between bride and groom as the wedding date approaches. Don't spend a single moment fretting about it, dear readers. It's nothing of substance, really, just details, and it doesn't reflect at all on how much you love each other.

And once you muddle through all the tears and recriminations and temper tantrums, you'll be free to enjoy your vows as you prepare for wedded bliss...

—The Sabina Charles No-Fuss Guide to a Wonderful Wedding

Alex was wearing a hole in the carpet outside her apartment. Where could she be?

"It doesn't matter," he said out loud, trying to stay calm. He clenched his jaw so ferociously he was afraid for a second he'd broken a tooth.

"I will be magnanimous," he muttered, "and overlook her lies. She doesn't deserve it, but that's okay. As long as she apologizes profusely and promises never to do it again—"

"Are we talking to ourselves?" Meg asked acidly.

His head snapped up. "Before you say anything," he told her in a stern, rigid tone, "you should know that I know. Everything. All the sordid details of your little Remington fun."

"Is that why—"

He held up a hand for silence. "Excuse me. I said before you say *anything.* May I finish?"

She bit her lip, looking insolent, but she nodded. "Go right ahead."

"Thank you. I want you to know," he declared, "that I know, but that I forgive you."

"You forgive me?"

"Yes." It was difficult doing this in his current frame of mind, but he'd thought it through and it was the only way, whether he was royally peeved or not. "I forgive you and I want you to marry me."

"What?" she cried. "What?"

He gave her a confused look. "Well, are you going to say yes?"

"No, I'm not going to say yes. Are you crazy?"

"I don't get this. I thought you'd be hap—"

"Is it my turn to talk now? Is it?" She was positively seething and he didn't understand why at all. He had every right to be furious with her, but he wasn't. So she was. What sense did that make?

"First," she said smartly, "where are your children?"

"My children?"

"Yes, you know, Sydney and Lolly." She scowled at him. "If you can remember their names. Did you or did you not promise to take them to the park today?"

"Well, yes, but—"

"Aha! That is point one," she said with a flourish. "Broken promise number one. Second," she continued, and her voice began to rise, "how *dare* you close down my job? Broken promise number two."

"I did not—"

"Oh, yes, you did." She punched a finger in his chest. "But if I don't have a job, I'll be more likely to say yes to your stupid proposal, won't I?"

"Stupid proposal?" he echoed. Now he was really getting mad.

"Yes," she shot back. "A stupid proposal. How dare you propose to me?" And she smacked him on the shoulder.

"Meg! Have you lost your mind?"

"I am holding on to my temper, but just barely," she whispered hotly. "All right, then, tell me, Thornhill, why are you proposing?"

"Why?" Shouldn't that have been perfectly obvious? "Because I want you to be a part of my life," he told her. "Or I did, before you started acting like a lunatic. And you're wonderful with my children. God knows, you're a lot better with them than I am." Stiffly, he added, "And now that I know you're the one who wrote all the books—well, I really think I knew it all along—but now I know you can handle my household perfectly and our life together can be quite wonderful."

"Wrong answer!" Meg shouted. "Did you ever think that maybe, when someone asks you why you're proposing, that maybe you should say, *Because I love you? Because I can't live without you?*"

"Well, I would've," he protested.

Meg gave him a nasty glare. "Well, you didn't, did you? You could have said that there is something about me, just *me,* no one else in the world, that you love more than life itself. But you didn't, did you?''

Oh God. He could see tears welling up in her eyes now. If she started crying, he didn't know what he was going to do.

"All my life," she said unevenly, "all I ever wanted was to be special, for people to respect me for my talents, for someone to love me for myself. So what do I do? I write books under someone else's name. I do all the work, Sabina takes all the credit. And now, I finally fall in love with someone, and he asks me to marry him, and why? Because he needs a baby-sitter!"

"Meg, that's not it," he began, but she was too fargone to hear him now.

"It isn't anything about me—not at all because I'm special—but because I happen to be *handy,*" she shouted. "Wife number one dies, so quick, let's plug in Sabina Charles, *No-Fuss* expert."

"What's that got—"

Meg charged on, circling him as she stomped back and forth in the hall. "But Sabina is a flake, and once you find that out, you drop her like a hot potato. So quick, let's plug in Meg."

"Plug in?" he ventured.

"I feel like a toaster or something!" she yelled, smacking him again. "One toaster doesn't work, you just plug in another one."

"Meg, don't be absurd." He caught her hands and held her still. "You're not a toaster. And I don't understand at all why you're so angry. I think I'm being pretty magnanimous to overlook all the stunts you pulled. You've had all kinds of chances to tell me the truth and you didn't. I asked you point-blank if you wrote the books and you said no."

"Well, you didn't exactly tell the truth yourself, did you?" she demanded.

"What does that mean?"

"I saw Fenn this morning." She spit the words out and shuddered. "She says you grew up on the wrong side of the tracks with a single mother. Is that true?"

Alex drew his eyebrows together. What this had to do with anything was really beyond him. But as long as they were airing all their dirty linen, he supposed he might as well launch into that sorry tale, too. "Actually, I grew up in a very wealthy household." He smiled thinly. "I just happened to be the cook's son."

Under her breath, Meg muttered, "That explains a lot."

Alex was hanging on to his self-control by a thread. He had asked this woman—this crazy woman—to marry him and she'd given him some bunk about not feeling special and had now turned to digging up ancient history.

"Are you referring," he said coldly, "to the fact that I'm a rotten father because I never had one? Well, maybe so. The one thing my mother wanted for me was to be rich and powerful, like the people she worked for. And I achieved that. But she never told me I might want more."

Was that a trace of sympathy he saw in Meg's wide brown eyes? It was the last thing he wanted.

"Meg, I never told you anything about my background. But I never lied."

"Yeah, but you kept it a secret, didn't you?" Her voice was softer, less fearsome now. "You let me fall all over myself feeling like I wasn't good enough for the great and powerful Alex Thornhill, when you come from just as ordinary a background as I do.''

He lifted an eyebrow. ''I never knew that what class I was from mattered to you.''

''It doesn't.''

''So why is this an issue?''

''Because I never really knew you at all!'' she tried to explain. ''You never gave me a chance. You have this superficial Alex Thornhill mask that you wear—slick and powerful and elegant—but it's not real. I fell in love with someone who doesn't exist.''

Now he was totally confused. He had one lifeline to hang on to and he laid it out before her, plain and simple. ''I need you, Meg. My children need you. I was angry that you lied to me, but I was willing to overlook it, to be magnanimous. I don't pretend to understand what exactly you're so angry about, but whatever it is, can't you overlook it the same way I did?''

The minute he used the word *magnanimous,* he saw thunderclouds gathering on her face.

''No,'' she said in a clipped little voice. ''You can just be *magnanimous* all by yourself, buster.'' And she began to march away from him, down the hall.

''Meg, this is your apartment.''

''Okay, then.'' She spun around, pointing a finger at the elevator. ''You leave.''

''Fine.'' Tucking his dignity around him, he strolled a few paces away.

''And if I were you, I'd learn how to be a father and stop looking for quick-fix servants and moms,'' she called after him. ''I'd take my kids to the park!''

Calmly, coolly, without any of the steam he felt coming out his ears, Alex returned, "And if I were you, I'd stop being so damned afraid."

"Afraid? Ha!" she said bravely. "I'm not afraid."

"You're afraid of not being good enough," he began. "Of not fitting in. Of people not respecting you. And that's why you don't take credit for your own work." He paused. He hadn't planned to say any of this, but it was too late. The words were already there. "And that's why you can't see how much I love you."

As Meg stood there with her mouth open, he took the stairs.

DAYS PASSED. WEEKS.

Every one of her sisters, including Anne-Marie, weighed in with an opinion on how to get him back. But she ignored them.

It was going to take something from him—some grand gesture to show her that he really did love her—before she was willing to overlook the baby-sitter thing. Didn't he realize that he had wounded her in her most vulnerable spot? Didn't he realize that the one thing she most feared in life was not being appreciated?

And what had he done? Lumped her in with any other willing female body who could look after his kids. He'd wanted someone a little classier, of course, but when he couldn't find a candidate, he'd had to turn to Meg.

She didn't want to think that was really it, but what choice did she have?

And so things proceeded pretty grimly. Until the day she got the call from Daybreak Books. Which just happened to be the same day—the same minute—she got the frantic call from Sydney.

"Meg? This is Oliver over at Daybreak. We wanted to talk to you about a new series of books to replace the *No-Fuss* line. We've been meaning to get hold of you for some time now—"

Just then the other line beeped and she put him on hold.

"Yes?"

"Meg, it's Sydney," the little girl wailed. "We're being held prisoner!"

"What?"

"Prisoner! Me and Lolly. Come get us, please? If you don't, we're going to escape," she cried. "Really. In the middle of the night. We'll just jump out the window, alone on the streets."

She did sound pretty agitated. "Where's your father?" Meg asked.

"Gone. Who knows?" In a very bitter voice, Sydney added, "You know him. He's always gone. Business or something. He went to Los Angeles, I think."

"Oh, dear." Her heart sank. She had hoped that Alex would take her advice to heart and mend his fences with his daughters. But it seemed he was playing the same old absent father games. "Listen, Sydney, where are you? I don't know if I can spring you, but at least I can visit you."

Quickly, she scrawled down the address. Brooklyn? What where they doing in Brooklyn?

BUT THE ADDRESS Sydney had given her was a school. A plain old public school, with kids running up and down the hall, with crayon pictures taped to the walls.

"Can I help you?" a nice-looking young woman asked. "Are you here for Parents' Day?"

"Parents' Day?" she echoed.

"Yes. Do you have a child here?"

"Sydney Thornhill?"

"Yes. That would be 3A." She smiled. "Right down the hall and to the left."

Utterly mystified, Meg followed the directions. There it was—3A. But she couldn't imagine anyone being held prisoner here. She pushed open the door.

The room was full of parents and children, including Sydney, who was sitting politely behind a small desk. When Meg came in, she glanced up and smiled immediately.

"Sydney, what's this all about? You're not being held . . ." But her voice died out when she saw him.

Alex, of course, although he didn't really look like himself. As gorgeous as ever. He was wearing jeans, of all things, with a casual shirt. And he needed a haircut.

"Meg?" he asked, with such hope in his beautiful blue eyes she couldn't believe it. "What are you doing here?"

"I think I've been the victim of a prank," she said slowly. "Sydney?"

The little girl shrugged. "You guys were taking too long. I wanted Meg to come and see my new school."

"I would've come," she said awkwardly. "But maybe not when your dad was here."

"But, Meg!" Sydney sighed, as if explaining to grown-ups were the worst thing in the entire world. "Meg, what good would it be if you came when he wasn't here?"

She just shook her head, unable to think of a thing to say. "But what are you doing in Brooklyn?" she asked finally.

"We moved!" Sydney said happily.

"You moved to Brooklyn?"

Alex shrugged. "All your family seemed happy here. I decided Fifth Avenue was not the best place to try to raise a family."

Meg was simply unable to take this in. "You moved? The kids are in public school? And your clothes? Your hair?"

"Well, I've made some wholesale changes." He gave her a dry smile. "I had this friend who convinced me my life was a mess and I was neglecting my children. I guess you could say I took her advice to heart."

"Alex . . . Well, I don't know what to say."

"Say you'll marry us," Sydney interrupted. "Please?"

This was incredibly embarrassing. She glanced at Alex. "I'm very glad that you've worked things out as far as the kind of father you want to be, but I don't see—"

"Sorry, Meg. I didn't put her up to that."

"Oh, I know," she said hastily.

"As long as Sydney dragged you here," he began, leading Meg aside to a quieter corner of the room, "I might as well take my chance. I'll admit it, I thought you would come back before this." His eyes held her. "I thought you would come to me."

"Well," she interjected, making a feeble joke, "I never would've thought to look for you in Brooklyn."

His gaze skittered away. He stuck his hands in his pockets. Did he have any idea how much she wanted to touch him, to drag those hands out of his pockets and pull them around her?

"So," he asked briskly, "are you going to do the books?"

"Books? What books?"

"The replacement for the *No-Fuss* books."

Meg felt very confused. "Did that come from you? Did you make them do that?"

"Well, actually, no. I mean, it was my suggestion, but they didn't have to—"

"Ouch," she said softly. "You convinced Daybreak to ask me, didn't you?"

"Don't you think it's time you stopped hiding your light under a bushel?" he asked quietly. But she saw a spark of intensity in his eyes. "You're talented and very special, and I think you ought to let the world know."

"Me?"

"Yes, you." He raked a hand through the dark, sleek strands of his hair. "Okay, look, I wasn't going to do this, but..."

With one swift motion, he took her shoulders in his hands. She jumped from the electricity of his touch. She had forgotten how it felt. How could she have forgotten?

"I got it, Meg," he said fiercely. "Maybe not that day, but later, when I had time to think it over. And I just want you to know that no matter what happens, I did love you. I do love you. And I never stopped thinking, not for one minute, that you were the most special woman I'd ever met."

She gulped. She could feel tears pressing behind her eyelids. "You did? You do? Really?"

"Absolutely."

"And you're not just saying this to—"

"If you call yourself a toaster again, I'll turn you over my knee," he vowed with a playful glint in his eyes. "And, no, I'm not doing it to get a baby-sitter. I'm do-ing fine with the girls all by myself. Well, maybe not fine, but we're coping."

She laughed and started to cry at the same time. "Oh God, Alex. I love you so much!" She threw her arms around him and buried her face in his chest before she disgraced herself in front of a classroom of children. "I missed you so much I thought I would die."

"That makes two of us," he whispered in her ear. "Will you come back to me, Meg?"

Her smile was wobbly, but it was still there. "Absolutely."

"Meg, Meg," Sydney yelled, pulling on her arm. "Are you going to marry us?"

She winked at Alex. "Maybe so, Syd. Maybe so."

Once in a while, there's a story so special, a story so unusual,
that your pulse races, your blood rushes. We call this

HART'S DREAM is one such story.

At first they were dreams—strangely erotic. Then visions—strikingly real. Ever since his accident, when Dr. Sara Carr's sweet voice was his only lifeline, Daniel Hart couldn't get the woman off his mind. Months later it was more than a figment of his imagination calling to him, luring him, doing things to him that only a flesh-and-blood woman could.... But Sara was nowhere to be found....

#589 HART'S DREAM
by
Mary Anne Wilson

Available in July wherever Harlequin books are sold. Watch for more Heartbeat stories, coming your way—only from American Romance!

HEART9

HARLEQUIN®

AMERICAN ♦ ROMANCE®

You asked for it...You got it! More MEN!

MORE THAN MEN

We're thrilled to bring you another special edition of the popular MORE THAN MEN series.

Like those who have come before him. Ambrose Carpenter is more than tall, dark and hansome. All of those men have extraordinary powers that made them "more than men." But whether they are able to grant you three wishes, or live forever, make no mistake—their greatest, most extraordinary power is of seduction.

So make a date with Ambrose Carpenter in...

#599 THE BABY MAKER
by Jule McBride
September 1995

MTM4

HARLEQUIN®
AMERICAN ◆ ROMANCE®

IT'S A BABY BOOM!

NEW ARRIVALS

We're expecting—again! Join us for a reprisal of the New Arrivals promotion, in which special American Romance authors invite you to read about equally special heroines—all of whom are on a nine-month adventure! We expect each mom-to-be will find the man of her dreams—and a daddy in the bargain!

Watch for the newest arrival!

#600 ANGEL'S BABY
by Pamela Browning
September 1995

HARLEQUIN®

Don't miss these Harlequin favorites by some of our most distin-
guished authors!
And now, you can receive a discount by ordering two or more titles!

HT #25559	JUST ANOTHER PRETTY FACE by Candace Schuler	$2.99	☐
HT #25616	THE BOUNTY HUNTER by Vicki Lewis Thompson	$2.99 U.S./$3.50 CAN.	☐
HP #11667	THE SPANISH CONNECTION by Kay Thorpe	$2.99 U.S./$3.50 CAN.	☐
HP #11701	PRACTISE TO DECEIVE by Sally Wentworth	$2.99 U.S./$3.50 CAN.	☐
HR #03268	THE BAD PENNY by Susan Fox	$2.99	☐
HR #03340	THE NUTCRACKER PRINCE by Rebecca Winters	$2.99 U.S./$3.50 CAN.	☐
HS #70540	FOR THE LOVE OF IVY by Barbara Kaye	$3.39	☐
HS #70596	DANCING IN THE DARK by Lynn Erickson	$3.50	☐
HI #22196	CHILD'S PLAY by Bethany Campbell	$2.89	☐
HI #22304	BEARING GIFTS by Aimée Thurlo	$2.99 U.S./$3.50 CAN.	☐
HAR #16538	KISSED BY THE SEA by Rebecca Flanders	$3.50 U.S./$3.99 CAN.	☐
HAR #16553	THE MARRYING TYPE by Judith Arnold	$3.50 U.S./$3.99 CAN.	☐
HH #28847	DESIRE MY LOVE by Miranda Jarrett	$3.99 U.S./$4.50 CAN	☐
HH #28848	VOWS by Margaret Moore	$3.99 U.S./$4.50 CAN.	☐

(limited quantities available on certain titles)

	AMOUNT	$
DEDUCT:	**10% DISCOUNT FOR 2+ BOOKS**	$
	POSTAGE & HANDLING	$
	($1.00 for one book, 50¢ for each additional)	
	APPLICABLE TAXES*	$
	TOTAL PAYABLE	$
	(check or money order—please do not send cash)	

To order, complete this form and send it, along with a check or money order for the
total above, payable to Harlequin Books, to: **In the U.S.:** 3010 Walden Avenue,
P.O. Box 9047, Buffalo, NY 14269-9047; **In Canada:** P.O. Box 613, Fort Erie, Ontario,
L2A 5X3.

Name: _____

Address: _____ City: _____

State/Prov.: _____ Zip/Postal Code: _____

*New York residents remit applicable sales taxes.
Canadian residents remit applicable GST and provincial taxes.

HBACK-JS2

PRIZE SURPRISE SWEEPSTAKES!

This month's prize:

BEAUTIFUL WEDGWOOD CHINA!

This month, as a special surprise, we're giving away a bone china dinner service for eight by Wedgwood**, one of England's most prestigious manufacturers!

Think how beautiful your table will look, set with lovely Wedgwood china in the casual Countryware pattern! Each five-piece place setting includes dinner plate, salad plate, soup bowl and cup and saucer.

The facing page contains two Entry Coupons (as does every book you received this shipment). Complete and return *all* the entry coupons; **the more times you enter, the better your chances of winning!**

Then keep your fingers crossed, because you'll find out by September 15, 1995 if you're the winner!

Remember: The more times you enter, the better your chances of winning!*

*NO PURCHASE OR OBLIGATION TO CONTINUE BEING A SUBSCRIBER NECESSARY TO ENTER. SEE THE REVERSE SIDE OF ANY ENTRY COUPON FOR ALTERNATE MEANS OF ENTRY.

**THE PROPRIETORS OF THE TRADEMARK ARE NOT ASSOCIATED WITH THIS PROMOTION.

PWW KAL